D0049393

ISLAND OF TEARS

The Mickey Rawlings Baseball Mysteries
Available from Kensington Publishing

MURDER AT FENWAY PARK

MURDER AT EBBETS FIELD

MURDER AT WRIGLEY FIELD

HUNTING A DETROIT TIGER

THE CINCINNATI RED STALKINGS

HANGING CURVE

Nonfiction Baseball by Troy Soos

BEFORE THE CURSE:
The Glory Days of New England Baseball, 1858–1918

ISLAND OF TEARS

TROY SOOS

KENSINGTON BOOKS
http://www.kensingtonbooks.com

KENSINGTON BOOKS are published by

Kensington Publishing Corp.
850 Third Avenue
New York, NY 10022

All Kensington titles, imprints, and distributed lines are available at special quantity discounts for bulk purchases for sales promotion, premiums, fund-raising, educational or institutional use.

Special book excerpts or customized printings can also be created to fit specific needs. For details, write or phone the office of the Kensington Special Sales Manager: Kensington Publishing Corp., 850 Third Avenue, New York, NY 10022, Attn. Special Sales Department. Phone: 1-800-221-2647.

Kensington and the K logo Reg. U.S. Pat. & TM Off.

Library of Congress Card Catalogue Number: 2001090975
ISBN: 1-57566-767-3

First Printing: November 2001
10 9 8 7 6 5 4 3 2 1

Printed in the United States of America

ACKNOWLEDGMENTS

It is a pleasure to thank Kate Duffy, my editor, for encouraging me to start a new series and for her invaluable guidance in the development of this work. I am also grateful to my agent, Meredith Bernstein, for her continuing efforts on my behalf.

For their assistance in historical research, I am indebted to Thomas M. Gambino of the New York City Police Museum, Barbara Mosqueda of the Lake Howell Media Center, and the staffs of the University of Central Florida Library, Stetson University Library, and Seminole County Library.

Finally, my thanks to Cindy Himmer for reviewing the manuscript and for her remarkable patience.

CHAPTER 1

The double eagle glowed like a miniature sun, a solitary beacon amid the murky shadows of the Hole. The saloon had no formal name—"The Hole" wasn't advertised on any signs, nor was it registered on city license rolls—but Bowery locals all knew the illicit dive by the same name used for the most notorious jail cells. The comparison to a dungeon wasn't quite a fair one, however. Prisons generally had better ventilation than the fetid Hole of Broome Street, and they certainly had a more reputable clientele.

Marshall Webb pried the twenty-dollar gold piece from the scarred tabletop where it had mired in a paste of stale beer and old cigar ash. He held the coin tightly against his palm for a moment, as if trying to absorb some warmth from its luster, before slipping it into his vest pocket.

Across the small table, Lawrence Pritchard eyed Webb with a look of concern on his drawn face. "We *had* agreed on twenty dollars, hadn't we?"

Webb shrugged, then continued to hunch his shoulders, trying to shake off the winter chill. The temperature of the Hole was maintained at the optimal level for business: a little warmer than the December air outside to attract customers, but cool enough so that once inside they would have to warm themselves internally with whiskey or rum. "Yes, twenty," Webb said with a cough. Smoke and dust hung thick in the low-ceilinged room, providing the ambience of a coal cellar.

"You don't look happy about it," said Pritchard with a frown that caused his Dunlap derby to duck low across his forehead. There was no hat rack in the Hole, since anything hung there would disappear faster than pickled eggs at a free-lunch counter.

The flickering gaslight from behind the bar was feeble, but Webb could see enough of his companion to notice that Pritchard was the one who didn't look happy. The middle-aged man's bony face, with sunken eyes and clean-shaven pale skin, had a spectral quality that was even eerier in the shadows. The occasional glint from his pince-nez was the liveliest aspect of his appearance. Webb reminded himself that Pritchard didn't look much different in any other venue, generally giving the impression of a nervous ghost.

After one last wriggle of his shoulders, Webb nestled within his overcoat. "The twenty is fine—it's what we agreed to for the last one." He toyed with his whiskey glass, debating whether to empty it at one gulp or make it last for two. "But the next one will cost you more—considerably more."

Pritchard hesitated before answering, "I'm a reasonable man. You know I have no objection to paying a fair price."

Webb stifled a laugh; to those in their trade, "fair" was often a matter of vigorous contention. He ended his debate about the drink by downing it at once, straining it through the thick mustache that overhung his lip, then launched into another debate about whether to exceed his customary limit of two drinks.

"The last one did very well for us," continued Pritchard. "If the next is at all comparable . . ."

"The next one will be a *peach*." Webb dabbed his tongue at the drops of rye clinging to his mustache. "I'm going to have some fresh material in three days."

Pritchard's expression instantly changed from worried to eager. "Care to give me some idea of what I can expect?"

"You've heard about Ellis Island?"

"One of Harrison's dumber decisions." Pritchard rolled his eyes. "What kind of idiot puts an immigration station where the water is too shallow for boats? Political, that's all it was—a way to get the Navy's munitions dump off the island and placate those New Jersey dunderheads who thought it would blow them all up some day." He shook his head. "We need to get Grover Cleveland back in the White House. Next election—"

Webb cut him off. "I don't care *why* the place was chosen. The point is: Ellis Island opens January first, and there are going to be thousands of immigrants coming in every day. . . ." His attention drifted to a nearby table, where two plug-uglies in shabby clothes of no discernible color or style were stealing glances at them. Webb discreetly surveyed the rest of the saloon. About a dozen other men, little more than shadowy figures in the dim light, were drinking the afternoon away; five of them stood at the bar while the others sat at small, rough-hewn tables. The two nearby weren't the only ones watching Webb and Pritchard with interest.

Webb suddenly slammed his palm on the table and leapt from his chair, yelling at Pritchard, "You ever try something like that again and I'll cut your heart out!" He reached into his jacket pocket, as if going for an implement to do exactly that.

Pritchard almost tumbled from his own seat, and his pince-nez fell into his lap as he jerked his head back. The look on his face was as shocked as if he'd already been stabbed.

With one hand on the table, and the other still in his pocket, Webb leaned forward until his face was inches from Pritchard's. He hissed as softly as the gas jets, "No offense, but I don't want anyone here thinking I'm an easy mark. There's men in this place who'd kill for a pair of old shoes without giving it a thought. Putting that twenty on the table the way you did was like waving red meat before a starving cur." Webb let go of the fountain pen that he'd hoped made a knifelike bulge in his pocket, and sat back down. "Good," he said in his normal baritone. "Now we understand each other."

When he'd recovered enough to speak, it was Pritchard's turn to whisper, "*You're* the one who insists we meet in places like this."

"In order to avoid being seen together. If you go attracting attention to us, that defeats the purpose, doesn't it?"

Pritchard paused to clean his glasses, then wiped the handkerchief across his forehead, having managed to break a sweat despite the cold. "You're quite right," he stammered. "I'm sorry." He neatly refolded the cloth, tucked it into his breast pocket, and took a moment to compose himself. "So . . . tell me about your plans."

Webb settled back in his chair, satisfied that he'd given any potential muggers reason to have second thoughts. "As I was saying, Ellis Island opens Friday. People from all over the world coming in. Some of them will be girls, on their own, expecting to find jobs as maids or cooks."

Pritchard shook his head with disapproval. "What kind of family sends a young girl alone across the ocean?"

No answer was expected, but Webb replied, "A poor one—perhaps a family that can only afford steerage for one. So they send a daughter to get her settled in some kind of work here. Maybe later they'll send a son, and if they can afford it, the rest of the family will follow." He smiled. "Anyway, that's the kind of girl I'm looking for: Thirteen or fourteen years old—maybe as old as sixteen but no more. Young, alone, and eager—that's what I want." An orphan would be ideal, he thought to himself—no one to help her in the strange new country, and no family to whom she could return.

"Pretty?" asked Pritchard.

"Of course. And if nature didn't make her that way, she'll be a doll by the time I finish with her." He smiled again. "I can do a lot with the right kind of girl. I guarantee you'll be happy with the result—*and* you'll be happy to pay."

The door to the Hole creaked open, letting in a gust of cold air and two ragamuffins, each about nine years old. Webb and Pritchard both watched as the boys made their way directly to the bar, their bare feet squishing in the swampy mixture of tobacco juice and sawdust that covered the floor. The taller of the two held open a small burlap sack, and began negotiating to sell the three live rats squealing inside.

"For the lunch spread, no doubt," said Pritchard in a rare attempt at humor.

Webb shook his head. "For the rat pit tonight." He then listened as the boys settled for two nickel beers a piece instead of the eight cents per rat they'd asked for initially. The saloonkeeper managed to convince them that they were coming out four cents ahead on the deal.

"I thought pitting dogs against rats was outlawed," said Pritchard. "Didn't the SPCA get that stopped?"

"For one thing," Webb answered, "neither the SPCA nor the law has any control over what goes on in here. For another, there are no dogs involved."

"It's rats against rats? I can't imagine that would be very entertaining."

"No, it's *man* versus rat. A man wearing leather boots steps into the pit against a hundred or so rats. He's got to stomp as many as he can before they bite through to his feet."

Pritchard's derby lurched up. "You can't be serious!"

Webb nodded solemnly. "A good terrier takes at least half a year of training, and the top ones can cost more than a hundred dollars." He gestured toward a group of toughs standing at the bar. "A man can be gotten for next to nothing."

Absently touching the vest pocket that held his gold piece, Webb thought of the new immigration center opening at Ellis Island. In a few days, human life would be even cheaper as a fresh supply poured into the city. It was a simple matter of supply and demand, and in New York City, as 1891 drew to a close, a human being could be had for less than the price of a good ratter.

CHAPTER 2

Edwin Crombie sucked at his lower lip as he cautiously turned back the crank. Half a turn more, he decided, then he'd play it safe and stop.

The shrill squeak of celluloid slipping off the rubber rollers immediately told him he'd gone too far. He frantically began cranking in the opposite direction, but in vain. The film strip rattled loose and useless inside the camera box, and Crombie sensed his plans unraveling along with it.

Letting go of the handle, he looked over the top of his moving-picture camera and gazed across the gray, choppy water of New York Harbor. Almost a mile to the north, at the mouth of the Hudson River, three steamships were anchored together, waiting to unload the steerage passengers they had carried across the Atlantic Ocean. Crombie was relieved to see that no transfer boats had left the steamers yet, so he had a little time.

Time alone wouldn't be enough to fix the camera, though. It would take technical ability, and Edwin Crombie was well aware that he had the mechanical aptitude of a puppy. He began to pace the landing wharf of the tiny island, breathing deeply of the brisk salt air and mentally kicking himself for not bringing Gus along. Gus could fix anything. "Damn it to hell!" Crombie suddenly began kicking for real, taking out his frustration on a mooring pile with his right foot. "Damn! Damn! Damn!"

"Somethin' the matter?"

Crombie cast a scornful glance at the burly, moon-faced young man slouched against another post. "Sure is, Butch," he sighed, thinking to himself that Butch would be of no help in remedying the situation. Crombie had found the dockhand in Red Hook, and hired him for the day to help lug the heavy camera on the ferry from Brooklyn. He had assumed that Butch's grimy denim overalls and stained flannel shirt were evidence that he was accustomed to hard work, but Crombie now believed that his assistant simply had an aversion to clean clothes. Butch had been of little help with the camera, instead concentrating most of his efforts on chewing the massive wad of tobacco that bulged in his stubbly cheek.

Crombie planted one more hard kick at the piling, then saw with dismay how badly he'd scuffed the toe of his cordovan boot. Letting out another long sigh, he turned to finding a more productive pursuit. *Okay,* he told himself, *Gus isn't here and Butch is a lazy dolt, so it's up to me.*

The problem Crombie faced was getting the film back on track without prematurely exposing it. To prevent himself from acting rashly, he dug his hands deep in the pockets of his heavy wool overcoat; he didn't want to risk touching the camera until he'd figured out what to do. He slowly walked around his "Kinemascope," an eighty-pound contraption mounted on a sturdy tripod, and examined the brass hardware that held it together. The only way to get at the film inside was to open the camera box—and that meant letting in light. Although little sunshine penetrated the thick, wintry clouds above, Crombie knew it was more than enough to destroy his precious negative.

It was the value and scarcity of the film stock that had gotten him into this predicament in the first place. He had turned back the take-up reel in order to use every possible frame for recording today's event. Now he might get nothing at all.

"Looks like it's startin'," announced Butch.

Crombie turned around to see a crowd of men filing out the immigration station's main door. Some were officials and dignitaries, identifiable by their black silk hats and Prince Albert coats. Others were clerks and guards wearing the stiff blue uniforms of the Immigration Service. Clad in gaudy red costumes with plumed hats, and carrying their instruments, were the musicians who made up a small brass band. There were also men in plain business suits and derbies whom Crombie assumed to be reporters here to document the opening of Ellis Island. They all remained huddled near the entrance, sheltered somewhat from the chill wind that gusted over the wharf.

Crombie knew that the first immigrants must be arriving soon, and he would have to act fast or miss his chance. In frustration, he burrowed his hands deeper in his pockets. *That's it—the coat!*

Stripping off his overcoat, Crombie ordered Butch, "Come here."

The young man spit a stream of tobacco juice at a low-flying gull, missing it by a good ten feet. "Where?"

"Here, Butch, here! I need help with the camera." Crombie's slight frame shivered in the chilly air, but now that he had a plan, he found the cold bracing rather than bothersome. Fishing a dime from his trouser pocket, he used it to partially unscrew each of the four bolts holding the side panel on the camera.

Butch finally lumbered over. "Whaddaya want me to do?"

"Exactly what I tell you to do." Crombie draped the coat over the camera and held it firmly to the top of the box. "Reach under the coat—*but don't lift it*. Can't let any light in."

"I dunno—"

"You're going to take this panel off. There are four bolts, one at each corner. They're already loose. Unscrew them and the panel should come right off."

Butch shrugged his shoulders. "Yeah, awright." Apparently it sounded like little enough work that he was willing to try. He slipped his hand under the cloth and fumbled with the bolts. "Got 'em." Pulling his hand back out, he fumbled again. "Ah, nuts!" One of the bolts had fallen to the wharf and bounced into the water.

"Never mind," said Crombie, struggling to hold his temper. "Slide the panel out, and put it down—carefully."

Butch did as he was told, and laid the slab of varnished oak against the tripod. "What now?"

"Hold the top of my coat tight on the top of the camera box. And don't drop it like you did that bolt." As incentive, Crombie added, "There'll be another dollar for you if this works."

Smiling so broadly that a clump of plug tobacco fell from the corner of his mouth, Butch laid a beefy forearm on the coat, pinning it firmly to the camera. "Got it."

Crombie pulled his own hands away, then worked them through the sleeves of the coat and into the camera's inner machinery. As his fingers grew stiff and numb from the cold, he groped blindly inside the box. Yes! He felt the reels. Working by touch alone, he turned the front spool to take up the slack film, and soon came to the end of the celluloid strip.

A piercing whistle blew from one of the steamships. "Looks like they're on their way," said Butch. "Just what we need: more o' them filthy foreigners."

Crombie didn't care to argue immigration policy; all he wanted was to capture the newcomers' arrival on film. And if he didn't get the camera back together in time, there was no chance of that. With his right hand, Crombie firmly gripped the end of the springy celluloid; with his left, he felt for the rubber rollers through which the strip had to be threaded. He tried to remember: Does it go straight through, or make an "S" around the rollers? Looking up, he saw a ferry pull away from the big ship; it would be only fifteen or twenty minutes before it docked at the island.

Crombie opted to thread the film straight through, and began carefully feeding the film between the rollers. Another blast of the whistle startled him and he tore the edge of the strip. "Damn!"

"You sure you know what you're doin'?" asked Butch.

Ignoring the question, Crombie renewed his efforts, finally getting the film threaded and onto the take-up reel. This time he gave it an extra turn to make sure it wouldn't unravel again. "There!" He pulled his arms from the jacket and held down the coat again. "Now put the panel back on."

Butch did so, finishing before the transfer boat was halfway to the island. To prevent light from getting into the hole left by the missing bolt, Crombie tore off a piece of his pocket handkerchief and stuffed it into the opening. He then donned his coat again despite feeling warm from his exertions. "Okay, help me move this thing. I want to aim it at the boat." The two of them supported the weight of the camera while kicking at the tripod's legs until the lens faced the oncoming ferry.

After giving the lens a quick polish with the remainder of his handkerchief, Crombie took hold of the crank and began turning. The ideal rate, Gus had told him, was twenty frames per second, but Crombie had no idea how to determine if he was cranking at that speed. He decided to err on the slow side and stretch it out; with seventy-five feet of film in the camera, he would only be able to shoot a couple of minutes today at most.

Butch spat into the water. "I seen photographers," he said, "and that ain't no way to take a picture. You gotta have a flash pan. And what the hell's that crank for, anyway?"

"Shut up," Crombie replied. He began counting off seconds, figuring he would take ten or fifteen of the arriving ferry and save the rest. As he cranked, Crombie watched the small craft with growing excitement. It rose and fell in the rough water, with dark smoke billowing from its tall stack and red-white-and-blue bunting fluttering from its rails. This was exactly what he wanted: *movement!* It was the selling point of the new invention. For the first time, people would be able to see realistic motion—and they would pay handsomely to do so, Crombie was sure. He could almost see money rolling in along with the boat—all of it for him and Gus. Not even Edison would have moving pictures of this day.

Crombie suddenly realized he was still cranking and removed his hand as if the handle had suddenly turned hot. How long had it been? Did he go twenty seconds? Thirty? How much film was left? At least a minute's worth, he hoped.

Stepping back from the camera, he continued to study the ferry boat. Individuals on the crowded deck were now visible, some excitedly waving hats and handkerchiefs, others standing stiff and motionless as if numb from their long journey. He wondered what they thought of the new world they were entering, and turned to look at the same views they might be seeing.

A mile to the north was the skyline of lower Manhattan, with the spire of Trinity Church, the city's tallest structure, visible through the leaden air. A couple of miles east, past Governor's Island, was the low bluff of Brooklyn Heights, and a few hundred yards to the west was the shoreline of Jersey City, New Jersey.

Crombie was sure that many of the immigrants had their eyes directed south, to that marvelous creation of Bartholdi and Eiffel: the Statue of Liberty. For five years, the "Lady in the Harbor" had been welcoming new arrivals to America, a shining beacon of hope. Although a few streaks of green oxide were beginning to color her gown, her copper face still glittered and the electric light in her torch burned brightly three hundred feet in the air—higher than anything in the city itself.

By comparison to Bedloe's Island, on which the glorious statue stood, Ellis Island presented a far less attractive sight, Crombie thought. Two years earlier, the tiny piece of land had been home to the Navy's Fort Gibson, and turning the site into an immigration station had involved practical considerations rather than aesthetic ones. Dirt from city subway excavations was used to enlarge the island from three to fourteen acres, and the channel was dredged to allow passage of ferry boats. Some brick buildings from the abandoned fort remained, clashing stylistically with the new receiving center built to process the immigrants. The enormous two-story building, which covered most of the island, was a wood structure of no particular architectural style; its boxy guard turrets gave the place the appearance of a frontier fort, while other embellishments were suggestive of a Coney Island hotel.

As the ferry drew closer to the island, officials and guards began moving down to the dock, and the brass band fell into formation alongside the flagstone walkway that led to the main building. One of the guards ordered Crombie to move his camera aside and "Get the hell out of the way." With a token assist from Butch, he dragged the machine a few yards back, but kept the lens aimed at the mooring area.

Minutes later, the immigrant transfer boat *John E. Moore* pulled alongside the wharf, with whistles and bells heralding the arrival of the first newcomers to Ellis Island. The brass band promptly added to the din, launching into a spirited, if uneven, rendition of Sousa's "Washington Post" march.

While crewmen tied up to the pier, a gangplank was laid across for the passengers. Several immediately pushed forward, trying to be the first off the boat, but they were unceremoniously shoved back by guards. Two officials boarded the ferry and began a search to select the lucky immigrant who would have the honor of being the first to enter the new station.

Edwin Crombie adjusted the position of his camera, carefully lining it up so that he could film the arrivals as they disembarked. The officials soon ushered a bouncy redheaded girl of about fifteen across the gangplank. Crombie cranked away at his moving-picture machine, capturing forever her first step onto American soil. She was a good subject for the camera, he thought, one audiences would certainly pay to see: pretty features, a broad smile, and a good figure well defined by a tight reefer jacket.

Others then began crossing from the ferryboat to the wharf. For many of them, the short trip across the gangplank was a cumbersome one. Since there were no porters for steerage passengers, they had to carry their own luggage, and some appeared to be carrying or wearing all of their worldly possessions.

Crombie briefly filmed each arrival, turning and stopping the crank as he tried to conserve his precious negative. He forced himself to focus on the filming process, but sensed that his celluloid was turning into pure gold. The moving images he was capturing would be sure to attract paying crowds eager to see the strange costumes of the arrivals and the expressions etched so vividly on their faces.

Crombie spent two or three seconds on each immigrant, until he finally heard the film rattle loose inside his camera, signaling that it was all used up. He lifted his head then and for the first time really looked at the newcomers, seeing them as people instead of subjects. It seemed he could read their stories in their eyes.

One young mother in a frayed tartan cloak carefully negotiated her way onto the wharf. She managed to balance an infant in one arm while dragging a small leather trunk behind her and talking soothingly in Swedish to the two crying toddlers who were tethered to her waist.

A wizened, toothless old man encumbered by several layers of clothing crossed the gangplank with the aid of a knotty cane. At his age, Crombie thought, his chances of surviving the journey hadn't been great, so there must have been a powerful attraction to coming to this country. Looking down at the island's soil, the old man smiled with satisfaction, perhaps thinking that American earth was a good place to be buried.

A few passengers later came a stooped, olive-skinned woman of about sixty years with three young children in tow. She was their grandmother, Crombie assumed, and he wondered what had happened to their parents. The woman wept with what looked like relief, giving the impression that she had accomplished a mission—perhaps to give her grandchildren a start in this new world.

All of the arrivals' faces were full of life: some with hope, some with fright. There were tears of joy and smiles of relief. No longer thinking of the commercial possibilities of his moving-picture machine, Crombie hoped only that the camera adequately captured the humanity in those faces.

There weren't many faces to Marshall Webb's liking. Of the hundred or so immigrants who stepped off the *John E. Moore,* only five or six had the qualities he was seeking. The pickings were slimmer than he had expected, but he held out hope that the next boatloads would carry more prospects.

Webb stood on the fringe of a sullen group of reporters and officials near the slate facade of the building's main entrance. His presence among them went unchallenged. A number of his companions were clearly suffering the aftereffects from New Year's Eve celebrations the night before, and were in no mood for talking. Webb had also carefully chosen an inconspicuous wardrobe, including a black frock coat and matching derby; his appearance was formal enough to appear official, but not fancy enough to attract unwanted attention. An occasional nod or tip of a hat was as much conversation as he had to endure.

Webb had arrived on the island early, giving him a chance to look around the place, speak with a couple of the officers, and establish the impression that he was supposed to be there. Because of his early arrival, the wait for the immigrants had become tedious for him; it was relieved only by the antics of the nervous young man on the wharf playing with something that looked like a cross between a camera and a Gatling gun.

Once all the passengers had disembarked from the transfer boat, they were gathered on the landing. An officer began reading names from the manifest of the steamer *Nevada* and organizing the newcomers into groups of thirty. While they were given instructions on the process they were to follow, an announcement was made to the reporters that ceremonies were about to begin inside.

The redheaded girl who'd been first off the boat was ushered inside, followed by the reporters. Webb trailed along, his eyes on the pretty young girl. She might be the one.

As they went in, Webb was struck by the strong smell of Georgia pine and fresh paint. Construction, he knew, had barely been completed in time for today's opening, and was still going on at some of the outer buildings.

Everyone was led up a broad staircase to Registry Hall on the second floor. This cavernous room was primarily open space, broken only by wire-screen pens and a maze of iron rails that gave the impression of a stockyard. High up, a gallery circled the hall, with uniformed guards pacing around it on patrol.

At the rear of the hall were half a dozen high desks staffed by immigration officials who would ultimately decide whether or not to issue landing cards to the newcomers. One of the clerks relinquished his desk to Colonel John Weber, superintendent of immigration, who wanted to personally register the first arrival. He introduced her to the assemblage as Annie Moore, fifteen years old, formerly of County Cork, Ireland. Weber presented the girl with a ten-dollar gold piece, then launched into a speech of welcome that soon turned into a self-congratulatory recounting of his achievement in establishing the new facility.

As the commissioner droned on, Marshall Webb ruled out Miss Annie Moore as a prospect. That ten-dollar windfall made her too affluent for his purposes; he preferred a girl more desperate for cash. Besides, all this fuss over her might result in continued attention later. Poverty and anonymity were qualities as essential to him as youth and beauty.

After the ceremony was over, the reporters departed with their stories, and the rest of the immigrants were herded in. They left their baggage on the ground floor and proceed upstairs to the hall.

Webb watched as they were processed, and again had the sense of being in a stockyard. Officials treated the newcomers like livestock, putting chalk marks on them like brands, prodding those who moved too slowly with their billy clubs, and bellowing at those who didn't understand English as if they could force them to comprehend by the sheer volume of their shouts.

The immigrants were put through a "hurry up and wait" routine. They were hustled through the aisles from one holding pen to the next, and detained at each one for various inspections and interrogations.

The first stops were for medical examinations, where everyone from infants to the aged were roughly poked and tapped and studied like horses being evaluated by draymen. In addition to checking for signs of heart disease and lung problems, everything from scalps to eyes to fingernails were examined. All diagnoses were written in chalk on the newcomer's outer clothes.

Those who passed the medical tests went on to be quizzed by immigration officers. Webb heard the same questions again and again: "Have you ever been in prison?" . . . "Who paid your ship fare?" . . . "Is anyone meeting you?" . . . "Do you have any money?" An affirmative answer to the latter query, Webb knew, would likely result in some of that money ending up in the officer's pocket.

It took a couple of hours for the process to be completed, during which hundreds of additional immigrants arrived, ferried to the island from the steamships anchored in the harbor. As they crowded into Registry Hall, the noise became more than Marshall Webb cared to hear. The cries of squalling children echoed throughout the room, above a rumbling undertone of hundreds of voices speaking a dozen languages; all the while, orders from guards to "Move!" or "Hurry!" punctuated the din. There were other shouts, too, as enterprising money changers, railroad agents, and vendors hawked their services and wares to the newcomers.

Webb also noticed as the hall filled with people that the fresh pine smell was gone, replaced by less agreeable scents; some were from the smoky coal-burning furnaces that heated the room, while others emanated from the immigrants themselves. Steerage conditions aboard ships didn't allow for much bathing, and ripe body odors began to hang heavily in the close air.

It was with relief that Webb saw the first immigrants begin the final stage of processing, lining up before the high desks where they would learn whether or not they would be admitted to the United States. The vast majority of those in line were of little interest to Webb, but whenever an unaccompanied teenaged girl reached one of the desks, he paid close attention.

Finally, he got the signal he'd been waiting for. An officer caught Webb's eye and nodded toward the young girl to whom he had just issued one of the prized landing cards.

Maybe too young, was Webb's first thought as she turned around. The blond girl was dressed in a childish style, wearing a tight, blue Zouave jacket over a checked gray dress that reached only to the tops of her high button shoes. Pinned to the back of her head was a small yellow straw bonnet that nearly matched the color of her long curls.

His second appraisal was more thorough, and he was pleased to realize that she was a bit older than she first appeared. Her slender body was definitely starting to take the shape of a woman. As the girl left the desk, with her entry pass clutched tightly in her hand, he noted that her face had the joy of a child in it. She was at that perfect transition point between girl and woman.

Webb quickly moved to intercept her as she headed to the exit door. Almost knocking over a vendor who was aggressively selling fried oysters, Webb stepped in front of the girl.

She stopped and looked up at him. "Yes, sir?"

For a moment, Webb couldn't bring himself to speak. He was transfixed by her startling blue eyes, which had the color and sparkle of sapphires.

"Sir?" The girl still stared up at him expectantly.

Webb forced himself to take his gaze off her eyes and pulled a small notebook from his pocket. In his best official voice, he said, "Just a few more questions if you don't mind, miss."

"I do not mind." She smiled a little more brightly, clearly eager to please. Webb noticed that she showed no sign of weariness, appearing as fresh as if she'd come from a leisure cruise instead of a long steerage crossing.

"Your name, please?"

"Christina van der Waals." Her pronounced accent was as Dutch as the name.

Webb didn't ask for the spelling. He'd rechristen her with a simple American name anyway—Katie, perhaps. "Where are you from?"

"Amsterdam."

Webb again hesitated. He had noticed the fine spray of freckles that dotted the bridge of her button nose. What an adorable face, he thought. And her skin—it was so smooth he almost wished he had thought to impersonate a doctor so he could touch her cheek.

Apparently a bit worried by his silence, Christina volunteered, "My English it is very good, and will be more good when I am staying in this wonderful country."

With a smile, Webb replied, "Your English is excellent. How old are you, miss?"

"I will be fifteen years old in May."

A good age, thought Webb. "And you've come to America alone?"

"Yes."

"Where are your parents?"

For the first time, Christina's smile faltered. "I have no parents. My aunt sent me here."

An orphan—perfect! Webb glanced back at the officer who'd alerted him to her. He had certainly earned his two-dollar bribe. Turning back to the young Dutch girl, he asked, "What will you be doing in this country? Do you have a job?"

"No, sir!" she blurted. "No job!"

Some of the other newcomers must have told her the correct answer to that question. To keep foreigners from taking "American" jobs, Congress had recently passed a law that only immigrants with no job prospects could be admitted. Many newcomers, eager to show their willingness to work, answered incorrectly and found themselves on ships back to their homelands.

"Very well," said Webb. "What do you *hope* to do?"

"I would like to work in a flower shop. Or to sing." The girl pushed away a lock of golden hair that had fallen over her eye. "My cousin Hendrika is a famous singer at the Baylor Opera House in New York. Her name here is Liz Luck. You have heard of her?"

The fact that the girl had a local relation might be a slight problem, thought Webb. "Liz Luck," he repeated. "I hear she has the most beautiful voice in the city." Christina beamed, and he was happy that his lie brought her such pleasure. "Will you be staying with your cousin?"

"Yes. I wrote to Hendrika. She will meet me and take me to her home."

Webb thought for a moment. "That's all the questions we have for you. Welcome to America."

"Thank you!" The girl flashed another smile, then almost bounced away to go meet her cousin.

As he watched her leave, Webb forgot there were hundreds of other people in the building. Katie, as he already thought of her, was perfect. He could do very well with her indeed.

CHAPTER 3

"How could you do something so foolish?" Gus Sehlinger's eyes were ablaze behind his tiny gold spectacles. "If you do such stupid things, you will ruin everything!"

"Ruin?" seethed Edwin Crombie. "I'm the one who's *building* everything."

Sehlinger flushed and his snowy beard quivered, giving him the appearance of an apoplectic Santa Claus. "Forgive the failing memory of an old man. I did not remember *you* building this camera."

Sehlinger was almost seventy, but Crombie knew there was nothing wrong with his partner's memory. He also knew that Sehlinger liked to use the forty-year difference in their ages to make him feel like an errant child. "I'm building a *business,*" Crombie replied. "Any mechanic can put together a camera."

"Mechanic!" Sehlinger let loose a guttural stream of his native German. The words appeared to leave a trail of smoke from his lips as his breath steamed in the unheated carriage house.

Crombie was happily ignorant of the language. He leaned back, a satisfied smirk twitching his lips; it wasn't often that he succeeded in getting under his partner's skin. When Sehlinger paused for air, Crombie asked him, "Whose name is that on the sign?"

Sehlinger made an exaggerated show of looking around the cluttered workshop. Plain wood benches lined the walls, all of them piled high with magic lanterns, stereoscopes, and other picture-viewing devices in various states of disassembly. Miscellaneous gears, sprockets, and springs were scattered about, some on the benches, others on the hard-packed dirt floor. Sehlinger finally directed his view to the elaborate brass plaque tacked to the lintel of the side door—exactly where he knew it was. He then made a production of cleaning his spectacles before putting them back on his round, red nose. Squinting, he read aloud:

American Kinemascope Company

Edwin D. Crombie, President

Looking at Crombie again, he said, "I forget, Mister President: What does the *D* stand for?"

Crombie regretted having once admitted to Sehlinger that he'd added the initial himself because he thought it appeared more dignified. "Nothing," he answered softly.

It was Sehlinger's turn to smile. "Ah, yes. Now I recall."

Enough of this nonsense, decided Crombie. "The point is, Gus, I have a lot invested in seeing this business succeed, and—" He saw Sehlinger open his mouth to interrupt, and cut him off. "We both have a lot invested, I know. But I did put in the money—"

Sehlinger refused to be silenced. "Where would you be without my camera? And is your money more important than what I am risking?"

Crombie replied calmly, "I want this to work for *both* of us. We can be rich men, Gus, if we're smart."

"Eddie, Eddie. How can you take the camera out in the open like that? What if Edison finds out?" Sehlinger shook his head. "So foolish."

Resisting the urge to remind his partner that he hated to be called "Eddie," Crombie answered, "Who would even know what it was? I only told the Ellis Island officials that I was a photographer; they have no way of knowing that I was taking *moving* pictures."

"*You* a photographer!" Sehlinger snorted. "Yah, and I'm a chorus girl." He slowly rose from the overturned milk can that he'd used as a stool. "Let me see if you have broken anything." The old man was still a few feet from the camera when he spotted the piece of cloth stuffed in the bolt hole. "What is this?"

"Don't pull it out," warned Crombie. "The film's still inside."

Sehlinger poked at the ragged bit of handkerchief with a wrinkled finger. "Where is the bolt that belongs here?"

"Lost it."

"Lost it! You think my machine will work with you losing parts? This is a precision instrument!"

"It's a damned *bolt,* Gus. Put in another and it'll be good as new." Crombie shook his head; he could never understand why Sehlinger treated a collection of springs and sprockets as if it were a favorite grandchild.

After a meticulous inspection, Sehlinger grudgingly admitted, "It does not appear that you did any other damage." His disappointment was obvious; no further damage meant there were no more reasons to chide his partner.

The door from the main house creaked open, and Crombie's eight-year-old daughter pushed through. She carefully balanced a tray that held a blue porcelain teapot and one cup. "Mama said to bring Mr. Sehlinger some tea."

The sight of his only child brought a smile to Crombie's face. While Sehlinger was often the bane of his existence, Emily was always his joy.

Sehlinger also beamed at the coltish girl. "Your mama is a very thoughtful lady. And you, my dear, are a little princess."

Emily wrinkled her nose in disgust and Crombie stifled a chuckle. His daughter didn't like being called a princess any more than he liked being called "Eddie." Emily's dream was to be a cowgirl when she grew up, and she often wore the Annie Oakley outfit that she had on now.

After she placed the tray atop an empty packing crate, Crombie asked her hopefully, "Did Mama say anything about bringing me a beer?"

She answered over her shoulder on her way back to the house, "No."

Too bad, he thought; Sehlinger's company was almost tolerable after a beer or two. The door had nearly closed behind Emily when he called after her, "Tell Mama we'll need the pantry again!"

"Yes, Papa."

To his partner, Crombie said, "Since we have the film, we might as well develop it."

Before pouring the tea, Sehlinger held his aged hands over the pot to warm them. "*We* develop it? You mean *me,* of course."

"There's a photography studio not far from here on Atlantic Avenue. I could take it there, if you prefer."

Sehlinger muttered a few unpleasant-sounding words of German, then gave the response Crombie expected. "I will do it. But be so kind as to permit me a cup of tea first, please."

After two cups—the second one out of spite, Crombie was sure—Sehlinger clamped an empty black briar pipe between his teeth and got to work. After draping an old horse blanket over the camera to keep out the light, he carefully removed the film and placed it securely in an empty wooden paint box.

Both men then went into the main house. Since the carriage house was too cold for film to develop properly, and using a heater was too dangerous with the chemicals that were involved, Crombie's wife allowed her pantry to be used as a darkroom. While Sehlinger went into the pantry to mix his developing bath among the pickles and canned goods, Crombie sneaked out a glass of lager and retired to the parlor to await the results.

As he waited, Crombie found himself engaged in a rare bout of uncertainty. The faces that he'd seen at Ellis Island had been so human, so alive, with strong emotions etched so clearly upon them. Could they really be captured forever on a strip of celluloid? Could moments of time be repeated again and again simply by running a piece of film past an electric lamp?

Crombie settled deeper into a plush armchair and put his feet upon an ottoman. The parlor was a cozy one, with a thick velvet carpet, polished mahogany woodwork, and upholstery dripping in fringe and tassels. Every room of the two-story frame house—one of the newer homes on Brooklyn's Nostrand Avenue—had a similar feel of utter comfort to it. But if this new invention didn't work, comfort would have to give way to survival. Although he would admit it to no one else, not even his wife, Crombie's savings were running out.

Carrying a fresh cup of tea and sucking at his empty pipe, Sehlinger joined Crombie in the parlor. "The print is drying."

"How does it look?" asked Crombie, realizing that he sounded more anxious than he'd intended.

Sehlinger didn't appear to notice. He pulled an ornate gold watch from the pocket of his tweed jacket and answered, "We will know in twenty minutes."

In part to convince himself, Crombie said, "I think we're really going to have something, Gus." He brought to mind the images of the day before. "Imagine people in Pittsburgh or Chicago being able to see the Atlantic Ocean—in motion, with the waves breaking, ships sailing by, seagulls flying overhead. They may never see those things in real life, so they'll happily pay to see moving pictures of them." His confidence returning, Crombie said, "Gus, we are going to be rich men."

Sehlinger smiled wryly. "I wish I were as young as you so I could enjoy the wealth." With a dismissive wave of his hand, he went on, "But for me, I will be content to know that this invention will make life better for people. Think of how much they can learn from moving pictures. A doctor can study surgery, a dancer can learn ballet. People will be able to learn about every part of the world without stepping foot on a train or a ship."

Crombie decided to bring up a subject he'd been meaning to discuss with his partner. "Whether we make these pictures for education or amusement, we'll need to protect them."

"What do you mean, protect?"

"I mean copyrights. I checked, and there's no legal protection for moving pictures yet. So what we—*you*—have to do is make a paper print of every frame of film. Then each frame can be copyrighted with the Library of Congress like a regular photograph."

Sehlinger peered over his spectacles. "Have you gone mad? We cannot do that. To make our pictures public now would destroy us before we make a single cent. Edison can*not* find out what we are doing!"

"I agree, Gus. We won't send the prints in yet; we'll just make 'em and file 'em. Listen, all I want to do is get a few things filmed and build up an inventory. Then, before we're ready to go public, we'll send the paper prints for copyright. That way nobody else can use our pictures—not even Edison."

Finding no way to argue, Sehlinger checked his watch again and stood. "Let me see if we even have any pictures."

Crombie hadn't considered that. What if light had gotten inside when he had the camera open? It could all be ruined. He worried for ten minutes before Sehlinger returned with a handful of film strips and a magnifying glass.

"Your photography is poor," the old man said with some pleasure. "But my camera worked perfectly."

Crombie eagerly took the magnifier and one of the film strips.

He held the three-foot ribbon of celluloid to a window for more light and began a frame-by-frame examination.

The first image was of the transfer boat *John E. Moore* making its approach to Ellis Island. Although he wouldn't admit it aloud, he saw that Sehlinger was right about his photographic skills. The ferry was in the upper left corner of the frame, its smokestack almost cut off. But the image was clear.

He grabbed some of the other strips, anxious to see how the immigrants' faces came out. Again, the images were clear, but the subjects were often in one corner or another of the frame. "You know what we need," he said, "is a better way to aim that camera. It's too damn heavy."

"It is lighter than Edison's."

"I know; I know. But it's still so heavy that one person can barely budge it. So all we can film is whatever happens to pass in front of the lens. We need to be able to aim the camera to follow the subject."

"Ach, you do not know what you are talking about. There must be adequate weight for stability. Otherwise, the camera will vibrate from the cranking and the images will not be clear." He proceeded to lecture Crombie about exposure times and film speed, but Crombie was no longer listening.

As he continued to study the film, Crombie realized that time *could* be captured. He found himself feeling exactly as he had when he was on the wharf, watching the newcomers first step off the boat. Their expressions were so clear that he again felt as if he could read their thoughts. "I have an idea, Gus."

Sehlinger grumbled, "Something to make more work for me, no doubt."

Crombie handed the magnifying glass and film strips to his partner. "No, it's part of *my* job—advertising. How's this for a slogan: 'Is your relative here?' Imagine how many people have relatives coming to America. Wouldn't they want a chance to see their arrival? Or how about the ones who came to Ellis Island themselves? I'll bet they'd be happy to pay a nickel to relive their first steps on American soil."

Sehlinger looked at some of the frames and slowly smiled. "When I came with my wife, rest her soul, it was to Castle Garden. We were so happy to be in America. I've been here almost fifteen years, Edwin, and I still think that was my happiest moment in this country. I would certainly like to see what we looked like that day." He looked at Crombie. "Others will, too. You were smart to do what you did yesterday. But next time you will tell me before you do such a thing, yes?"

Crombie agreed not to take the camera out again without telling his partner first, and they both settled silently back into their chairs.

"I wish I could have taken more pictures," Crombie finally said. "We need a camera that can hold more film. Or a way to change reels outside. I had the damnedest time trying to get the film back on the roller when it came off."

"Why did it come off? What did you do?"

"You know how hard it's been to get film. I was trying to save every frame, and I took too much off the take-up reel." Before his partner could scold him for the mishap, Crombie suggested, "Maybe you could get some more negative from Edison."

Sehlinger's teeth tightened on the pipe stem. "I am a scientist, not a thief."

"You take his ideas. Why not a little piece of film here or there?"

"*His* ideas! All he thinks of is his phonograph. I do the work on his moving-picture machine." Sehlinger was sputtering. "First you insult me by asking me to steal. Now you don't even credit me with what *is* mine—my ideas."

Crombie quickly said the right things to mollify Sehlinger, but silently wished that he really could find a mechanic to replace him.

CHAPTER 4

Almost every city and town in America had at least one opera house, Marshall Webb knew, but few of them ever presented the works of Verdi or Mozart. "Opera House" was used as a name for entertainment venues ranging from burlesque houses and brothels to concert saloons and dance halls. Webb had made some inquiries and learned that the Baylor Opera House was probably not the kind of cultural establishment that young Christina van der Waals imagined.

From his seat aboard the lurching Sixth Avenue el, Webb stared out the window at one of Manhattan's most notorious neighborhoods. A light, steady snow fell, cloaking the soot and cinders on the ground below, but even the shroud of white couldn't make this area look clean.

As the elevated train progressed north of Twentieth Street, man-fishers appeared in the second-floor windows of hotels and bagnios. These scantily dressed prostitutes did their brazen best to attract the attention of men in passing trains. Some held placards listing the prices for their affections, while others pulled aside their garments to give previews of what could be had for less than a dollar. The fact that it was mid-afternoon did nothing to inhibit the whores, for the Tenderloin—often called "Satan's Circus" by preachers who sermonized against the vice district—was their territory.

Webb got off the el at Thirtieth Street and adjusted his silk muffler to keep the biting cold from the back of his neck. The fallen snow wasn't deep on the sidewalk, but there was enough to be slippery, and he trod cautiously. Slipping was the only hazard that concerned Webb, for this was the better part of the Tenderloin and its streets were safer than most in the city. Recognizing that violence and thievery were bad for business, the north-end establishments hired enforcers to ensure that their turf was kept safe for "respectable vice." Here, a man could get drunk with little fear of being drugged, play games of chance that weren't rigged, or have his sexual urges slaked without having his watch and billfold stolen.

Despite the relative safety, there were few other pedestrians braving the weather this day. Webb passed only half a dozen men and one shivering newsboy before arriving at the Baylor Opera House.

The three-story yellow-brick structure was in the shadow of the el between Thirty-first and Thirty-second Streets. A gilt-trimmed marquee and garish posters on either side of the entrance advertised:

NEW FRENCH REVUE

The Latest Exotic Dances!
The Most Beautiful Chorines Direct From Paris!

Webb walked up to the ticket booth, which was staffed by a prim silver-haired woman who looked as if she should have been home knitting booties for her grandchildren. Instead, she was absorbed in the latest issue of the *Police Gazette*. Without glancing up, she told Webb, "Twenty-five cents, sir."

"I'm not here for the show. I'm looking for one of your, uh, singers: Miss Liz Luck."

Her eyes still on the pink pages of the sensationalistic weekly, the ticket clerk said, "Singer? Miss Luck works here, but she's no singer."

That came as no surprise to Webb, who didn't think much singing went on in the "opera" house. "What *does* she do?"

"Dance. But if you want to see her, you'll have to come tonight, after ten. She won't be on till then."

"I'm not looking to see her dance. I only need to talk to her. Could you tell me where she lives?"

The woman chuckled. "No, sir. Even if I knew, I couldn't tell you that. Have to protect our artists' privacy, you understand."

"Certainly. But this is a family matter."

Finally looking up, she studied Webb for a moment. "Well . . . I really don't know where she lives. But one of the other ladies might. Don't have many working this afternoon." She pursed her lips. "Try Eva; I believe she's friendly with Miss Luck."

"Is Eva here?"

"Yes, sir. Working the boxes. Stage left, most likely."

Webb put a quarter on the counter.

"Fifty cents for a box, sir."

The extra quarter was probably compensation for having interrupted her reading, but he paid and went inside.

The Baylor's small lobby was papered in solid red and decorated with prints of women in various stages of undress. The stained carpeting had long ago lost all traces of its original pattern, and the oil-burning chandelier overhead was missing several of its decorative globes. Webb thought the place looked familiar, but there were many theatres just like this one, and he wasn't sure if he'd been here before.

He climbed a narrow staircase to the balcony and found an unoccupied box with two armchairs. The stench of body odors—and bodily fluids—was so bad that he found the smoke wafting up from the seats below to be almost refreshing. Ignoring comfort, Webb tried to sit lightly on one of the chairs to minimize contact with whatever substances the cushion might have absorbed. He looked over the rail and saw that the crowd in the lower level was sparse, with only twenty or thirty men scattered among a couple of hundred seats. Near the stage, an upright piano and bass fiddle comprised the orchestra; the musicians played with little enthusiasm and even less accuracy.

On stage, three buxom women in circus tights performed an acrobatic act that involved combining their limbs into the unlikeliest positions. Most of the men cheered loudly at their antics and occasionally tossed coins at their feet.

A few men, however, paid more attention to the women in the audience. In the row below him, Webb saw a female head bobbing over a man's lap, while not far away, another couple were sprawled across three seats, engaged in their own acrobatics.

Within five minutes of his arrival, a plump brunette of about thirty, wearing only striped stockings and a black sateen corset stretched nearly to the breaking point, whisked into the box. Her rouge and powder were so thick that they might have been applied with a trowel. She immediately hopped onto Webb's lap, sinking him deep into the cushion. He wasn't sure which contact was more objectionable, that of the soiled chair or the pressing weight of the painted woman.

Tickling Webb's whiskers, she said, "What a handsome gentleman. Tall, too. I *like* 'em tall."

Webb gagged momentarily on the cheap perfume that seemed to emanate from her fleshy body. "Are you Eva?" he coughed.

"I'll bet you're tall everywhere." Her hand dropped to his crotch. "I'm Annie, dearie. Anything Eva can do, I can do better—*much* better." As if to prove it, her fingers began a deft massage. "Only two dollars for a private room—and that includes my *complete* attention."

Webb found, with more annoyance than pleasure, that her practiced hand was starting to bring him to attention. "Thank you, but it's Eva I want to see."

Annie gave him a painful squeeze that immediately reversed the effect of her previous ministrations. "Your loss, dearie." She stood and pulled the top of her stocking away from her thigh. "But you'll put a dime in my stocking for luck, won't you?"

Relieved to have her bulk off his lap, Webb pulled out a quarter and pressed it against her skin. "Will you tell Eva to come see me?" When Annie agreed, he let the coin fall into her stocking, and she left with a smile.

As he waited for Eva, Webb again directed his attention to the floor show. The acrobats had been replaced by a line of six chorus girls purportedly doing the cancan. The music was that of the salacious French dance, but their dancing consisted of little more than leg kicks and hoisted skirts. A couple of the girls had trouble lifting their thick legs, but the skirts came up readily enough. Since none of them wore undergarments, they were rewarded with coins for almost every lift of their dresses.

"You must have heard good things about me," said a smoky female voice behind him.

Webb pulled his gaze away from the entertainment below and focused on his visitor. Although dressed basically the same as Annie, this woman was younger and prettier, with clear skin and radiant auburn hair. She wore her corset in a different style than

Annie, using it as a shelf on which to rest her full breasts rather than confine them.

"Eva?" he asked.

She eased onto his lap. "That's me."

Trying in vain to ignore the bare breasts inches from his eyes, he said, "You're a . . . you're a friend of Liz Luck, I understand?"

"Did Liz tell you to see me? She's a dear." Eva began gently running a finger over Webb's forehead.

"No." Webb tried harder to keep his eyes on her face. "I'm looking for Miss Luck. They told me downstairs you might be able to tell me where she lives."

The sweet facade on Eva's face was quickly replaced by wariness. "What do you want with Liz? She don't entertain at home."

"I'm not looking for entertainment. It's a family matter."

Studying him, she asked, "You a copper?"

"No." Webb smiled and plucked a silver dollar from his vest pocket. "Would a cop be willing to pay you?"

After a moment, she answered, "No, a cop would more 'n likely use his billy club."

He pulled open the top of her stocking. "Do you know where Miss Luck lives?"

She nodded. "Twenty-eighth Street, between Sixth and Seventh. Next to the Gold Mine Pawnshop—you can't miss it. Name you got to ask for is Gleason. Liz Luck is only her stage name."

Webb tucked the dollar under her stocking and was surprised to find that he enjoyed the brief contact with her skin.

"Only a dollar more," Eva coaxed, "and we can go to a private room."

Webb shook his head. "Thank you, but I really have to go."

As he left the theater, Webb began to tally all the expenses he was incurring: Two dollars for the Ellis Island official who'd pointed out Christina van der Waals, one dollar to Eva, and a quarter each to Annie and the ticket taker. He'd have to remember to get Lawrence Pritchard to reimburse him.

The way turf was divvied up in the Tenderloin, with specific streets catering to particular vices, Twenty-eighth Street was the domain of the gambling houses. And since gamblers often needed quick cash, pawnshops were conveniently located along that street as well.

As Eva had predicted, Webb found the Gold Mine Pawnshop without any difficulty. A nickel to the proprietor—which would be added to Pritchard's bill—got him directions to Liz Luck's home.

The third-floor walkup was in a dilapidated building that appeared to have been built by a drunken carpenter. Almost nothing was straight: the ceilings sagged, floors were buckled, and walls bulged from crumbled plaster pushing out against faded wallpaper. The only redeeming quality was that almost no daylight reached into the hallway and the gas jets were unlit. Struggling to see in the darkness, Webb finally spotted the door to apartment 3B.

His knock achieved two results. One was to cause a chunk of plaster to fall onto the hall floor. The other was to stir a man inside to yell, "Get the damn door, would ya? I'm tryin' to sleep!"

Light, rapid footsteps approached from within, and a female voice asked softly through the flimsy door, "Who is it?"

"Immigration Bureau," answered Webb, electing to maintain the pretense of being an Ellis Island official.

"You must have the wrong place."

"I'm looking for . . ." Webb struggled to recall the Dutch girl's real name; he had already decided that it would be "Katie" from now on. Finally remembering, he said, "Christina van der Waals."

The door cracked open a few inches, and a bright blue eye peered at him. *"Christina?"*

"Yes, ma'am. She arrived at Ellis Island on Friday. I'm doing a follow-up visit. You're her cousin, I presume—Miss Luck? She mentioned she'd be staying with you."

"Yes, that's me." The door opened a few more inches, enough for Webb to see an attractive woman of about twenty, with a slim figure and hair the same shade of blond as Katie's—Christina's. "Come in. But quietly, please. My husband is sleeping." She had a hint of the same accent as Christina, too, but it was almost masked by a New York brusqueness.

"Thank you." Webb stepped inside and removed his derby. No offer was made to take his hat or coat, but it was just as well, for the temperature inside wasn't much warmer than outside. He cast a quick eye around the small apartment. Faded prints, mostly of flowers or birds, adorned the walls in the unlikeliest spots—probably to cover up holes, Webb assumed. The parlor furniture was sparse, cheap, and worn.

Almost as worn was the flannel lounging robe draped around Liz Luck. "There must be some mistake." She tightened the belt and modestly raised her hand to hold the collar closed. "Christina's in Holland." Luck's brow furrowed and Webb saw fine creases around her eyes. "Are you *sure* you have the right girl?"

"Yes, ma'am." Although he knew the details by heart, Webb pulled out his notebook and read, "Christina van der Waals. Arrived January first from Amsterdam. Fourteen years old—fifteen in May. Blond hair, blue eyes." Looking at Luck again, he saw that her eyes were almost as blue as Christina's, but without the sparkle. He found himself wishing that he had met Liz Luck when she was Christina's age.

"Yes, that's my cousin. But she isn't here. I haven't had so much as a letter from her in almost a year." She shook her head. "I just don't understand."

It was Webb's turn to be puzzled. "She said that she wrote you—and that you would be meeting her to take her home."

The same gruff voice that he'd heard earlier called from an adjacent room, "Who the hell is it?"

"Immigration!" Luck answered. To Webb she said, "I wish Christina *was* here. I haven't seen her in six years, since I left Holland myself." She held her hands open. "But she isn't. You're *sure* she's in New York?"

Webb nodded, but was starting to feel uncertain himself—not about having seen Christina, but about her whereabouts. He expected the girl to be safely here by now. Where could she have been for the past three days?

The bedroom door opened and a small bull of a man with a magnificent red walrus mustache came out wearing the uniform of the New York City Police Department. "I better go in," he grumbled. "My shift started an hour ago, and I can't sleep with all this talk anyway."

"I'm sorry," Luck said, biting her lip. "Warren, this is . . ."

"Marshall Webb." The name came out before he had a chance to think of a false one. The sight of the uniform had caught Webb by surprise.

Luck continued the introductions, "This is Mr. Webb from immigration. Mr. Webb, this is my husband, Warren Gleason."

Gleason took his navy greatcoat from a peg by the door and eyed Webb suspiciously. "What is it you want?"

Webb returned the scrutiny. He couldn't tell if the stern expression on Gleason's pasty face was normal or if it had been adopted as part of the uniform. As for the uniform itself, there was a mustard stain on the tunic and the buttons and badge needed to be polished. "I was looking for Christina van der Waals, Miss Luck's cousin. But there seems to be a mix-up." He regretted the immigration story, but there was no way out of it now.

"Warren," Luck said meekly, "Mr. Webb says Christina came to Ellis Island Friday. What if something happened to her? Maybe you could ask about her at the station house."

"Immigration is federal now," he answered, placing a tall helmet on his bullet head. "New York police don't have no authority."

Luck turned to Webb. "I haven't seen Christina in so long. Could you tell me what she looked like? Is she all grown up? Is she pretty?"

Warren Gleason didn't give Webb a chance to answer. "I'm goin' and that means *you're* goin'. This is a respectable household. Can't be leaving my wife with another man." His only courtesy was to hold the door open.

Webb began to say a polite good-bye to Liz Luck. He barely had time to see the tears welling in her eyes before Gleason prodded him out the door.

CHAPTER 5

"Perhaps next time we can meet in some cozy opium den in Chinatown," Lawrence Pritchard said, surveying the squalid interior of Bassett's Tavern. The Mulberry Street dive was similar to the Hole, but with a less pleasant ambience. Pritchard held up his glass of port, eyeing it skeptically in the scant light. Scowling at what he saw, he used his handkerchief to clean a smudge from the rim before bringing the glass to his lips. He grimaced, the taste obviously no more agreeable than anything else in the place. "Why on earth can't we meet near my office—in a nice hotel bar, with waiters and napkins?"

"Because every bar on Park Row is full of editors and publishers," Marshall Webb answered. "You know I can't be seen with you."

Pritchard smiled tightly. "I'll try not to take that personally."

"You know it's not personal," said Webb. "I've told you before: if anyone from *Harper's Weekly* finds out about my sideline with you, they'll fire me."

"You make more money writing for me than you do for *Harper's*. You only get a piece in there about once a month, right? And they don't even give you writing credit—I've never seen your name in print. So which job is the sideline?"

"It's not about money. It's about reputation. *Harper's* is a respectable publication. What I do for you is . . ." Webb held his hands open. "Let's just say my family would not approve. I've disappointed them enough in the past; I don't intend to bring them any further shame."

Pritchard drank some more wine, this time pouring it into his mouth so that his lips didn't touch the glass. "I think you still like these hellholes, and *that's* why you insist on meeting in places like this. Oh—" He reached into a pocket of his overcoat. "I thought you might like a copy of your latest." He pulled out a thin paper-bound publication and handed it to Webb.

Unfolding it, Webb strained to read the cover in the dim light:

Pritchard's Dime Library Presents

THE COURAGEOUS CAVALRYMAN

or

How Sergeant Frazier Saved The Day

by David A. Byrd

"Good artwork," Webb commented on the lurid full-color illustration of a Union cavalryman about to slash a Confederate soldier with his saber. He quickly thumbed through the thirty-two-page novel and handed it back to Pritchard.

"Don't you want it?" the editor asked.

"No. I know what happens. I wrote it." Webb reached into his pocket. "I have something for you." He gave Pritchard three sheets of foolscap covered with meticulous handwriting. "This is the new one I was telling you about."

Pritchard made a facetious show of hefting the pages. "Where's the rest of it?"

"It'll be a while. Months maybe."

"*Months?* I need a new story every two weeks!"

"You have other writers."

"They don't sell as well as you."

Webb was pleased at the compliment. "Sales will be even better for this one. And it's going to be a *real* novel—I want it clothbound."

Pritchard removed his pince-nez and rubbed the bridge of his nose as if Webb had just punched him on it. "Do you have any idea what it takes to print a clothbound book? The money is in dime novels: easy to print, cheap, available at any newsstand." Putting the eyeglasses back on, he looked at the top sheet that Webb had given him and read the title aloud: "*From Amsterdam to New Amsterdam*. Hmm, I'm not sure I like that."

"I'm not sure *I* like it either, but I can't write without a title. We can change it later."

Pritchard continued to read, his thin voice barely reaching across the table:

"The welcome sight of the Statue of the Liberty signaled that the long, trying voyage across the stormy sea was at last coming to an end. But for Katie, the young golden-haired Dutch girl, a new journey was about to begin. She would be starting a new life in the New World."

He went on to skim the rest before handing the pages back to Webb. "Not bad for a start. But you'll have to convince me that there's enough for a book."

"It'll be a wonderful rags-to-riches story—"

"Like Horatio Alger?"

"More like Dickens." As soon as the words were out, Webb realized how immodest he sounded. "The story, not the writing. Anyway, Katie's an orphan, new to the country, no money, no job. She comes to New York City full of hope but completely naive. How is she going to survive? What will she do? Every reader will be pulling for her to make good. And here's what's going to make the story unique: It's going to be factual. I'm going to keep track of what Katie actually does, and tell her true story."

"Just like you watched a real Civil War battle for *The Courageous Cavalryman*?" Pritchard kidded.

Webb smiled; he'd been a toddler when the war ended. "No, and I didn't witness a scalping to write *Chief Wingo on the Warpath*, either."

Pritchard swirled his remaining wine, then put it aside without drinking. "I'm not necessarily opposed to publishing a full-length book. We have done a few clothbound. But I'll have to see more. When do you think you can get me the first five or six chapters?"

"I'm not sure. I've run into a bit of a problem: Katie seems to have vanished somewhere between Ellis Island and Manhattan."

"Vanished?"

Webb nodded. "She was expecting to be picked up by her cousin, a dancer who goes by the name Liz Luck. Last week I went to see the cousin. As far as she knew, Katie was still in Holland. I talked to her briefly again yesterday—still no sign of

Katie, and the cousin seems to think I'm playing some kind of cruel joke on her by telling her she's here in America."

"She's been missing *ten days?*"

"Yes," Webb answered grimly. He was acutely aware of how long that was—and of what might befall a girl who was alone on the streets of New York for any length of time. He had wanted to look for Christina immediately after he'd spoken with Liz Luck, but *Harper's* had other plans for him. With only a day's notice, the publication decided that he simply had to go to the state capital to interview party leaders about their picks for the presidential nominations. Webb had had to endure five dreary days in Albany, listening to dreary politicians, all the while hoping that Christina would turn up safely at her cousin's apartment.

"You'd better give up on her, then," Pritchard said. "Find another girl. There are a million and a half people in this city, and boatloads more coming in every day. Your story idea is a good one. Simply find another girl for your main character."

Webb couldn't abandon his first choice as easily as Pritchard did. "No," he said emphatically. "There's too much about Katie that I like: coming from Amsterdam to the city that was once called New Amsterdam . . . arriving on New Year's Day to start her new life . . . being one of the first newcomers to set foot on Ellis Island." Webb thought for a moment. No, those circumstances weren't the qualities that he liked about Christina van der Waals. It was the way her face radiated hope and optimism. And the determination that glittered in her stunning blue eyes. "There's just something special about this girl. I have the feeling that her life is going to be a story worth telling."

"Not much of a story if she doesn't turn up again."

"She will," said Webb with more hope than confidence. "Besides, obstacles are good for drama—the more she has to overcome, the more compelling her tale."

"So where do you go from here?"

Webb hesitated. He'd been trying to determine the answer to that question ever since he came back to the city. "I have a couple of ideas," he finally said, wishing desperately that he could come up with a single one.

CHAPTER 6

It was less than twenty miles, almost due west, from downtown Manhattan to the Orange Valley in New Jersey, but it took Marshall Webb more than two hours to complete the multi-stage journey. First, he boarded a streetcar that carried him across lower Manhattan to Pier 30 at the foot of Chambers Street. There, he caught the late-departing Pavonia ferry across the North River to the Erie railroad depot in Jersey City. Next was a slow train to Orange, past the factories and office buildings of Newark, and, finally, a wobbly, two-horse omnibus bound for the rural village of West Orange.

Although he knew his visit to West Orange was a long shot, there was a chance that it might help him track down Christina van der Waals. And, at this point, Webb figured that he couldn't afford to let any possibility be ignored, no matter how slim the odds.

As the jostling carriage neared his destination, Webb was struck by the difference between the city he'd left this morning and the peaceful New Jersey countryside. The quiet Orange Valley was dabbed with patches of recent snow, and the ice-coated limbs of bare oak trees shivered in the brisk air. It was a view that could have appeared in a Currier and Ives Christmas print. All that intruded on the pastoral scene was a cluster of boxy brick buildings, one of them three stories tall.

The omnibus creaked to a halt in front of the larger structure, which housed the main offices and workshops of Thomas Edison's new laboratory.

Webb hopped off the coach, the lethargy of the long journey quickly lifting, and went to the front entrance. There, a nervous male receptionist asked his business; Webb replied that he was here to see Mr. Edison, and presented his card:

Marshall Webb

HARPER'S WEEKLY
Harper & Brothers, New York

Since Webb was merely an occasional contributor, the publication didn't provide him so much as a desk in their office, but they did provide him with a calling card that often worked like magic in opening doors and loosening tongues.

The receptionist promptly disappeared into an inner office and came out with another man, somewhat older, taller, and, judging by the cut and cloth of his suit, of a substantially higher income.

"I'm Alfred Tate," the second man said, introducing himself to Webb, "Mr. Edison's secretary. May I ask your business with Mr. Edison?"

Webb handed his card to Tate. "Marshall Webb, with *Harper's Weekly*. I'm here to interview Mr. Edison about his kinetograph machine."

Tate examined the card as if it were a banknote suspected to be counterfeit. "Do you have an appointment?"

"I believe my office made one," Webb lied.

"I'm not aware—I don't recall—" Tate stammered. "Let me see if Mr. Edison is free to see you." He walked away shaking his head and muttering, clearly annoyed at having been uninformed of the appointment.

Webb waited, confident that Edison would find the time. The "Wizard of Menlo Park," now transplanted to West Orange, was a notorious publicity hound and never passed up an opportunity to talk to the press.

The great inventor appeared in less than five minutes, with Alfred Tate trailing along at his heels. Edison's face was easily recognizable from a hundred photographs and drawings, and his clothes evidenced his well-known disregard for his personal appearance. He wore a moth-eaten black business suit that looked as if he'd been sleeping in it, and around his neck a grimy white handkerchief was loosely knotted. Grooming wasn't Edison's strong suit, either. A shaggy mop of hair starting to gray at the sides crowned his head, and, although he had no whiskers, he couldn't exactly be called clean-shaven since there were streaks of stubble that his razor had missed.

Edison greeted him warmly in a thick Midwestern accent: "Mr. Webb, so good of you to come."

Webb was momentarily speechless with awe, as he realized he was shaking hands with a genius. By the time Edison was Webb's age, he had already invented the stock ticker, the incandescent lamp, and the phonograph. Now forty-five, his mind continued to conjure up devices that were changing the world, and his Edison General Electric Company provided the power that ran them.

"It's a privilege to meet you, sir," Webb finally said. Recalling that the inventor was partly deaf, he spoke louder when he added, "I appreciate you taking the time to see me."

"Glad to, glad to." Edison ran a hand through his hopelessly unruly hair. "I understand you're from *Harper's*."

"Yes, sir. Last summer we ran an article about your latest invention, the kinetograph, as you call it." Before coming to West Orange, Webb had reread the article so that he could speak credibly about the new device that was supposed to record motion on film.

"Oh, I certainly remember that article! My lawyers insisted that I file for additional patents when it was published." He smiled sheepishly. "I'm afraid I sometimes talk a bit more than is prudent."

"Well, it should be a marvelous instrument, sir, even better than your phonograph."

The inventor briefly scowled. "No, nothing is of greater value than the phonograph. The main reason I'm interested in this moving-picture machine is to accompany the phonograph—to provide images along with the sound."

Webb said, "That sounds like a wonder, sir. And I'm here to see what progress you've made. When Mr. Lathrop wrote his article last year, you were still working on the camera. I saw it in use at Ellis Island on New Year's Day, so I thought I would come and see how it worked. I'm sure our readers will be interested." But not as interested as Webb himself, who had remembered that he wasn't the only one to show an interest in the immigrants that day.

Edison appeared at a loss. He cupped an ear and repeated, "You *saw* the camera?"

"Yes," said Webb. "It certainly looked like the device Lathrop described. A young man was using it outside the new immigration station."

"Outside?" Edison shook his head. "I have to admit that we've not yet reached that point of development." From his tone, he clearly didn't enjoy having to say there was something his inventions couldn't do. "We are making great progress, but it is all done within this building. We have never tried taking the equipment outside." Scowling again, he said, "Let's go to the laboratory. I want to speak with my assistants about this."

Edison escorted Webb to the second floor of the main building. Every room they passed was a hive of activity; some men were laboring amid glassware and jars of chemicals, others worked with wires and dynamos, and many more were using equipment that Webb couldn't recognize and didn't understand.

Stopping to unlock a closed door that was simply identified as "Room Five" in stenciled black paint, Edison said, "This is where we are developing the kinetograph."

There was less activity in room five than in most that they had passed, for it was staffed with only two men. Compensating for the lack of manpower was an excess of equipment: cameras, phonographs, and dozens of instruments too incomplete to identify were lying about the cluttered laboratory in no apparent order.

"Mr. Dickson," Edison called.

A dapper, dark-haired man of about thirty promptly answered in an English accent, "Yes, Mr. Edison," and hustled over. He sported a trim mustache and goatee so impeccably groomed that Webb was almost envious.

Edison made the introductions. "Mr. Webb, this is my assistant, Mr. William Kennedy-Laurie Dickson; he knows more about the kinetograph than I do. Mr. Dickson, this is Mr. Marshall Webb of *Harper's Weekly;* he's interested in writing another story about our little invention."

The two men shook hands. No introduction was made to the second worker in the room, an elfin old man with thinning white hair, a bushy beard, and gold spectacles. He was painstakingly winding a long strip of material onto a spool, but his attention was obviously fixed on Webb.

"There seems to be a little confusion," Edison said to Dickson.

"Mr. Webb believes that he saw our camera operating outdoors—at Ellis Island—a few weeks ago. That couldn't be possible, could it?"

The spool the old man had been turning fell onto the floor and the strip raveled off with the sound of a sheet of paper being torn.

After casting a sharp glance at his coworker, Dickson shook his head. "Absolutely not. We have never taken the camera outside these walls."

"Very well." To Webb Edison said, "If you'll excuse me, I have to meet with my lawyers—more confounded patent business. Mr. Dickson will be happy to explain the kinetograph to you." He turned to go, but before closing the door, he cautioned Dickson, "Your explanation will of course be limited to what is protected by our patents."

Dickson assured him that he understood. Left with Webb, he said, "I am at your service, Mr. Webb. What would you like to see?"

The only things Webb really wanted to see were the pictures from Ellis Island—specifically, any that might include the image of the young Dutch girl. But now that he was here, he felt he had to carry through with the pretense of reporting on the new invention. "Could you begin with the basics?" he asked. "I understand little about how the device works."

"Certainly." Dickson led the way to a desk piled high with books, photographs, and drawings. "The object of the kinetograph is to capture images of motion and then reproduce that motion exactly. We accomplish this by means of a series of photographs taken very quickly—forty-six exposures per second, to be precise."

Webb knew that portrait photographs were often ruined because the subjects moved during exposure. "Why don't they all blur together?" he asked.

Dickson hesitated. "I am not at liberty to give the details of our technique. But the principle that is involved is called 'persistence of vision.' Here, let me show you." He reached for a small drum-like device on a shelf behind him and placed it on the desk. "This is a zoetrope. It has been around for many years, and is really nothing more than a child's toy, but it is based on the same principle as our kinetograph. Look through this slit."

Webb had already seen that a series of images was painted on the inside wall of the drum. He lowered his head as directed, looked through a narrow slit in the side of the instrument, and Dickson began to spin the drum. Webb smiled as he saw a monkey jump up to a tree branch and grab a banana. "It's looks like continuous motion."

"Exactly," said Dickson. "That is because of persistence of vision—the eye briefly retains an image even after it has passed. So a series of still pictures can appear to move with complete fluidity." Dickson went on to tell Webb about early efforts at capturing motion on film by Eadweard Muybridge and others, and described the primitive devices they invented.

Webb tried to feign an interest in the discourse, but he was still thinking about what he had seen at Ellis Island. He interrupted Dickson, "Do you have any competitors? Could it be one of *their* cameras that I saw at Ellis Island?"

Dickson answered thoughtfully, "No serious competitors, no. Mr. Edison is quite vigilant about protecting his ideas. Could you describe the device that you saw?"

Webb gave him a description of the apparatus, as well as what he had seen of its operation. As he spoke, he noticed that the old man was continuing to turn a spool that was already empty.

"That sounds like a type of camera, certainly," said Dickson. "But not one of ours."

"May I see yours?"

"I'm sorry, no." Dickson smiled politely. "I would be happy to show you the reproducer, but I'm afraid the camera is still unavailable for public inspection." He then led Webb to an oak cabinet the size of a large bread box. A crank was attached to its side and a viewing hole was cut into the top panel. "Look through here and turn the crank."

Webb did as instructed and was awestruck to see a lifelike *moving* photograph. The scene was of a mustachioed man in baggy workman's clothes who jumped around, acting more like a monkey than the one in the zoetrope. The film loop lasted only seconds, but it was enough to convince Webb that he had experienced pure magic. "It's so *real*," he said. "May I see it again?"

As Webb watched the workman go through precisely the same routine, Dickson told him, "That is Fred Ott, one of the mechanics here. He does a wonderfully comic sneeze, too; in fact, it is going to be the subject of our next film."

After two more viewings, Dickson led Webb to a table that supported a phonograph and another oak cabinet. An iron axle ran from the phonograph into the cabinet. "This is what Mr. Edison calls the 'kinetophonograph.' It is a marriage of sound and sight." He then went into a long description of their attempts to synchronize the film strip with the phonograph cylinder.

Overwhelmed with the technical jargon, Webb's thoughts again wandered. The new invention was certainly a marvel, but all he wanted was single image of Christina van der Waals, something that he could show to others who might recognize her and help him track her down. How was he going to go about finding her now?

CHAPTER 7

East Fourteenth Street near Union Square was lined with a mix of entertainment, commercial, and residential buildings. The neighborhood was so diverse in its businesses and architecture that Edwin Crombie could glean nothing about the character, occupation, or social status of those who lived there.

The area had once been the heart of New York City's entertainment district, and although many of the old theatrical houses had moved up Broadway to Herald Square, enough attractions still remained to give the neighborhood a strong theatrical presence. They covered the cultural spectrum from Huber's Dime Museum and Tony Pastor's variety house to Steinway Hall and the Academy of Music. There were also numerous dining and drinking establishments, with rathskellers and Luchow's Restaurant providing a German flavor. The residences interspersed between the theaters, restaurants, and office buildings were mostly well-kept brownstones, and it was up the steps of one of these that Crombie purposefully marched.

Before knocking on the door of the second-floor apartment, he held back a moment, reminding himself to be civil and remain calm. Just because August Sehlinger had been in such a panic last night was no reason for Crombie to act rashly. He proceeded to knock twice, politely, proud of himself that he'd resisted his initial urge to simply break down the door and barge inside.

When the door swung open, Crombie again restrained his hand, this time resisting the urge to throw a punch with it. At first sight, he decided he didn't like the lanky man who stood in the doorway with his hand on the knob. His clothes were too formal, for one thing: a charcoal gray cutaway suit, with a black silk Windsor tie knotted neatly against a high wing collar. Awfully stiff attire for home wear, Crombie thought. And those impeccable brown whiskers, with the thick mustache swooping down to merge smoothly into the side whiskers, leaving the chin bare—they belonged on a Czar or an Englishman, not an American.

"You Webb?" Crombie asked.

"Yes." The man frowned quizzically, as if he recognized Crombie from someplace but couldn't remember where.

"Just who the hell are you?" As he said the words, Crombie could almost hear his wife's voice reprimanding him, *Now be nice, Edwin,* and he told himself that he would do better to follow her advice.

Webb answered calmly, "Who the hell is asking?"

Crombie found himself momentarily speechless; Webb's imperturbable manner had thrown him. Crombie was well aware that he had a knack for making people defensive, or angry, or at least irritated; he wasn't used to someone responding to him with utter calm. He elected to simply answer Webb's question. "Edwin Crombie." As an afterthought he awkwardly stuck out his bony right hand.

"Marshall Webb." The handshake was returned firmly. "Would you care to come in?"

"Uh, yes, thank you." *Why is he being so hospitable?* Crombie wondered as he scraped mud and slush off his boots before stepping inside.

He quickly sized up the combination parlor, library, and dining room. It was decorated in a manner that matched Webb's attire: a bit formal, spare, and with little warmth or adornment. A massive rolltop desk, stained dark, was the largest piece of furniture, with matching glass-door bookcases on either side of it. Near the single window that overlooked East Fourteenth Street was a small dining table and a pair of bent-backed chairs. Crombie was struck by the lack of decoration; there were no paintings or tapestries on the walls, the mantle of the small fireplace had only an enameled iron clock upon it, and there wasn't a single photograph to be seen anywhere. The only images on the drab beige walls were a few framed Civil War woodcuts that might have been taken from the pages of *Frank Leslie's Illustrated Newspaper*.

Webb gestured to a leather easy chair that could comfortably seat a giant. "I was about to have a glass of port, if you'd care to join me."

Still bewildered by Webb's gracious manner, Crombie agreed and sat down.

Webb went to a sideboard and reached for a decanter. "This building has one of those infernal steam heating systems that makes more noise than warmth. I can't stand to listen to all its hissing and clanging, so I still use the fireplace." He turned around with two filled wine glasses. "Or, when it's just a bit nippy like today, I find that a glass of port usually provides sufficient warmth."

Crombie accepted the drink, Webb settled onto a horsehair sofa, and both men took healthy sips of the wine. Somewhat relaxed, by both the drink and Webb's demeanor, Crombie felt almost friendly to his host. Then it occurred to him that he was being soft-soaped, and he didn't like it at all. "My question remains," he said. "Who *are* you?"

Webb's mustache twitched in a smile. "I believe I've already answered that."

"No, you only gave me your name. I want to know what you do—and why you were at the Edison laboratory on Wednesday."

"I'm a writer, for *Harper's Weekly*. I was thinking of doing a story on his kinetograph machine."

"Hogwash! I went to the *Harper's* office this morning. They've never heard of you."

An embarrassed flush crossed Webb's face. "With whom did you speak?"

"The receptionist, of course. He said there's no Marshall Webb working there." Crombie's tone became demanding. "So what is it you're after? You a detective for Edison?" He almost slammed down his wine glass. "I swear that's how he keeps his competition down—with spies and lawsuits . . . and sabotage, more'n likely."

"I can see why that would concern you, since you have a kinetograph of your own." Before Crombie could decide whether to deny the statement, Webb continued, "I saw you on New Year's Day, taking pictures at Ellis Island." He smiled again. "It took a moment before I recognized you at the door. When I saw you at the immigration station, I assumed you were with Edison, since his was the only kinetograph of which I was aware. That's why I visited his laboratories to inquire about it."

"And why would you be interested, since you're not really a writer?"

"I am indeed a writer for *Harper's*. But I'm not on the permanent staff there, so that's probably why the receptionist didn't know of me. But I *am* a regular contributor." Webb went to his desk, retrieved some papers, and handed them to Crombie.

Crombie quickly scanned the correspondence, which was on *Harper's* letterhead. The subject of the letters was a proposed article on the construction of the General Grant National Memorial on Riverside Drive. "All right, I believe you." Then he asked hesitantly, "About seeing me with a camera . . . are you planning to mention that in your story?"

Webb looked for the answer in his wine glass. "I see no reason why I should have to." Shifting his piercing gaze to Crombie, he added, "I assume you would prefer that I *not* mention it?"

Crombie fought the urge to blurt, "For chrissake, please don't!" Trying not to betray any concern in his voice, he answered, "I would prefer that my own efforts at developing a moving-picture machine remain confidential for now, yes."

Webb nodded agreeably. "I understand." Leaning forward, he went on. "But I am interested in the subjects from Ellis Island. I would very much like to see the pictures you took."

Crombie thought for a moment. He didn't want to expose any more of his enterprise to Webb, but if he didn't cooperate with him, he might find himself in a *Harper's Weekly* story—and that could alert Edison. "We haven't developed a viewing system yet," he said, hoping to discourage Webb without offending him. "I'm afraid they would only look like regular photographs, not *moving* pictures."

"That's all I need," said Webb.

"I don't understand."

Webb's confident manner appeared to fade. "I'm hoping to find an image of one particular girl who arrived at the immigration station that day."

"Why?"

Taking too long to answer, Webb finally said, "To show to one of her relatives."

Crombie was skeptical that that was the entire reason. "We tried to develop the film, but it didn't come out well."

Webb persisted. "I would still like to see what you have." He looked directly at Crombie. "That is my only interest in *your* kinetograph. Once I see the pictures, I'll limit my article to Edison's instrument."

It didn't take long for Crombie to agree to the implied blackmail. What difference did it make why Webb wanted a picture of some girl, as long as he kept Crombie's secret. Besides, when he and Sehlinger were ready to go public with their invention, perhaps Webb might remember the favor and do an article to promote their American Kinemascope Company.

As they rode together on the rocking cable car over the Brooklyn Bridge, Marshall Webb found himself unable to get a clear read on his companion. He couldn't tell if Crombie was still worried about the implied threat of exposure or if he always fidgeted so nervously.

Crombie kept poking his finger inside his celluloid collar as if to loosen it, even though his neck was so scrawny that the collar barely made contact with his skin. He also picked at his sloppily tied four-in-hand, crossed and recrossed his arms over his baggy Norfolk jacket, and repeatedly nudged up the brim of his soft-fur fedora. Overall, he was as unrefined in his appearance as he was in his mannerisms. Crombie's thin, angular face was clean-shaven, revealing old acne scars and a few active pimples. His thick hair, a color that would be called "strawberry blond" on a woman, was slicked down with brilliantine. Although Webb assumed him to be in his mid-twenties, Edwin Crombie could almost pass for an adolescent.

The cable car ground to an unexpected halt midway across the bridge, and a conductor hopped onto the track to check the problem. When it became apparent that they might be stuck there for some time, Webb asked Crombie, "How long have you been working on your camera?"

Crombie crossed his arms again. "For a while."

Webb silently hoped that the trolley would be repaired soon if this was the kind of conversation that he could expect.

"Actually," Crombie went on, "my expertise isn't the camera

itself. I'm a showman. I'm the one who's going to make moving pictures popular."

"How are you going to do that?"

"By giving people what they want. I know what they like."

To Webb's relief, the car jolted forward and resumed its squeaking journey. "What makes you such an expert?" he asked.

Crombie tugged at the brim of his hat. "Years of experience," he answered. "I left home when I was fourteen to tour with Doc Caulfield's Medicine Show. My job was to convince the suckers that his snake oil had cured me of chronic self-abuse. I did a good job of it, too; we sold a lot of bottles to a lot of very nice ladies who wanted to keep their boys from falling victim to the same 'affliction.' Then I worked for a magic-lantern show. We'd travel around the country, pitch our tent, and set up a show projecting glass slides of all kinds of subjects. That's how I came to know what people like to see. And that's what the American Kinemascope Company is gonna give them."

After the cable car touched ground in Brooklyn and the two men switched to a Nassau Railroad streetcar, Crombie continued to describe his plans. "People want to see something special, a scene that lets them in on a part of the world they'd never get to see otherwise. So the first pictures we're going to make will be like the one at Ellis Island: historical events, things that happen only once. I want to take the camera to the World's Exposition in Chicago and then, after the conventions, film the presidential candidates. . . . Maybe go to the Polo Grounds for opening day of baseball season." He was looking out at the streets of Brooklyn, but obviously seeing a future that was much brighter. "I'm gonna be rich."

They got off at Fulton Street and Nostrand Avenue and walked a couple of blocks north to a whitewashed two-story house with cheerful green shutters. As they strode up the walkway, Crombie said, "I was lucky to find a place in this area with a carriage house. A doctor used to live here and he had it added on—kept a phaeton in it for making house calls. We use it as a workshop now."

That was the second time he'd said "we." Webb asked, "Who else are you working with?"

Crombie grunted, "I have a partner." Then his mouth clamped shut, indicating he would say no more about it.

Webb had already suspected as much. Somebody must have told Crombie about his visit to the Edison laboratory—probably somebody who shared Crombie's concern about being discovered. Webb guessed that the white-bearded old man he'd seen in room five was the most likely candidate, but he didn't press Crombie.

After letting Webb inside, Crombie ushered him into the parlor. "Helen!" he called.

An attractive brunette, who appeared a few years older than Crombie and about fifty pounds heavier, soon came in from the kitchen, trailed by the aroma of baking bread. "Did you remember to wipe your feet?" she asked Crombie.

"Yes, dear." To Webb he said, "This is my wife, Helen."

Webb made a small bow.

"You married, Webb?" Crombie asked.

Somewhat taken aback by the personal question, Webb hesitated before answering, "No."

"Well, you should be." Crombie glanced around his home with satisfaction. "It's good to be married."

"I almost—" Webb began, before cutting himself off. He didn't care to discuss his former fiancée any more than Crombie wanted to talk about his secret partner.

"Where's Emily?" Crombie asked his wife.

"In the backyard, climbing the elm tree. You want me to call her in?"

"No, that's okay." To Webb he explained, "My daughter. Prettiest little girl you've ever seen." Addressing his wife again, Crombie said, "I'll be showing Mr. Webb some pictures."

"Shall I put on a pot of coffee?"

"No, don't go to the bother," said Crombie. "We'll just have a couple of beers."

Helen flashed a smile that said, "Nice try." As she headed back to the kitchen, she said aloud, "The coffee will be ready soon."

Crombie shrugged at his defeat, apparently used to it, and pointed Webb to a chair. "Let me get you what we have from Ellis Island. Be right back."

Webb's wait was a short one. Clutching a handful of film strips and a small stack of prints, Crombie returned and placed the materials on a mahogany parlor stand. "Here you go. These prints are the same as the film—we're making a copy of every frame.

Don't have them all done yet, but we will soon. I don't know which you want to look at first, but the prints might be easier to see. For the film, you have to hold it up to the window."

Taking Crombie's suggestion, Webb reached for the photographs. His first reaction was disappointment; the images were grainy and only about an inch square. "Maybe I better try the film," he said.

"Oh, I forgot the magnifying glass. Let me get it. That'll help."

It did. By the time Helen Crombie came in with two steaming cups of coffee, Webb was looking at a photograph of Christina van der Waals crossing the gangplank from the transfer boat onto Ellis Island. He easily recognized the Zouave jacket she'd worn that day, but her face was tilted down and partly obscured by her bonnet.

Webb then scanned the film strips, and found several frames adjacent to the one that had been printed. Christina's features were identifiable in these, and Webb focused on the clearest of the views. Even with the magnifying glass, her image was a bit blurry, but the face that he'd first seen two weeks ago today still seemed to radiate a special brightness. Although he could see into the print what he remembered of the girl, Webb wasn't sure that the image was large or clear enough for anyone else to be able to identify her. "Would it be possible," Webb asked, "to make a large print of this one?" As an afterthought, he added, "Two prints."

"I suppose so," Crombie answered. "My partner will be here tonight; I'll ask him." He paused. "But now let me ask you something: Will you promise that you won't write—or tell anyone—about our venture?"

Without hesitation, Webb answered, "You have my word."

"At least," added Crombie, "until we *want* the public to know about our moving pictures. Then if a story about us was to appear in *Harper's* it might be quite a boon."

There wasn't much that was subtle about Edwin Crombie, Webb decided. But it did seem as if they could help each other. "I'm only a writer," he said. "The decision to publish what I write is up to the editors. But I can try."

Crombie accepted the answer. "You'll have the pictures tomorrow."

CHAPTER 8

Webb was impressed with the enlarged photographs that Crombie's partner had printed. Alone in his apartment, he leaned back in one of the dining chairs near the window, stretched out his long legs, and held up one of the prints to catch the afternoon sunlight on Christina van der Waals's image.

He wasn't sure if it was the photograph alone, or if it was the memory that it triggered of seeing her in person, but Webb could swear she looked as fresh and bright as when he'd met her in Ellis Island's Registry Hall. The grainy sepia print couldn't show the sparkling blue of her eyes, of course, nor the gold of her hair, but in Webb's mind he could see them.

After studying the photograph for a while, he slowly lowered it and stared out his window at bustling East Fourteenth Street below. There were the usual shoppers and theater-goers, as well as office workers hurrying home and early diners going into restaurants. Those were the people in ready view. Webb knew that there were many others on the city streets who were less visible, some of them predators and some of them prey. Compared to the harsh reality that a girl alone on the streets faced, the rags-to-riches plots he'd been contemplating for his book seemed silly.

Again looking at her cheerful face in the photograph, Webb refused to accept that this might be the last view he would have of Christina. But it was now more than two weeks since she'd arrived in America, and she seemed to have totally vanished. Even with this photograph to identify her, to whom would he show it? Who would notice one girl on these crowded streets?

As the winter light began to fade, Webb decided that at least he knew what to do with the second print he'd asked Crombie to make: Give Liz Luck a picture of her cousin.

Having no desire to run into her husband again, Webb decided not to risk visiting Liz Luck at her apartment. He wasn't sure if representing himself as an immigration official was even a crime, but if Warren Gleason discovered the ruse, he might find himself under arrest—or at least subject to more questions than he cared to answer.

Webb instead caught the Sixth Avenue el and arrived at the Baylor Opera House shortly before midnight. He again tried explaining to the ticket seller that he'd come to see Liz Luck on a family matter, not for the show, but he again had to purchase a ticket.

In the seedy lobby, he gave the same explanation to the manager, who brusquely rejected his request to speak with Miss Luck backstage. "But if she's in the mood," the manager said with a leer, "maybe you'll get a private audience with Lizzie in one of the boxes."

Although he'd paid for a box in order to avoid mingling with the rest of the audience, Webb found that all of the boxes were already occupied. Saturday night was the busiest in the Tenderloin, and the Baylor Opera House was packed with rowdy patrons. The back of the main auditorium was also filled, with so many couples engaged in various sex acts that it looked like a carnal circus. Webb opted for a second-row seat, where the crowd was sparser and the activities in the back rows less audible.

He had to endure two acts—the first a contortionist in a flesh-colored union suit who could lock her feet behind her head, and the other a trio of chemise-clad "acrobats" whose only demonstrable skill was playing leapfrog—before Liz Luck took the stage.

From the moment she came out, swathed in the diaphanous veils of a Turkish harem girl, it was clear that Luck was different from the other performers. For one thing, the four musicians who comprised this evening's orchestra began to play more skillfully, as if they believed she was worth the extra effort. Also, some of the other men in the audience ceased their conversations and cast expectant eyes upon the stage.

As Luck began her solo dance routine, Webb saw that she had some talent. Her dance developed into an enticing performance that was more ballet than burlesque. Although suggestive, Liz

Luck's movements weren't as vulgar as those of the previous girls, and she never completely disrobed.

Webb became so entranced by her routine that he was annoyed when a corseted brunette who smelled of cigarettes stopped in front of him. "Handsome gentleman such as yourself shouldn't be sittin' alone," she said. "A nickel for my company."

"No." Webb twisted his head to look past the girl to the stage. She moved on to the next man in the row and began repeating her pitch when Webb changed his mind. "Wait. Come back, please."

She sidled back to him, again blocking his view of the dance. "Nickel is for my company. It's fifty cents for—"

Webb cut her off. "How much to give a note to Miss Luck?"

"Two bits?" Her tone suggested that she expected to be negotiated down.

Webb nodded, took out his notebook, and scribbled a brief message. Handing the note and a quarter to the girl, he said, "It's very important."

The girl smiled and retreated backstage.

Liz Luck finished her dance to some applause and a small shower of coins. She scooped them up as gracefully as possible and left the stage to be replaced by the same "French" cancan dancers that Webb had seen during his first visit.

Webb didn't have to wait long before the brunette returned. "Miss Luck will see you. And I told the manager it was okay for you to be back there." She held out her palm to be rewarded for this additional service. When an extra dime was placed into it, she kept her hand out. "I can show you to her myself if you like, sir." Webb agreed and paid out another ten cents.

She quickly led him backstage and into an unheated dressing room, then left to resume her solicitations in the auditorium.

As Webb stepped inside the harshly lit room, he felt as if he'd walked into a wall. The air was so dense with dust, powder, and smoke that he had to make a conscious effort to continue breathing. Almost as thick as the atmosphere was the clutter of costumes: garish, filmy garments were heaped in piles on the floor, draped over stools and dressing tables, and hanging from pegs on the walls.

A dozen women in various stages of undress were chatting, smoking cigarettes, and applying rouge. None of them appeared self-conscious at the entrance of a man, except for Liz Luck, who was seated at the cleanest of the dressing tables, wearing a faded silk dressing robe that completely concealed her harem costume. She modestly pulled the robe a little tighter and blushed slightly when Webb approached her.

She greeted him with, "Have you found Christina?" The initial flush of embarrassment in her eyes had given way to a flicker of hope.

"No, I'm sorry, Miss Luck." He added as a question, "I was hoping that you might have heard from her by now."

Her expression collapsed to one of sadness, and she gave her head a small shake.

Hoping that a picture of her cousin might cheer her up, Webb said, "I do have something for you." He reached into his pocket and handed her one of the prints that he'd gotten from Crombie. "This is Christina, on New Year's Day, getting off the boat at Ellis Island."

Liz Luck took it from him, holding the photograph lightly by the edges. "Oh, my God, it's really her." Her breath caught. "She *is* here." She looked up at Webb with fear and bewilderment in her eyes. "But she's not *here*."

Webb didn't know what to say; he had no answer and knew no way to comfort her.

Luck dropped her gaze to the image of her cousin again. "Christina's all grown up," she said, more to herself than to Webb. "And so pretty."

While Luck studied the picture, Webb studied her and again noticed the resemblance to her younger cousin.

"We were more like sisters than cousins," she went on wistfully. "Christina's parents were killed in a fire when she was only two, and my family took her in. I always thought of her as my little sister." Looking up at Webb, she asked, "When you spoke to her, what did she say? How did she sound?"

Webb recounted their brief conversation, including the fact that Christina had wanted to work in a flower shop or be a singer like her cousin Hendrika.

"Nobody's called me 'Hendrika' in years," Luck said. "And as you saw, I'm not a—"

The short, chubby manager barged into the room and interrupted them. He said to Luck, "You need to be gettin' ready for your next dance."

"I'll be ready."

"You gonna be workin' the boxes later? It's a full house—plenty of customers if you wants."

Luck grabbed a scuffed jewelry box that jingled with coins when she lifted it. "No, I should have enough from the shows. Not tonight."

Clearly unhappy with her answer, the manager left, grumbling about "goddamn prima donnas."

Her face red, Luck avoided Webb's eyes when she said in a soft voice, "Like I was saying, I'm not really a singer. But that's what I told Christina in my letters home. I suppose I made a lot of things about my life in America sound better than they are." She choked back a sob. "I do need to change for my next performance. Please turn around."

Webb did so and found himself facing two of the acrobats who'd been playing leapfrog earlier. They'd divested themselves of their chemises and appeared in no hurry to don any other garment. One was brushing her hair while the other rolled a cigarette.

Liz Luck went on. "I fear that whatever happens to Christina is my fault—I gave her false hopes about life in America. If it wasn't for what I wrote in my letters, she'd be safely home in Holland."

"About those letters," said Webb, trying to ignore the naked distractions in front of him. "Christina told me she'd written to tell you she was coming. And she expected you to meet her."

"I haven't gotten a letter from home in more than a year. I still write, but their mail doesn't find us; we don't stay in one place very long."

Webb said, "Whatever brought Christina to America, the fact is that she's been here for two weeks now. Where do you think she would go, if not to your apartment?"

Luck hesitated before answering. "She might have come here. I told her where I was working. But if she did . . . " She drew a hard breath. "If she did, then she saw what kind of 'opera house' this really is. Maybe she decided she didn't *want* to see me again."

That could be, thought Webb. But then where would she go from here? Hopefully, she didn't stay in the Tenderloin for any length of time.

"You can turn around."

When he did, Webb saw that Liz Luck now wore a skimpy outfit of fringed leather and feathers, making her look like some kind of exotic Indian princess. "Has your husband asked about Christina at the police department? Maybe they could find her."

"I've pleaded with him. He says everybody knows police only investigate if you pay them to."

"They won't do it for a fellow officer?"

"Warren's only a patrolman. No detective is going to do him any favors." Liz stood up. "I have to go back onstage." She eyed Webb directly. "I'm going to do all I can to find Christina. Will you still look for her, too?"

Webb felt that the two of them somehow shared the loss of Christina. "Yes," he answered, wishing that he knew *where* to look.

CHAPTER 9

Webb decided that if he couldn't figure out where Christina vander Waals had ended up, he would start by looking for her where she'd arrived. On Monday morning, despite bitter winds and an icy rain, he took the ferry from lower Manhattan to Ellis Island.

At the receiving station's administrative office, Webb showed his *Harper's Weekly* card and was promptly introduced to Assistant Superintendent Jacob Ivins. The barrel-chested immigration official had the chin whiskers of a sea captain, the navy blue uniform of a streetcar conductor, and the manner of a bureaucrat.

Webb explained that he had been on hand for the first arrivals to the island and was returning to write a story about the operations at the new facility.

"I'm glad you came back," said Ivins. "Things are going much smoother now. Don't get me wrong—there were no difficulties with the opening. But not all the construction was completed yet." He reached for a navy blue pillbox cap with a black leather visor. "If you'd care to join me for a tour, I think you'll be very impressed with our facility."

Webb accepted the offer and was led outside. On their way to the landing dock, Ivins pointed out several brick buildings that were dwarfed by the enormous receiving station. "Those were left over from Fort Gibson. We've refurbished them, saving taxpayers the cost of new construction. One of them serves as a dormitory, another's a laundry, and that small one is a bathhouse. On the other side, there's a hospital and a power plant."

"Sounds like you've covered all the needs here," Webb said, giving Ivins exactly the positive response he sought.

"We have to. There are entire towns with smaller populations than we have on any given day. We only took in a thousand or so immigrants the first day—wanted to make sure our procedures were all worked out, you understand—but we're getting almost five thousand a day now, and Colonel Weber says we can handle up to seven thousand."

Maintaining the pretense that he was here for an article, Webb dutifully recorded the information in his notebook.

At the wharf, Webb saw ample evidence of the increased numbers. Two transfer boats were docked, with dozens of immigrants tramping over both gangplanks. Some of the arrivals were dressed in the finest costumes of their native lands; others looked plump from the many layers of clothing that they wore so they wouldn't have to carry as much luggage.

Leading Webb to the main entrance, Ivins pointed out the hundreds of people awaiting entry to the building. "More than what you saw before, isn't it?"

"Sure is. Are they all going to be able to get through today?"

"Absolutely," Ivins answered with pride. "Let me show you the processing."

Back inside, the two men worked their way past a line of weary immigrants and climbed the broad staircase to the second-floor Registry Hall. Webb noticed the distaste on Ivins's craggy face whenever the assistant superintendent came close to one of the newcomers. Upstairs, they moved on to another, narrower staircase that led them to the gallery above the main floor. Judging by his expression, it was clear to Webb that Ivins was more comfortable looking down on the immigrants than walking among them.

"Quite a lot of people," said Webb, surveying the long queues and packed holding pens. There were easily four times as many newcomers as he'd seen on New Year's Day.

"I know." Ivins wrinkled his nose. "And I don't think one of them has had a bath in two weeks."

Understandable, thought Webb, since steerage was the equivalent of a ship's basement and didn't provide washing facilities. "You don't get many first-class passengers here, I guess."

"None," answered Ivins. "First and second class disembark in Manhattan. The Immigration Bureau only inspects steerage passengers. They're the ones who bring in the problems." He shook his head. "Can't imagine if we had to process *everybody;* there's just too damn many of them. That's why the federal government took over immigration; New York couldn't handle it."

"I understood there to be other reasons," said Webb. "Bribery of officials, immigrants being robbed by inspectors—"

Ivins turned on him sharply. "None of that goes on anymore. And anyone who says it does—"

"*I'm* not saying it does," Webb quickly reassured him. But he knew that the officials were still open to bribery; after all, it had cost only two dollars for a registry clerk to put him in contact with Christina van der Waals. Trying to get back on Ivins's good side, Webb looked about the hall and commented, "It appears you have quite an efficient operation here."

"Thank you. We do." Ivins seemed to welcome the change back to their original conversation. "The biggest improvement over Castle Garden has been in our baggage handling. As you saw, the entire first floor is restricted to baggage, leaving this room uncluttered so we can process the people faster."

Although he knew the basics of the operation from his previous visit, Webb asked, "How do you process them?"

Ivins began walking along the gallery toward one end of the hall. "Basically, we sort out who stays and who gets sent back." He pointed down to an area near the staircase. "First they get questioned. Everyone has to answer the same set of twenty-nine questions, and they have to answer satisfactorily."

"What if they don't speak English?"

"Our officers speak several languages. But if you ask me, we shouldn't. People want to come to this country, they ought to speak English." He moved farther along the gallery and directed Webb's attention to a group of men clad in white uniforms. "Those are doctors from the Public Health Service. Once an immigrant passes questioning, he gets a medical examination. That's where we get the most rejects."

"Because they're sick?"

"We sure as hell don't want them bringing their diseases here." He pointed to a line of immigrants standing along one wall; they all had chalked letters on their coats. "See? They got all kinds of things wrong with them. The *H* means a bad heart, *E* is for eyes, *K* for hernia, and the worst is *X*—those are retarded or insane."

"Where are they being taken? To the hospital you mentioned?"

Ivins stared at Webb as if *he* should be marked with an X. "The hospital is for our staff. Why should we give free medical care to foreigners?" He shook his head. "No, they get moved to the dormitory and undergo additional tests. If they fail those, we send them back to wherever they came from."

"How many have to go back?"

"About twenty percent are detained for a while, and half of those end up being deported."

All right, Webb thought; he had let Ivins talk long enough to maintain the pretense that this was an interview. What he wanted to know was where Christina van der Waals might have ended up, and he knew that she'd successfully passed all the tests. "What about the ones who pass?" he asked. "Where do they go?"

"There," said Ivins, with a nod toward the front of the hall, where the high registration desks were lined up under an enormous American flag. "That's where they get their entry passes."

"I mean after that. Where do they go when they leave Ellis Island?"

"Depends." Ivins shrugged, indicating that where they ended up wasn't his concern. "We have a ferry to New Jersey for those going west, and the railroad companies have ferries going straight to their depots."

"What if somebody was expecting to be met by relatives? Where would they be picked up?"

"Not here. Nobody gets on the island for a pickup—we're crowded enough as it is. No, they'd have to take the *J. H. Brinkerhoff* to the Barge Office and be picked up there. The ferry runs every hour, and it's usually full."

A short time later, after thanking Ivins for the information, Webb stepped aboard that very transport boat.

The Barge Office, at the foot of Whitehall Street in the east end of Battery Park, was visible from Ellis Island. In fact, the tower of the Roman revival edifice could be seen from much of lower Manhattan. Built of granite block, the Barge Office was solid and stable—and in complete contrast to the chaotic movements of the people and vehicles that milled about it.

There were fewer immigrants here than at Ellis Island, but no organization, and they wandered through the office and around the streets without direction. Only a handful of uniformed

Immigration Bureau officials staffed the Barge Office, and it was half an hour before one of them, a pinch-faced young man who looked like an adolescent Lawrence Pritchard, agreed to speak with Webb.

The two of them stepped outside and into a swarm of humanity. Immigrants, speaking in a dozen tongues, huddled together or walked around looking for relatives. Vendors tried to sell them their first American meals: popcorn, peanuts, fried oysters. Money changers offered to convert foreign currency to dollars. Hackmen and railroad agents loudly advertised the availability of transportation while other men tried to entice the newcomers with promises of jobs and housing.

Webb asked the beleaguered officer, "If an immigrant expects to be met by relatives, this is where they come, right?"

"Yup, but as you can see, the system for finding them needs some improvement." The young man stuffed a plug of tobacco inside his cheek and began working it with his tongue.

"What if somebody isn't picked up, or doesn't know where to go?"

"We try to help. Give them directions, provide information on transportation—basically tell them whatever it takes to get them started on their way."

"But where do they go *to?*"

The immigration official gave Webb a baleful look and spat a thin stream of tobacco juice. "I don't give a damn where they end up. There's thousands coming in every day. All I care about is getting them out of the Barge Office so we can make room for the next boatload."

"What about a lost girl? Who would help her find a place to go?"

The officer nodded at a couple of men, dressed like Tenderloin sports, who were lounging by a lamppost. "*They'll* sure help her find a place to go."

That wasn't the answer Webb had been hoping to hear. "Isn't there anyone from the government to help? Surely we can't have children roaming the streets on their own."

That earned Webb another look. "You sure got some peculiar notions, mister. It's more than enough that the government lets them into this country. They got to make their own way once they're here."

Webb took out his photograph of Christina. "This is the girl I'm talking about. She arrived on New Year's Day. Do you remember if she came here?"

With scarcely a glance, the officer laughed. "I don't look at them. Like I said, I just try to get them out of here."

Webb tucked the photo away. "Okay. Let's say you were looking for a girl who was coming here and she got lost. Where would you go to look for her?"

The young man spat again, this time for distance, and appeared pleased with the result. "I dunno. A few years back, somebody took a lost girl to the ASPCA. Maybe that's the place to check."

Webb couldn't believe his ears. The American Society for the Prevention of Cruelty to Animals? Was that the best refuge this modern city—this rich country—could offer a lost child?

CHAPTER 10

"It really don't hurt so bad, Miss Davies." The trembling girl tried to pull her arm away. "I got lots worse'n this before."

Rebecca Davies kept a firm hold of the slender wrist, while trying at the same time to be as gentle as possible. "This needs to be treated." The fresh burn on the back of the girl's hand was starting to blister, and the skin around it was an angry red. Lifting the ragged sleeve a little higher, Rebecca saw the scars of older burns, most of them in the shapes of circles or crescents. "Cigar?" she asked.

The girl hesitated. "Yes, ma'am." She ran the back of her free hand over her tear-streaked cheek.

Rebecca didn't ask how she got it. She'd seen enough similar scars, and heard enough reasons: a husband's dinner hadn't been hot enough, or there was no beer in the house for father, or a girl failed to bring home enough money from her job. *This poor thing couldn't be a day over sixteen,* Rebecca thought, *and she's already been hurt more than any human should be in a lifetime.* Delicately tugging the sleeve back down, she called, "Miss Hummel!" To the frightened girl she said, "We'll talk later, after you've had a chance to eat and rest a little."

Within a few minutes, a short gray-haired woman, dressed as usual in a starched dress and apron that made her look like a combination nurse and maid, came to the sitting room door. "Yes, Miss Davies?"

"Could you please take Miss Yost to the infirmary?" She gave the girl's forearm a soft pat. "And she will be staying with us tonight, so we need to get a bed made up for her."

"Yes, ma'am." Miss Hummel took the orders with perfect composure. It was all part of the routine at Colden House. "And ma'am, there's a gentleman for you in the foyer."

Rebecca stifled a groan. "What does he want?" She had far too much work to do to waste time on a caller.

"He says he's looking for a girl."

Well, we certainly have enough of those, thought Rebecca. The addition of Miss Yost brought the current number of female guests to more than twenty. "Very well," she sighed. "I'll see him." She smoothed her serge bell skirt and mentally braced herself to be ready for anything. Men who came to Colden House "looking for a girl" were often the same ones the girls were trying to escape. Other times, they were police officers looking for "suspects"—whenever a woman was spotted at a local crime scene, the police assumed she might be hiding in Colden House.

Miss Hummel led the young girl to the narrow staircase of the old Federal-style row house while Rebecca stepped out to the foyer.

A tall dark-haired gentleman in a caped mackintosh had his back to her, absorbed in a seascape on the wall. Rebecca's first assessment was that he was too well dressed to be with the police. He didn't look like an angry husband or father, either. "May I help you?" she asked.

He turned around, revealing a face that wasn't classically handsome, but attractive enough for Rebecca to take notice. His clear eyes had the light of intelligence in them, and there was a hint of a well-mannered smile on his lips. The brown Franz Josef whiskers, with a carefully cultivated mustache over a clean-shaven chin, were a bit old-fashioned but quaintly charming. She had to remind herself that good-looking men could be every bit as troublesome as homely ones—often more so.

"I hope you can," he said. "Miss Rebecca Davies, I presume?"

She nodded.

The visitor glanced about as if expecting a butler to take his coat and hat. He could wait forever, as far as Rebecca was concerned, for there were no servants at Colden House. Besides, she didn't intend for him to stay long enough to remove his coat. Receiving no encouragement, he finally ventured, "I have been told that this is the place where a lost girl might come for assistance."

"We do have a number of young women as our guests," she said.

"I'm looking for a girl—a Dutch girl, about fourteen years old—named Christina van der Waals. Has she been here?"

"The name is unfamiliar to me," Rebecca answered honestly. "And you haven't given me yours."

"Forgive me." He blushed slightly, which Rebecca found rather endearing. "My name is Marshall Webb."

"What is your interest in Miss van der Waals?" When he didn't answer promptly, she prodded, "Are you a relation? Employer?"

"No, ma'am. I'm a—My interest is . . ." He slipped his hand up under the cape of his overcoat and fumbled for something inside. "I'm a writer. I was hoping to do a story about her, but she's been missing for the last three weeks." He withdrew a photograph and held it out. "Could you perhaps take a look at this and tell me if you've seen her?"

Rebecca stepped closer to take the photo from him and examined the grainy, slightly out-of-focus image. "I hope you're a better writer than you are a photographer, Mr. Webb." She immediately felt a twinge of guilt about teasing the man; he was gentlemanly enough, but a bit stiff, and maybe lacking a sense of humor. Before she could say anything more, her attention was diverted by the chiming of the hallway clock: six o'clock. "I'm sorry," she said, handing the photograph back to him, "but I have to supervise dinner preparations. I've never seen this girl before."

"I understand. Thank you for your time." He tucked the picture back in his pocket and added with a small smile, "And, yes, I am."

"You are what?"

"A better writer than a photographer." The smile turned slightly mischievous. "I didn't take this picture."

Rebecca couldn't help but smile herself. "If you'd like to come with me to the kitchen," she offered, "we can continue the discussion—if there's anything left to discuss."

"I do have a couple questions more."

She nodded toward the rack near the front door. "You may be more comfortable without your coat."

As Webb hung up his outer clothes, Rebecca noticed that he looked even slimmer and taller without them. Six feet, perhaps an inch or two more, she guessed.

On their way to the kitchen in the rear of the house, Rebecca asked him, "Who suggested that you come here?"

"Oddly enough, I began at the ASPCA."

"To find a missing *girl?* Why on earth—"

"An official at the Barge Office told me they take in children."

"Ten or fifteen years ago they did, yes. There were very few aid societies for children back then."

"Well, there sure are plenty now. I've been everywhere from the Wetmore Home for Friendless Girls in Washington Square to St. Zita's Temporary Home for Friendless Women on East Fifty-second Street. I tried the Shelter for Respectable Girls on Fourteenth, the Night Refuge for Homeless Women on Fifteenth, the Asylum for Destitute Young Christian Girls on Sixteenth . . . "

"And no one had seen Miss van der Waals?"

"No. To be honest, none appeared overly concerned, either, once they learned she was an immigrant. The matron at the last place I visited suggested that I try Colden House. She said you take in 'all kinds.' "

Although she doubted that it was intended as such, Rebecca took the matron's statement as a compliment.

They entered the kitchen, which had ample space but few laborsaving devices; some of the fixtures looked as if they'd been installed when the house was originally built more than a hundred years earlier. Ready to provide the necessary manual labor were four apron-clad women awaiting instructions. Rebecca gave them their assignments and they fell to work, chopping vegetables, mixing dough for bread, and filling kettles of water.

"Looks like you're feeding an army," commented Webb.

"We have anywhere from twenty to thirty women staying here at a time," Rebecca said. She eyed one of the ancient wood-burning ranges and reminded herself that they really had to get a coal stove. "If you would be so kind, Mr. Webb," she said, "there's a cord of wood outside the back door. Could you bring some in?"

Without hesitation, he answered, "Certainly."

By the time he came back in with an armload of firewood, he'd risen a notch in Rebecca's estimation. Webb hadn't asked for an apron or gloves, and didn't seem to mind the dirt and wood chips that now dusted the front of his smartly tailored suit.

After stacking the wood next to the stove, Webb joined Rebecca at the table where she was chopping carrots. "Quite a job, feeding this many," he said.

"Feeding is the easy part," said Rebecca. "Our goal here is to provide our guests with skills that will last them longer than one meal. We try find them decent jobs so they don't have to go back to the sweatshops, provide medical treatment when needed, teach reading and arithmetic. I hope to institute some other educational programs, too."

"Like Chicago's Hull House?"

Rebecca glanced up at him with surprise. Hull House had opened only three years earlier; the fact that Webb knew of it boosted him another notch. "We're not like it yet," she said. "I am interested in adopting some of Jane Addams's methods, but I never seem to have time to do long-term social planning." She thought to herself that there was always some urgency that required her attention, like the new girl, Miss Yost. She'd have to remember to speak with her later.

"Excuse me, Miss Davies. I have the towels for washing."

Rebecca was surprised to see Theresa standing right next to her with a basket full of laundry. She hadn't seen her come in and was a bit annoyed with herself for having had her attention so focused on her visitor. "We'll do them after dinner," she said. Looking at the towels, so threadbare they could almost be mistaken for gauze, she was embarrassed again, this time at Webb's seeing their poor condition. Quickly she asked him, "So tell me, Mr. Webb, what kind of story were you planning to write about Miss van der Waals?"

"A success story, about how an immigrant girl, coming alone to America, can make her way to a new life. She starts with nothing but dreams, works hard, and finally—"

"And finally marries a wealthy man and lives happily ever after?" finished Rebecca.

"I suppose that would be the ideal ending." He sounded serious.

Could this man be so naive? Rebecca's regard for him began to falter. "That sounds like a Horatio Alger story, Mr. Webb. You must have read too many dime novels."

He muttered a reply that was barely audible but sounded like, "Worse. I write them." Before she could respond to that curious statement, Webb said, "I've started writing, but without the girl, I'm at a loss to continue. Do you have any suggestions where else I might go to try to find her?"

Rebecca thought a moment. "I honestly don't know. It sounds as if you've already been to the other homes I might have suggested." She looked around at the women laboring to get dinner ready, and suddenly wondered how much real work this writer ever had to do. *Maybe that's why he can think of a poor lost girl as nothing more than a character for a story.* "If you're looking for a story to write," she said, "we have twenty of them here right now. One of our guests, who arrived a short time before you did, is about sixteen years old and has been used as an ashtray—somebody's been burning her arm with cigars. We have another girl who was sold into prostitution at age twelve, right here in Manhattan. And then there's Samantha, who was kept prisoner in a sweatshop, chained to a sewing machine because she was fined more for broken needles than she earned in wages." Rebecca's voice rose with anger, although she wasn't really angry at anyone in particular; it was the anger of frustration. She told the stories of a few more residents of Colden House, giving the worst cases to drive it into Webb's head as she wished she could drive it into society's consciousness.

Finally taking a breath, she looked at Webb for his reaction. His expression was distant, as if he simply didn't care to hear about such things. Now she was angry at herself for having been attracted to him earlier. "I'm afraid that's all the time I can spare, Mr. Webb." She wiped her hands on her skirt. "I need to check on the girl who came in earlier."

"I understand," Webb said. "Thank you for all the time you have given me. I can see myself out." He hesitated. "The girl with the burns . . . will she be all right?"

Rebecca was taken aback by the note of genuine concern in his voice. "I don't know. But if there's anything I can do about it, she will be."

With a final good-bye, Webb went out to the foyer. Rebecca fought back the urge to see him to the door. She was generally a good judge of people, but she didn't know what to make of this man.

CHAPTER 11

Just south of the Tenderloin was one of New York's fastest-growing shopping districts. Although not nearly as fashionable as the "Ladies' Mile" over on Broadway, the half-dozen blocks running below Twentieth Street on Sixth Avenue were home to a number of fine department stores. Among them was Tyner's Dry Goods Emporium, a block away from its chief competitor, B. Altman. The day after his visit to Colden House, Marshall Webb walked into Tyner's, making his first entry there in several years.

The store looked largely as he remembered it. Sturdy, dark wood tables and shelves were stacked high with linens, bedspreads, dress materials, curtains, and a variety of other home furnishings. The sales clerks, all male, were identically attired in square-cut blue sack suits and bow ties, and served a clientele almost exclusively female. Although clean and well-lit, Tyner's was plainly appointed and lacked carpeting on the floor. Webb had heard Mr. Tyner speak often enough about his policy of keeping operating expenses to a minimum: "You keep down costs, and you can keep down prices. Low prices mean more customers, and more customers mean more profit." Profits had been high, Webb knew, since before the Lincoln administration.

He approached an aged clerk whose appearance hadn't changed in the twenty years since Webb had first encountered him. "Excuse me. Do you know where I might find Mr. Paul Tyner?"

The clerk showed no sign of recognizing him, which was fine with Webb. "I believe he's in silks, sir." The old man tilted his long nose in the direction Webb should take.

After making his way past a couple of matronly women quarreling over a lace bed set—each claimed to have seen it first—

Webb found his younger brother standing before a stack of brightly colored silk bolts.

Paul Tyner looked every bit the successful merchant. His enormous belly, the hallmark of every thriving businessman from Diamond Jim Brady to J. P. Morgan, appeared to require the massive watch chain draped across his vest to keep it from bursting. The suit he wore was the same navy blue as those of the clerks, but of a finer weave and more elegant cut.

At Webb's approach, Paul eyed him with a mix of curiosity and worry. It was a distrustful expression that Webb had come to dread, and part of the reason he seldom saw his brother anymore. Several years earlier, when Webb had hit bottom, it was to Paul that he had gone for help, and his brother had given it willingly. The two never mentioned the past again, but ever since, Paul always scrutinized Webb with suspicion, as if expecting that he'd relapsed into old habits.

As they politely greeted each other and shook hands, Webb was struck by how different they were. Paul, several years younger, looked at least ten years older; his hair appeared to have fallen, with only a few thin brown strands on top and a spade beard jutting out from his jawline, and the concerns of business had etched themselves around his sunken eyes. The difference extended to their names and family connections; although full brothers by birth, Paul had taken their stepfather's name when their widowed mother remarried, and happily went into the Tyner business before he'd turned twenty-one.

Mildly irritated at the probing look Paul continued to give him, Webb wanted to say, "I'm doing fine on my own, thanks, and don't need a thing from you." Instead he said, "I was shopping for some towels and thought I might as well buy them here." He didn't add that the main reason for coming to Tyner's was that he intended to count it as a family visit, thereby letting him decline any other family functions for a while.

"I'm glad you did," said Paul. Clearly relieved that Webb hadn't come because of a problem, he added, "It's good to see you again, Marshall."

"You too, Paul. You're looking prosperous."

Paul beamed. "Business has been good. And Father has promoted me to manager, you know."

Webb winced at hearing "Father." To Webb, who, unlike Paul,

remembered their real father, their mother's new husband remained "Mr. Tyner." He said with a forced smile, "Yes, congratulations." It was about the fourth time in the past six months that he'd congratulated Paul on the same "news." "Like I said, I'm here to give you some more business. I want about a hundred towels and—"

"What are you doing—opening a hotel?" Paul chuckled at what he thought was a hilarious joke.

"No, they're not for me. There's a place down on State Street, Colden House, that shelters lost and hurt girls. I was there last night and saw they could use some new towels. Probably need blankets and linens too. I want—"

Paul interrupted, "Are you"—he cleared his throat—"*involved* with one of these girls?"

"No." Another reason Webb didn't care for family visits were the inquiries—never subtle—as to whether there was a woman in his life. "I just saw that they're doing some good there and I want to help out."

After a brief pause, Paul said, "If they don't have to be fancy, I got a terrific deal on some huckaback towels from a jobber in Philadelphia—bought his entire stock. Good quality, all linen, hemmed but no fringes. And no patterns, only plain white. They're marked at a dollar thirty-five a dozen."

"They'll do," said Webb.

"What I'm thinking," continued Paul, "is that nobody's buying them anyway. Everyone wants the fringed damask towels these days, so my great deal isn't doing me any good." He again cleared his throat. "So how about if the store simply donates eight or nine dozen to this Colden place."

Webb was surprised. "I didn't know Tyner's Dry Goods was doing charity work now." He immediately regretted how ungracious that sounded, but Mr. Tyner was notoriously stingy.

"Father will never know. I'll take them off inventory."

"Thank you," said Webb, truly grateful. If Paul's generosity was discovered, he would probably get in trouble for it.

"You mentioned blankets," Paul went on. "We're overstocked on some wool blankets. Plain gray, but warm enough—five-pound weight. Marked at one-fifteen a pair, but I'll throw in a couple dozen of those, too. You want to pick them up yourself, or have them delivered?"

"Delivered to Colden House, if you don't mind. I'd just as soon keep the donation anonymous."

Paul smiled. "So would I."

Webb again thanked his brother.

Before letting him go, Paul asked, "You *will* be coming to Sunday dinner tomorrow, won't you?"

So this was a quid pro quo, realized Webb. "No. But please give mother my love."

"You haven't come in months," Paul sternly reminded him.

"I was there for Christmas."

"You *had* to come for Christmas. That doesn't count."

Webb didn't like to refuse. He owed his brother—he would always owe him, for far more than the towels and blankets. But he wasn't up to facing the family right now. "I'd like to," he said. "Honest. But I'm working on something important."

Paul again looked quizzical but didn't press for details. Webb had never told him about writing dime novels, and sometimes he thought Paul suspected that he made a living through illegal means. Paul was certainly a good enough businessman to realize that Webb's infrequent pieces in *Harper's* didn't pay enough to support him.

"I'll come to dinner soon," Webb promised. "I'm in the middle of a terrific story and have to get it finished." He didn't mention that the story wasn't for *Harper's Weekly*.

CHAPTER 12

Wednesday morning, Webb found himself called on the carpet in the office of Harry M. Hargis. And an expensive carpet it was—Oriental, picked up on a visit to Persia, as the dapper *Harper's Weekly* associate editor was happy to tell visitors. The entire office was expensively furnished in a manner that Webb considered more arrogant than tasteful. But that suited the publication, whose masthead bore the immodest motto "A Journal of Civilization."

Hargis's personal appearance matched the ostentatious decor. The waxed tips of his dainty mustache were curled up, and his well-groomed hair was plastered down. His stiff wing collar was so high that it could have served as a chin rest. A carnation the same shade of red as his silk cravat was pinned to the lapel of his alpaca coat.

From behind his carved mahogany desk, Hargis said, "I've been hearing a lot about you, Webb—far more than I care to hear."

"How so, Mr. Hargis?"

The editor drew deeply on his long cigar. "Monday, I received a telephone call from a fellow name Tate, Alfred—or Albert or something—Tate. He's Thomas Edison's personal secretary, and he was interested to know when *Harper's* would be publishing Mr. Webb's article on the kinetograph." He leaned toward Webb. "Imagine my surprise; I had no idea we were doing another story on Edison's moving-picture machine. Would you care to explain?"

Webb thought fast and answered slowly. "I didn't say that the article had been commissioned, nor did I promise anything would be published." He decided not to mention seeing the camera at

Ellis Island. "The article we ran last year made it sound like a marvelous invention, and I was curious as to whether there had been any further developments."

"So you presented your card, implying that you were there on *Harper's* business."

Since that was exactly what he had done, Webb shrugged in affirmation.

"Mr. Edison is a highly respected man. And news of his inventions always sell a lot of papers. We don't want you wasting his time on fishing expeditions, or he may not cooperate with us in the future."

There was little chance of that, thought Webb, since Edison positively craved publicity, but he answered meekly, "Sorry, Mr. Hargis."

Hargis leaned back, rolling the cigar between his manicured fingertips. "Yesterday I received another phone call. This time it wasn't to ask when we'd be publishing a story, but to make sure we *wouldn't* be."

Webb didn't understand. "From Mr. Edison's office?"

"No. This was from the government—the United States government!" Hargis referred to a sheet of paper on his desk. "Mr. Ivins, a superintendent with the Bureau of Immigration, said you were recently at Ellis Island, and that you were doing a piece on the new receiving station for us."

"I didn't say anything definite about—"

Hargis waved him to be quiet. "The point is, Mr. Ivins made a complaint about you. He said you asked some most impertinent questions, implying there was bribe-taking and other improper activities taking place on the part of immigration officers."

"I said there *used* to be, back when New York ran immigration. Everyone knows it." Webb was astonished that Ivins had taken his comment so seriously. For the most part, he thought his questions had been perfectly appropriate.

"He claimed you suggested such practices were continuing."

"But I—"

Hargis held up a hand. "The point is: Did anyone here ask you to do a story on Ellis Island?"

"No."

"Then stay away from there. And that's not only me telling you. As far as the Immigration Bureau is concerned, you are persona non grata." Hargis sighed a stream of cigar smoke. "Look Webb, I like you. You've never given us any problems before, and your occasional contributions are perfectly . . . adequate. But let's be blunt: You got your position, such as it is, as a favor to your family." He planted the cigar back between his teeth. "You've been here two years, is it?"

"Almost three."

"And you're doing very nicely. In time, maybe you'll even develop into a real writer. Perhaps get a staff position."

Webb resisted the temptation to tell Hargis that he was already a real writer and didn't need his charity. But the editor wasn't likely to be impressed with such literary works as *The Courageous Cavalryman* or *Chief Wingo on the Warpath*. "I hope so, sir," he said.

"Then keep your nose clean, and don't ever again use the *Harper's* name unless you have an assignment from us. The name has meant a lot in this town—all over the world—since eighteen fifty-seven and I intend to protect it. If that should require that I sever your relationship with us, I would do so without hesitation. Do we understand each other?"

Webb said that he did and was dismissed like a schoolboy who'd been kept after class.

Rebecca Davies knew it was petty and childish, but she took pleasure in the shoddiness of Lawrence Pritchard's office. She truly didn't care about a person's possessions or status, but she had heard so many comments and criticisms about the poor furnishings of Colden House that it was almost a relief to see that there were places even less well appointed.

The cramped one-room office of Pritchard's Dime Library made Colden House look almost opulent in comparison. Several mismatched bookcases overflowed with books and manuscripts, the file cabinet was missing a drawer, the small throw rug in front of the editor's chipped pine desk was moth-eaten, and the two chairs that were squeezed close to the desk belonged to a kitchen set.

"I'm not sure I understand your purpose in coming here," said Pritchard. He blinked rapidly behind his pince-nez.

"I am here to speak to you about Mr. Marshall Webb," she told him again.

Pritchard fidgeted in obvious discomfort. "Why do you think I know—"

"And about the story he's writing." Rebecca was certain that Pritchard was the publisher of Webb's work. She had telephoned most of the dime-novel publishers in New York; all except Pritchard readily said they had never heard of Webb. Lawrence Pritchard didn't admit it, either, but he was so hesitant and evasive that he might as well have.

"I, uh . . ." Pritchard's sepulchral appearance and jitteriness made him look like a rattling ghost.

"Mr. Webb came to see me at Colden House," Rebecca continued, hoping to put the unfortunate man at ease. "He told me that he wrote dime novels"—muttered it, actually, as she recalled—"and that he was writing a story about a girl named Christina van der Waals, who'd arrived at Ellis Island some weeks ago. He hadn't been able to find her since, and thought I might be able to assist him."

"Very well, Miss Davies." Pritchard took out his handkerchief and dabbed the back of his neck. "I hope you don't think I was being impolite. It is Mr. Webb's desire that his work for me be kept confidential, and I was merely trying to respect his wishes." He creased the fold of the handkerchief and put it back in his pocket. "Since he has already discussed this book with you, however, I assume I may speak freely with you as well."

"Thank you." Rebecca gave him the same smile she used when trying to coax donations for Colden House. "I can see we're both cautious people, Mr. Pritchard. That's why I'm here. Before I help Mr. Webb with his book, I would like to know something about his work. Do you have any of his other novels that I may see?"

"Certainly." Pritchard stood and began rifling through a stack of publications on one of the shelves. He pulled out five or six thin paperbound volumes and laid them on the desk before her.

Rebecca almost winced at the garish covers depicting soldiers, cowboys, and Indians in various acts of violence. "David A. Byrd," she read aloud.

"That's Mr. Webb's nom de plume," explained Pritchard. "As I said, he prefers that no one know of his authorship of these books."

The sanguinary covers and titles led Rebecca to think that perhaps Webb wasn't the man she had hoped he'd be. "What about Mr. Webb personally?" she asked.

"He's . . . well . . . " Pritchard frowned slightly. "I'm not sure that I understand the question."

"Is he a man of integrity? You understand, I have a number of young women for whom I feel responsible, and before I decide to cooperate with Mr. Webb—to allow him in Colden House—I would like to know that he is a man of good character."

Pritchard hesitated. "I believe he is."

The tone failed to convince Rebecca. "Could you be more specific?" she pressed.

"Well, he is honest. Our business dealings have always been straightforward, and I have found him to be a man of his word." Pritchard thought a moment. "He's a bachelor, and as far as I know his work is the most important thing to him." He opened his mouth to say more, then closed it.

What is he leaving out? Rebecca wondered. *A man gets to be in his early thirties, never married or started a family, and all he cares for is writing juvenile dime novels?* There had to be more. "How long have you known him?"

"A few years." Pritchard began to fidget again. He finally said, "To be honest with you, Miss Davies, Marshall Webb is not an easy man to know. In the time that I've dealt with him, I have always found him to be a gentleman. What he was like before that"—he spread his hands—"you'll have to ask someone else."

CHAPTER 13

Webb crumpled up the sheet of foolscap and dropped it into the wicker wastebasket next to his desk. To his dismay, the basket now contained more balls of paper than there were sentences on those discarded sheets.

He began again, his gold-nibbed pen scratching away on a fresh sheet of paper:

> *Her first month in the new country certainly wasn't what Katie had expected, but she had survived it bravely, with pluck and optimism. She still knew that America was the place for her, and that she would achieve her dreams.*

Later, he could fill in the details of what happened during her first month, Webb figured. Right now, he wanted to pick up her story from the present—a task that would be infinitely easier if he could locate Christina. He'd begun sketching out a dozen possibilities this morning, but never found one convincing or satisfying.

Webb knew that part of the reason he'd renewed his work on the novel was that it was a way for him to sustain hope. He truly didn't care whether Katie's story ever made it into print. He simply didn't want to concede that Christina's story might already be over.

As he put pen to paper again, the doorbell startled him and the sentence he'd begun turned into a messy splotch of black ink. No matter; it probably wouldn't have turned out any better than his earlier efforts.

Webb went to the door and opened it to see the woman from

Colden House, Rebecca Davies. Surprise and curiosity got the better of his manners, and he stared at her without speaking. She was stylishly clothed in an emerald green reefer jacket and a plaited black mohair skirt. The gold brooch on her jacket lapel and the pearl pin in her brocade scarf were elegant and understated.

"Perhaps you don't remember me?" she prompted.

"Oh, I'm sorry, Miss Davies. Of course I remember you. It's just that I wasn't expecting . . ." Webb wondered if she had looked this attractive at Colden House. Perhaps it was the color in her face from being out in the February air that made her appear more radiant. Or the cluster of silk lilacs sprouting from her small bonnet like a splash of springtime.

"My apologies," she said. "I shouldn't have called on you without notice. I hope I'm not intruding."

In fact, Webb had become so accustomed to a solitary existence that almost any visitor seemed like an intruder. "Not at all. Please come in."

She did so, and began to eye the apartment in a manner that Webb found thoroughly invasive. He glanced around quickly to see if he had left a pair of trousers on a chair or his socks on the floor. No, the place was entirely presentable. It occurred to him that she was studying the room so intently to learn something about him, not because the furnishings were all that fascinating.

"Would you care for—" began Webb, before realizing that he didn't have much in the way of refreshments to offer. And he wasn't entirely comfortable having a woman in his apartment unchaperoned. "As a matter of fact, I was about to go to lunch. I'd be delighted if you would join me."

Her response wasn't what Webb had hoped. "Lunch? It's not even eleven o'clock." The words were clipped, the same as when she'd terminated his visit to Colden House and had left him to believe that there would be no further contact between them.

"Oh, right." Webb tried to think of a plausible explanation. "I was up quite early; I suppose my schedule is a bit off."

The puffy sleeves of her jacket lifted in a shrug. "Late breakfast, early lunch . . . either way, I'd be happy to join you."

Webb found himself more pleased than he expected at her acceptance. "Very well," he said, smiling. "Let me get my hat and coat, and we'll take a hansom cab. The St. Denis serves an excellent lunch—or breakfast, if you prefer."

"That's not far," she replied. "And it's the first sunny day we've had in weeks. Do you mind if we walk instead?"

Webb didn't mind at all; in fact, he quite enjoyed walking about town with an attractive young woman by his side. And based on the glances he kept stealing as they strolled over to Broadway, she was indeed a handsome woman; with some more attention to her appearance, she would even be pretty.

Miss Davies was tall, about five-eight, with a trim figure, and Webb judged her age to be somewhere between twenty-five and thirty. Her honey blond hair was in a chignon, with a number of loose strands dancing about her fair face. She had fine features, but they were somewhat sternly fixed; her lips were a bit tight, and there was a rather impudent tilt to her jaw. Altogether, thought Webb, with a little face powder to soften her look, and a more relaxed demeanor, Rebecca Davies could be quite a vision.

"Mr. Webb?" she asked expectantly.

"Yes?" It occurred to Webb that she had been saying something, but he hadn't been listening.

"I asked about your search for Miss van der Waals. Have you found her?"

"No. And I'm at a loss for where to go next." He thought of his writing attempts this morning. "I will keep trying, however."

"You're interested in her for a story, not because you care about her, is that correct?" asked Miss Davies.

It sounded to Webb like an accusation. He wasn't sure how to answer. "That was my original reason for pursuing her, yes. But now . . ." After a thoughtful pause, he continued, "I would like to know that she is all right."

"Ah, still hoping for the happy ending."

Webb tried to see her expression to determine if the comment was intended to be good-natured or if she was ridiculing him, but his attention was suddenly diverted by a passing coal wagon. Throughout their walk, Webb had had to keep a wary eye on the street. The morning sun was melting the accumulated ice and snow, which proceeded to mix with the horse excrement on the pavement. The result was a foul slush that was sprayed up by the wheels of passing carriages and wagons. Webb did his gentleman's duty, walking on the curb side of the sidewalk to protect Miss Davies from the vile showers.

He got off lucky with the coal wagon; it was traveling slowly enough that the wet spray only reached his boots. By the time he looked back to his companion, she was opening her mouth for her next question. "Tell me," she said, "how long have you been a writer?"

From her demanding tone, Webb could tell that Miss Davies wasn't merely passing the time with friendly conversation. Her questions had a purpose to them, and if she wanted answers, he thought, she ought to have the decency to tell him that purpose. "For a while," he replied.

"What did you do before that?" She sounded like a prospective employer.

"I tried my hand at several vocations." Webb then tried to turn the interview around. "Have you been at Colden House very long?"

"A little over ten years."

"How did you come to start working there?"

"Family connections."

She could at least answer with complete sentences, thought Webb.

"But about you," she said. "I imagine you must need some education to be a writer."

Webb grunted noncommittally. If Miss Davies wanted to compete for the shortest responses, he'd be happy to play that game.

By the time the waiter came to take their orders, Webb was inclined to eat lightly so that he could be sooner done with lunch and Rebecca Davies. Then he reconsidered; perhaps he should instead order the best fare available so that at least the food would be agreeable, if not the company. He finally decided on the latter course, opting for turtle soup and roast duck while Miss Davies ordered toast with tea.

Seated across from her in the stylishly appointed dining room of the St. Denis Hotel, Webb tried to make up his mind whether his companion's eyes were green or hazel. Whatever the color, they were marvelously expressive; Webb had the sense that they could turn fiery angry or steely cold in a split second. Fortunately, he wasn't subjected to either of those extremes, and he found that he rather enjoyed looking at Miss Davies's face. Her relentless questions, however, continued to grate on him.

When the soup was served and Webb lifted the first spoonful to his mouth, she asked him, "Do you prefer to be called Mr. Webb or Mr. Byrd?"

His gaze jerked upward and he saw that the expression in her eyes had turned mischievous. After coughing clear some of the soup that had gone down his windpipe, he answered, "I prefer Marshall."

Miss Davies appeared disappointed that he didn't register more alarm. "I thought you would be curious about how I know of your other identity."

Webb was intensely curious, but determined not to let it show. "I assume someone told you."

"Your editor, Mr. Pritchard, was kind enough to give me some of your novels." She added quickly, "Please don't think he betrayed you. I'm afraid I deceived him somewhat—I led him to believe that you'd already told me about your books."

Webb silently cursed Pritchard for giving him away, then cursed him again for not informing him afterward that he'd spoken to Miss Davies. "I'm not ashamed of what I do," he said quietly. "But I do prefer to keep that part of my life confidential. I would be grateful if you would keep it such."

"I have no interest in revealing your secret," she said with an easy smile. "I only wanted to know more about you."

Webb flushed, flattered at the admission. He could think of nothing to say in response.

Rebecca Davies went on. "I've read some of your stories. Rather melodramatic, and too much blood and gore for my taste. An awfully simplistic writing style, too." She took a bite of toast. "But I suppose that's what people like to read."

Webb flushed again, this time with annoyance. *This woman came to see me because she wanted to critique my writing?* "They seem to," he said through clenched teeth.

Apparently oblivious to Webb's irritation, Miss Davies ventured, "I was hoping that I could talk you into writing a new book."

There was positively no rhyme or reason to the questions and statements that came out of this woman's mouth, thought Webb. He put down his spoon, wishing that he had opted for a smaller lunch so that he could sooner make his escape from her. "I don't understand." It was a totally truthful statement.

She looked at him directly, earnestly. "I would like you to write a realistic story about the awful things that can happen to some of the immigrant girls who come to this country. I want it to be something like Jacob Riis's *How the Other Half Lives*."

"Why do we need another *How the Other Half Lives* when the original came out only a year or two ago?"

"I think we can use a different one. Riis used photographs for his portrayals, and most of the illustrations that were published were only sketches from his photos. I think a *story*, with characters that readers can follow, might capture people's attention better. Also, the people in Riis's book weren't like us. They were the 'other half,' people living in Bowery tenements or Chinatown. I want you to write about what's happening all over New York to these immigrant girls—in sweatshops and brothels and on the streets."

"Why would you think I'm the person to write such a book? After all, I specialize in gory melodrama." Still smarting from her assessment of his work, Webb added, "*Simplistic* gory melodrama."

Miss Davies ignored his sour tone. "Dickens wrote melodrama, too. And not simplistic, but accessible. He wrote for people, and that's what I'm looking for you to do. If you can capture the story of these girls as vividly as you wrote about Sergeant Frazier in that cavalry battle, people will read it."

Dickens was a flattering comparison, thought Webb, and he was pleased that she'd read *The Courageous Cavalryman*. But he warned himself not to feel too flattered again. This woman had a maddening way of tugging his spirits up and down.

She went on, "There's another reason why I think you're the one to write this book: I believe you would be sympathetic. You did seem concerned about Miss Yost—the girl who'd been burned with cigars. Also, two days ago, you sent a generous gift to the House: some very nice towels and blankets, for which I'm most grateful."

"What makes you think—" Webb cut himself off. She seemed to know everything else about him, so he shouldn't be surprised to find that she knew about that, too. "I intended for the donation to be anonymous."

She smiled. "I know. And that's all the more to your credit. I coaxed the name of the store from the deliveryman. Then I contacted Tyner's Dry Goods and was told by a Paul Tyner that they were donated at your request." A touch of pride colored her smile when she added, "I can be rather tenacious when I'm after something. I assure you, neither of those men had much of a chance with me."

"Why would you go through all that trouble?"

"It's routine. I try to identify all of our benefactors. We rely on donations, and I've found that the more you thank someone, the more likely they are to give again."

The waiter came with the duck. Webb sighed, knowing that it would be going largely to waste. Miss Davies had a terribly unsettling effect on his stomach.

Idling poking at the orange-glazed bird with his fork, Webb said, "I've already been working on a story about Christina van der Waals—'Katie' in my book. But without her, there is no story anymore."

"Every girl is a story."

"Not like Katie. She would have made it. If you'd met her, you'd have seen how spirited she was, how full of hope. Katie would have overcome anything and made a success of herself."

"You *really* only want stories with happy endings?"

"That's the way they're supposed to be."

"Mr. Webb—Marshall . . ." She appeared uncertain if he'd meant it when he said he preferred to be called by his first name. "*Everyone* comes to this country with hopes and dreams. I have a dozen Katies at Colden House right now."

"You don't understand. There was something *special* about this girl." He put down the fork. "*Is* something special. I want to continue looking for her."

"How long has it been now?"

"Just over a month."

"Why not do both?"

"Both?"

"Look for Miss van der Waals—perhaps I can help with that—*and* talk to some of my girls about their lives. Just consider writing about them. That's all I ask."

For the first time, Miss Davies was sounding reasonable. How could he not agree to consider what she'd asked? He looked at her again. With her sales pitch done, she had relaxed, suddenly appearing less intense and much softer. Her eyes were inviting. "Certainly I'll consider it," he answered. Surprised to find that his appetite had returned, Webb dug into his lunch.

CHAPTER 14

"You will? I'm very pleased to hear that." As well as a bit surprised. Rebecca had been left with the impression that Mr. Webb wasn't interested in her proposal. She bent slightly, bringing her mouth closer to the transmitter of the wall telephone, and asked, "How soon can you start?" *Ease up,* she immediately cautioned herself, *you're pushing him again.*

Webb's voice crackled over the line, giving the best answer she could have hoped for: "Right away."

"Would you care to come here this afternoon?"

After agreeing to a time of three o'clock, Rebecca hung up the receiver and began considering how to handle Mr. Webb. So far, he was willing to work with her, but he had sounded a bit skittish about the prospect. Her task would be to maintain his interest without overwhelming him. It would require considerable restraint on her part, for Rebecca was well aware that the subtle approach was not her strong suit. She'd lost more than one potential ally over the years by being too aggressive, too passionate, and—she freely admitted—too tactless.

After relinquishing supervision of the daily tasks to Miss Hummel for the afternoon, Rebecca went upstairs to speak with some of the guests. She had decided that the best approach with Mr. Webb was to have him meet some of the girls personally rather than ply him with statistics. He seemed to respond to individuals, such as Miss Yost and Miss van der Waals. Besides, what she wanted him to do in his book was give a human face to the victims of exploitation and abuse, not a litany of facts.

She also decided to start with immigrant girls; Webb might feel that she was helping him in his search for Christina van der Waals, and be more agreeable to helping her in turn.

Webb noticed quite a difference in Rebecca's demeanor. She had politely invited him into a clean, plainly furnished sitting room, and made him feel like a welcome guest, even taking his coat and offering a cup of tea.

Once they were both comfortably seated, and had warmed themselves with a few sips of Earl Grey, Rebecca said, "I thought I should tell you a bit about what we do here at Colden House."

"I'm curious to learn," said Webb. Another refreshing change from their lunch meeting was that this time she was speaking with him, not interrogating him.

"I know you've been to a number of other homes for women during your search for Miss van der Waals. Although I am sure that many of those are run by people with the best intentions, too many of them, in my opinion, are overly restrictive in whom they will accept. At Colden House, we take in women who need help and who are willing to make an effort to help themselves. Whether she has an 'acceptable' religion or nationality, or a sufficiently 'virtuous' past is not a requirement." Rebecca's voice had started to rise, and she paused for a deep breath. "That's one difference," she continued. "Another is the house itself. We try to make it both a home and a safe harbor for the women who stay here. Today you'll meet a couple of them, but their stories are not easy for them to tell. So speak with them briefly, please, and don't press for details if they don't wish to discuss them. I'll be present during your conversations to make them more comfortable, if you don't mind."

"On the contrary," said Webb. "I would prefer it."

Rebecca smiled warmly. "Very well. I thought I would introduce you to a few of the girls who are recent immigrants. They may provide you with some idea of what Miss van der Waals might have experienced."

While she went upstairs to get the first girl, Webb thought about the difference in Rebecca's manner. Previously, she had been pushing him; now she'd adopted the opposite tack: pulling him, trying to coax him to where she wanted him to go. Usually he didn't take well to any kind of manipulation, but Rebecca Davies was quite appealing in her new approach. Webb had the feeling that she could easily coax him into almost anything, and he would go willingly.

Rebecca soon returned, and Webb noticed that in the time she'd been gone a few of her stray blond locks had been tucked into place. Accompanying her was a short, dark-haired young woman in a plain black wool skirt and an equally plain white-linen shirtwaist. She probably wasn't quite twenty years old, and from her coloring Webb guessed that she was probably Greek or Italian.

"Mr. Webb," said Rebecca, "this is Miss Gia Serrano. She's been in America less than a year, but she speaks English very well and has agreed to chat with us." The young woman bit her lip and nodded shyly. She kept her heavy-lidded eyes directed down at the carpet and clutched a handkerchief in her hand.

Webb stood, and with a small bow said, "It's a pleasure to meet you, Miss Serrano." He received another nod in response.

Rebecca led the young woman to the sofa and sat down next to her while Webb took the armchair facing them. "Tell Mr. Webb about your arrival in America." She patted the girl's forearm. "You can tell him everything."

"Yes, Miss Davies." Her voice was soft, and her Italian accent so light that it was almost a lilt.

"Where did you come from?" Webb asked.

"Sardinia. I have a mother and two younger sisters still there. My father I don't have anymore. He was a fisherman; he drowned in a storm three years ago." She stared down at the handkerchief in her folded hands.

When she hesitated to go on, Rebecca prompted, "So you decided to come to America."

"Yes. To support my mother and sisters. There was no work in our village except to fish, and that is only for the men. Everybody says that in America it is easy to become rich, so I came here to work, to make enough money to bring my mother and sisters. From my uncle, I borrowed the money for the fare to come here. It was supposed to take ten days, the trip, but we were at sea for two weeks." She tugged and twisted the handkerchief. "We finally came in to Castle Garden and I was so excited to be in America. But the immigration officer, he tells me I can't have permission to come into the country yet. He tells me I have to meet him later, in the city, to get my entry pass. He says it's a rule for women traveling alone." She lowered her head further. "I didn't know . . . so I believed him. He said to come to the Graney Hotel, where all the new girls stay. I did, and he took me to a room, and he—" She began to sob. "I am *such* a stupid thing."

Rebecca said to her, "It wasn't your fault." To Webb she said quietly, "He forced himself on her."

Miss Serrano brought the handkerchief to her eyes, dabbed at the tears, and caught her breath. "When he finished, he said to me, 'Welcome to America.' Then he took all the money I had and left me there. I didn't know what to do; I only wanted to leave quickly in case he came back. But the hotel manager stopped me in the lobby. He says I can't leave until I pay for the room. When I tell him I can't because I have no money, he has me taken to jail."

Webb asked, "Didn't you tell the police what happened?"

"I tried. They said I was making up a story. And that I had to pay my bill or I stay in jail. Then the manager says I can work it off for him by cleaning. I didn't know what to do—I had no job, no money, no place to stay. I had to agree."

Rebecca said to Webb, "She was there eight months before she came to us."

"Eight *months* to work off a hotel bill?"

"I kept owing him more money," Miss Serrano said. "He charged me rent to stay there, and charged me for food. When I said I would work somewhere else to pay him, he said he would take me back to jail. So I stayed—until I heard about Miss Davies and how she helps girls like me."

"What are you going to do?" Webb asked.

Rebecca answered for her. "She'll stay with us for now. Then we'll try to find her a decent job in another city, maybe Boston."

"I would work very hard," said Miss Serrano.

"I know you will." Rebecca Davies stood. "Let me take you back upstairs."

The two left Webb alone to ponder what he'd heard. He knew that the rampant corruption at Castle Garden was one of the reasons the federal government had taken over immigration from the New York authorities. But he'd thought that bribery and theft were the usual offenses. Rape went beyond anything he could have imagined.

Rebecca returned with a gaunt young woman in a faded gingham dress. She had high Slavic cheekbones, hair a slightly darker shade of blond than Rebecca's, and her eyes had the squint of someone with poor vision. Rebecca introduced her as Vanessa Drobosky and ushered her to the same spot where Miss Serrano had sat.

"Miss Drobosky came to America from Poland almost three years ago," Rebecca began. She turned to the young woman. "Tell Mr. Webb what happened when you arrived."

"My father had heard the stories about this country," she said in precise English. "He didn't believe that the streets were really paved with gold, of course, but so many people talked about how good life was in this country that he decided to take us all to America. My mother, father, brother, and me. A good, strong family, my father said, could accomplish anything together.

"We came to Castle Garden and my father bought our entry passes—he didn't know until later that you don't have to pay for them. But he said it was a small price to pay to come into this country. The officer who took his money then told him how he could get a good job right away; all he had to do was see a certain man outside the receiving station." She pursed her lips distastefully but, unlike Miss Serrano, kept her head proudly high as she spoke. "There were many men outside Castle Garden. Some offered jobs and rooms; others were money changers or railroad agents."

"Everything for a price, of course," Rebecca commented.

"Yes," said Miss Drobosky. "But how is somebody new to this country supposed to know what is the proper amount to pay for things? Or what is the proper way to get a job?"

"You can't be expected to," answered Webb.

"My father," she went on, "found this man, who offered to get us a house and give us all jobs—if we paid him five dollars. After buying our passes, it was almost all the money my father had left, but he gave it to him. Then we were put in an open wagon with some other people from our ship and taken to Ludlow Street. The 'house' turned out to be a tenement; it was a dreadful, filthy place that looked like prison. The man wanted fourteen dollars a month for a two-room flat on the six floor. There wasn't even a window—only an air shaft that everyone used as a garbage dump." Miss Drobosky appeared nauseated at the memory of it. "But with no money left, we couldn't go anywhere else. We didn't have enough to pay the rent in advance, but since we were going to work for this man, he said he would take it out of our pay. My father had no choice but to agree; he thought we would soon be able to afford a real home." She shook her head sadly. "The jobs turned out to be as bad as the rooms. We had to work on another floor of the tenement that had been turned into a workshop for making knee-pants. My father did the cutting, my mother and I worked the sewing machines, and my brother was assigned a pressing iron. We worked twelve hours a day, sometimes more, and turned out hundreds of knee-pants. But we never really made money; the boss would fine us for broken sewing needles, or talking, or not working fast enough. Then the rent was due, and again we had to owe most of it. We tried to save—lived on almost nothing but bread and pickles—but never could get ahead. Two months ago, my brother couldn't take it anymore; he ran away. Now there's one less worker to make money, so we owe the boss even more. My mother and father are heartbroken that Tadeusz is gone, and wish we had stayed in Poland. We were poor there, but we weren't slaves."

Webb wondered what her parents were going to do with their daughter gone as well. "How long have you been at Colden House?" he asked.

"A week. Miss Davies says I can learn to be a telephone operator. Then I can get a good job and pay what my parents owe, so they can move out." She turned to Rebecca, "Will that take very long?"

"I don't know, but we'll do everything we can." To Webb Rebecca said, "The man they met outside the Barge Office is a 'sweater.' They're like vultures, the way they prey on immigrants to get them into their sweatshops and tenements." After telling Miss Drobosky she could go, Rebecca added, "Believe it or not, there are even worse 'agents' than the man the Droboskys encountered. Some pretend to be officials and put newcomers into carriages telling them they're going to another immigration building; but they're often taken to trains bound for the Midwest, where the immigrants end up working in factories or slaughterhouses as slave labor. And for young women arriving alone, it's often worse than that: they might be taken to brothels and forced into prostitution. I have another guest who went recently went through that ordeal, if you'd care to speak to her."

"No," said Webb. He'd been given enough to think about for

one day. He began considering all he had heard, then felt Rebecca's expectant stare upon him. She obviously wanted him to share his thoughts. "I'm wondering," he said, "if Christina van der Waals might have run into a situation like these girls did."

"Very likely, I'm sorry to say. Young women alone are the most vulnerable to the procurers and sweaters—and to crooked officials."

Since he assumed Rebecca would find out anyway if she chose to, Webb volunteered that he also wrote for *Harper's Weekly*. "I visited Ellis Island after Christina arrived, and talked to an official—said I was writing a story for *Harper's*. He didn't care for some of my questions and called my editor to complain. I wonder if it's because there are still crooked officers there and they don't want the attention."

"There will always be some corruption," said Rebecca. "Whether federal, state, or city, some officials will always to use their positions for personal gain. I do hope that Miss van der Waals didn't fall into the hotel-room trick."

"I doubt it," answered Webb. "She already had her entry pass."

"She might have been lured away by someone at the Barge Office, then."

"But why would she go off with a stranger? She was expecting to be met by her cousin." He remembered his conversation with Liz Luck. "Her cousin didn't know she was coming, though, so Christina must have given up waiting for her at some point and gone off on her own."

"She hadn't written to tell her cousin that she was coming?"

Webb filled Rebecca in on his discussion with Liz Luck. "I believe what she told me," he said, "about not knowing that Cristina was here. But I don't know about her husband. He's a policeman, by the way. He's making no effort to look for Christina. He should be able to do *something* to find her. I'm going to have a talk with him, I think."

"Do you mind if I speak with Miss Luck?" Rebecca asked. "We can compare notes then."

Webb doubted that there was more to learn, but he liked the idea of working together with Rebecca.

CHAPTER 15

Rebecca Davies wasn't certain that she would learn anything more from Liz Luck than Webb had, but she knew that the woman might find it easier to talk with someone of her own sex, and perhaps reveal more than she had to Webb.

A little past noon, a time when she figured that Miss Luck was likely to be at home and her husband walking a beat, Rebecca went to see her. Walking along Twenty-eighth Street past the gambling houses, pool halls, saloons, and pawnshops, she noticed a number of women, both young and old, who were clearly down and out. Some were living under stairways or on fire escapes, with rags for bedding and nothing at all for protection. Rebecca had the urge to invite every one of them to come to Colden House, but reluctantly resisted it. *Don't be foolish,* she told herself; *you're already swamped with women coming in on their own, and simply* can't *offer shelter to everyone.*

When she came to the same ramshackle apartment building that Webb had described to her, next to the Gold Mine Pawnshop, she thought that at least it wasn't as bad as some she'd seen—certainly better than the tenements on the East Side. The residents of this area were probably working people, she figured, most likely making their livings here in the Tenderloin.

Rebecca groped her way along the darkened hallway, almost tripping over a sleeping old man, and found apartment 3B.

Her knock was answered by a frightened female voice. "Who is it?"

"Miss Luck?"

"Yes. Who are you?"

"My name is Rebecca Davies," she answered through the flimsy door. "I would like to speak with you, if I may."

"No. I'm not seeing anyone. Go away."

"It's about your cousin, Christina van der Waals."

The door cracked open and a woman's red, puffy eye peered at her. "Do you know where she is?"

"No, I'm sorry I don't. But I hope we can find her soon. Please, may I speak with you?"

The door creaked open. "Come in."

Rebecca did so, and Liz Luck quickly closed the door behind them. When Luck turned around, she held a hand over the right side of her face. Despite the woman's attempt to hide it, Rebecca could see her swollen cheek and black eye; she elected to pretend that she didn't notice.

"I won't take much of your time," Rebecca began. "I run a shelter for women, Colden House, and I've had an inquiry about your cousin, Miss van der Waals. I would like to help find her, if possible, and I'm hoping that you might give me some information."

"I'd tell you *anything* to help Christina, if I knew anything. But I don't." Luck pulled her worn lounging robe more snugly around her. There was no heat in the shabby apartment, and little sunlight came through the one small window. "Who was it that asked about her?"

"A Mr. Webb," Rebecca said. "According to him, Christina was expecting you to meet her when she arrived. Why didn't you?"

"Because I didn't know she was coming!"

"She wrote to tell you."

"I never got her letter." Her uncovered eye began to water. "We've had to move four times in the last year—we sometimes have trouble making the rent. Her letters never caught up to us."

"When was the last time that you did get mail from her?"

"About a year ago. She didn't say anything about coming to America."

Rebecca believed what Liz Luck was telling her. She'd heard enough stories to have a sense of when someone was telling her the truth. "Okay," she said, "but if you didn't go to meet Christina, why didn't she come to you? She knew you worked at the Baylor Opera House, didn't she?"

Luck walked over to the kitchen table and slumped into a chair. "Maybe she did go to the theater. If she did, she saw what that damned place really is, and probably didn't *want* to see me."

"Are all the dancers there also, uh . . . ?" When Liz didn't respond, Rebecca said, "Don't worry. I have no intention of telling your husband."

The woman snorted and for the first time showed anger. "Warren Gleason is not my husband. He's never thought it necessary to go through the formality of a wedding." She dropped the hand from her face. "And he knows exactly what I do. He's the one who says I have to earn twenty dollars a week—if not by dancing, then by working the private rooms." She pointed to the bruised skin around her eye. "I was two dollars short this week."

Rebecca was appalled. She knew that police officers tolerated vice, often partook of it, and accepted graft for protecting the bagnios and dance halls. But she had never heard of a policeman pushing his own wife—even if a common-law wife—into prostitution.

Liz Luck went on, "I don't know if Christina ever came to the Baylor. I've been all over the neighborhood, showing the photograph that Mr. Webb gave me. Nobody's remembers seeing her." Sobs began to interrupt her breathing. "And I'm almost happy about that. I'd hate to think what could have happened to her if she came into the Tenderloin. But if she didn't come here, then where *did* she go? Where *is* she?"

"I wish I could tell you," Rebecca said softly.

Luck's sobbing slowed; she appeared to lack the strength to continue crying. "Whatever's become of Christina is my fault. I never told the truth about my life here. I wanted my family to think I was doing well in America—told them I had a husband and sang in an opera house. So what I'm choosing to believe is that Christina came to the Baylor and ran off when she saw what it was. Maybe that's a good thing; as much as I'd love to see her, I don't want her to see me. Not like this."

Rebecca decided not to mention the possibility that Christina had never made it to the theater. There was no need to say what everyone in this part of the city already knew: Lives were lost every day to the brutality of the environment and the cruelty of men. She said, "Thank you for talking with me. As for that eye, put some ice on it to get the swelling down." She would have said beefsteak, but it was unlikely that there was any in the house. "And if you ever need a safe place to stay, Colden House is in the Battery, on State Street. There will be a bed for you."

Luck nodded her thanks at the offer, and Rebecca let herself out.

Since Warren Gleason lived in the Nineteenth Precinct, Webb figured that he was most likely assigned to that precinct as well. So, while Rebecca went to speak with Liz Luck, Webb went to the station house at 137 West Thirtieth Street to talk with her husband.

The interior of the reeking, raucous police station was in keeping with its neighborhood. The dingy institutional waiting room was packed with denizens of the Tenderloin. Among them were flamboyantly dressed streetwalkers, pimps, and gamblers, as well as less conspicuously garbed pickpockets and muggers. Hunkered along the walls were the area's most destitute individuals. These men and women, who could afford no better shelter, spent their winter nights in "police lodging houses," sleeping in station house cellars. The ones here were probably waiting for evening, when the cellars would be opened up for them again.

Webb worked his way through the crowd to a high desk manned by a sergeant with bushy black side-whiskers. "I'd like to see Officer Gleason," he asked.

"We got a Jack Gleason and a Warren Gleason." The sergeant paused to spit a gob of tobacco juice on the waiting room floor; it splashed onto the bare foot of one of the paupers. "Which one you want?"

"Warren."

"Whaddaya want him *for?"*

"Information," Webb answered, hoping the sergeant would take that to mean he was an informant of Gleason's. "He said I should only talk to him."

"Well he ain't here. Gleason's a patrolman; he's out patrolling his beat."

"Where exactly *is* his beat?"

A fight suddenly broke out between a couple of the prostitutes, and the sergeant slammed his nightstick on the desk to get their attention. "You break it up, or I'll break your goddamn heads!" After the women were separated, he answered Webb, "Gleason patrols especially hard around the northeast corner of Twenty-ninth and Seventh. Try there."

Ten minutes later, Webb reached that intersection and found no police officers in sight. A few doors from the corner, though, on Twenty-ninth Street, was a narrow brick saloon with "Cutter's" painted over the door and "Beer" advertised on a grimy window.

Webb stepped inside and quickly sized up the place. It wasn't quite as repellent as the dives where he met Lawrence Pritchard. The gaslight was adequate, and the air, although smoky, was breathable. There was even music provided by an old man playing an Irish fiddle tune. Several women, who from their dress and conduct were either practicing or aspiring prostitutes, were talking to men at the bar and sitting with them at the tables. There were several card games going on, but Cutter's appeared to be the kind of saloon where a winner stood a reasonable chance of walking out alive and in possession of his winnings.

Standing at the bar, his boot propped on the foot rail and his meaty hand wrapped around a schooner of dark beer, was Patrolman Warren Gleason. Except for his helmet, which was resting next to an empty shot glass on the bar, Gleason was in full uniform. He was talking and laughing with a buxom woman who was as scantily dressed as the man-fishers on Sixth Avenue. She didn't appear the least concerned about his badge.

As Webb approached Gleason, he noted that the burly officer's expression wasn't quite as hard as it had been when they'd first met, and he was stroking his full red mustache as if trying to draw the woman's attention to the one graceful feature on his otherwise porcine face. From what Webb could hear, though, it sounded as if the officer and his companion were simply having a friendly chat rather than a negotiation for her services.

"Officer Gleason," Webb said. "May I speak to you for a minute?"

Gleason looked Webb up and down with pale, deep-set eyes. "You're the fella that was talking to my Liz."

"About her cousin, yes."

The officer took a swallow of his beer. "I suppose I can give you a minute, but not much more." He smirked. "I'm on duty, you know."

The woman he'd been speaking with cackled so hard that beer sprayed from her lips.

Gleason gave her a playful pat on her ample bottom. "Go get us a table, Rosie, and find me a lucky deck of cards. I won't be long." As Rosie sashayed away, Gleason told the bartender, "Give her another brew, Cutter. Put it on my tab."

The bartender scowled, but began drawing a glass of lager. Webb knew that New York police officers didn't have tabs—saloonkeepers were expected to provide them with all the free beer and food they wanted in order to remain in business.

Gleason turned his attention to Webb. "You said you was from immigration." It sounded like an accusation.

"That's right," answered Webb, realizing after he said it that he hadn't put much conviction in the statement.

"Now why would the U.S. Government be worried about one little Dutch girl?" Gleason switched from stroking his mustache to tugging at it.

Webb decided to pretend that the concern wasn't his. "Oh, some high muckamuck at the Treasury Department got the idea to track down some of the first arrivals to Ellis Island and see how they're doing. There were a lot of problems with the old immigration station at Castle Garden, and I suppose he's trying to show how well everything's working with the new system—to make himself look good, no doubt. So they pulled a few names from the first boatload, and Christina van der Waals is one of the ones I was assigned to find. But I'm not having any luck."

Gleason appeared satisfied with the story. "That's the damn government for you," he said. "If you ask me, there's too much concern about immigrants. The government ought to be worryin' about *Americans*, not these goddamn foreigners."

The bartender came back and asked Webb, "What'll it be?"

"Rye." Webb didn't think beer would be strong enough to help him tolerate Gleason's company.

"Put it on my tab," the policeman said again. "And I'll take another shot, too."

"Of course," muttered the bartender as he reached for the bottle.

Webb said to Gleason, "I thought you'd be concerned about *one* of the immigrants. After all, Christina is your wife's cousin."

"Well, yeah, of course I am. But I never met the girl in my life;

she's no blood kin of mine. Who knows why she really wanted to come here, or where she decided to go off to?"

"You weren't expecting her?"

"No." Gleason picked up his beer glass.

"She thought someone was going to meet her. She must have written to Miss Luck."

"I'm a cop, not a damn mailman." Gleason polished off the beer. "I didn't know nothin' about her coming here."

Two shots of whiskey were put on the bar before them. Webb drank his slowly, taking the time to think. He was getting nowhere with Gleason, and more polite questions weren't likely to get him any further. Putting his empty glass back down, he asked, "Where were you January first?"

The officer put down his own glass. "You government boys sure got cheek, dontcha?" He forced a smile, but there was no hint of amusement in eyes. "You're lucky I ain't the sort to take offense at a question like that. And the answer is, I was right here. We celebrated through the night New Year's Eve, and I decided to sleep it off in the back room." He beckoned to the bartender. "Ain't that right, Cutter? After that New Year's Eve party we had, I was here all the next day."

The bartender, who was half Gleason's size, wiped his hands on the bar rag and gave the cloth a hard twist. "Yeah, that's right." He sounded as unconvincing as a man who'd been beaten into confessing to a crime that he hadn't committed.

"You know," said Webb to Gleason, "I'm not a detective. I was told by my boss to find Christina, so that's what I'm trying to do as best I can. But it's really a job for professionals. Can't you get the police department to help find her?"

Gleason hunched his big shoulders. "Nope. Ain't no reward bein' offered. The detectives ain't gonna go looking for somebody if there's nothin' in it for them."

"Not even for a fellow cop?"

"Only if the fellow cop is puttin' up cold, hard cash."

"All right," said Webb. "I'll keep looking on my own. I'll let you know when I find her."

"You do that." Gleason picked up his helmet from the bar, indicating the conversation was over. "Cutter, bring Rosie and me a bottle. We're gonna play a little cards."

As Gleason moved away from the bar, Webb dug for a quarter and put it next to his empty shot glass.

Cutter said glumly, "Your drink is on Gleason."

"Then it's a tip."

The bartender nodded his appreciation and quickly pocketed the coin.

CHAPTER 16

Marshall Webb had fallen behind in his work, both for *Harper's* and for Lawrence Pritchard, so he cloistered himself in his apartment over the weekend and did nothing but write.

He worked on his *Harper's* article first, since it was shorter and more quickly gotten out of the way. Webb's assignment was to write a brief memorial about Brigadier General Henry A. Barnum of the Grand Army of the Republic, who had recently died of pneumonia. Unfortunately, there wasn't much to write about Barnum, whose inconsequential military service had been followed by an equally inconsequential career as a New York "public figure." The only reason for giving Barnum's death such prominent notice was because it had become standard practice to document the passing of each Civil War general and tally the number of those who still survived. Webb would have preferred to write about a heroic private rather than a privileged officer, but he managed to grind out enough words about Barnum to satisfy his editor.

It was then on to a Western story for Pritchard. Since his proposed book on Katie was taking so long, Webb had agreed to write another dime novel in the meantime. His heart wasn't in it, but he followed the basic plotline of one of his earlier books, changing the names of the characters and places. By mid-morning on Monday, he wrote "The End" to *Shady Sam, the Scourge of Snake Canyon*.

When he finished, Webb found that the coffee he'd been living on for the past two days was still affecting him. Unable to sleep, he pulled out his interrupted story about Katie and scanned the sparse pages. He wished that this book could be completed as easily as *Shady Sam,* and that he could determine the fate of its main character. But by now he didn't believe that he would ever see Christina van der Waals again.

Webb decided to go out for a walk in the hope that some fresh air and exercise would make him sleepy. It was a good day for a walk; the bright sunshine and warmer temperatures signaled that spring was fast arriving. There were even a number of bicyclists wheeling along Fourth Avenue. To Webb, they were an unwelcome sight; he hadn't succumbed to the bicycling craze and didn't see anything positive about adding yet one more type of vehicle to the trolleys, trucks, wagons, and carriages that already clogged the city's streets.

After aimless walking a couple of dozen blocks, Webb headed back home. At a Union Square newsstand, he stopped to buy several papers so that he could catch up on what he'd missed over the weekend.

Once he settled in his parlor easy chair, he skimmed the front pages of the newspapers and saw that they all reported on an astonishing sermon by the Reverend Charles H. Parkhurst, outspoken minister of the Madison Square Presbyterian Church. Parkhurst, who also served as head of the New York Society for the Prevention of Crime, a citizens' group, had delivered a virtual declaration of war against corruption in city government. According to the minister, the corruption was rampant, extending from the patrolman on the beat to the Mayor himself.

The *New York World* provided the most detailed coverage of the sermon, so Webb followed its account of Parkhurst's opening salvo:

> *In its municipal life our city is thoroughly rotten. . . . Every step that we take looking to the moral betterment of this city has to be taken directly in the teeth of the damnable pack of administrative bloodhounds that are fattening themselves on the ethical flesh and blood of our citizenship.*

The minister's rhetoric was full of fire and brimstone, and he came close to equating the city's political managers with Satan's minions:

There is not a form under which the devil disguises himself that so perplexes us in our efforts, or so bewilders us in the devising of our schemes, as the political harpies that, under the pretense of governing this city, are feeding day and night on its quivering vitals. They are a lying, perjured, rum-soaked and libidinous lot.

He specifically targeted Mayor Hugh Grant and his administration for attack, blaming them for the fact that Manhattan brothels and gambling houses were "as thick as roses in Sharon":

Every effort that is made to improve character in this city, every effort to make men respectable, honest, temperate and sexually clean is a direct blow between the eyes of the Mayor and his whole gang of drunken and lecherous subordinates. While we fight iniquity they shield and patronize it.

He also identified police graft as the system by which the municipal government profited from the vice industries:

All people ought to understand that crime in this city is entrenched in our municipal administration, and that what ought to be a bulwark against crime is a stronghold in its defense. . . . I should not be surprised to know that every building in this town in which gambling or prostitution or the illicit sale of liquor is carried on has immunity secured to it by a scale of police taxation that is as carefully graded and as thoroughly systematized as any that obtains in the assessment of personal property or real estate.

Parkhurst concluded that the Mayor, under the control of Tammany Hall, and his subordinates including the police, were linked in "official and administrative criminality that is filthifying our entire municipal life, making New York a very hotbed of knavery, debauchery and bestiality."

As he put the newspapers aside, Webb wondered what might result from Parkhurst's broadside. With so much coverage about the one sermon, perhaps the newspapers would follow up with their own investigations into vice and corruption. Yesterday might well have marked the first shot in a campaign to change city politics. He looked at the date on the paper: February 15. So the sermon had been delivered on Valentine's Day, a holiday that Webb had spent writing, alone.

He decided that maybe he'd talk to Rebecca about that book again.

CHAPTER 17

Rebecca Davies always had mixed emotions when one of her residents moved out, and that was never more true than at this morning's departure of Gia Serrano. After what Miss Serrano had endured as a virtual prisoner in the Graney Hotel, Rebecca wished that she could keep the young woman in her protective care a while longer. But she also realized that the sooner Miss Serrano began her new life, the happier she would be.

As Rebecca sat at her small corner desk in Colden House, writing a thank-you note to the Boston shop owner who had agreed to give Miss Serrano a job, she mentally checked to see if there was anything else she could do for the immigrant girl. Rebecca had already arranged for her to move into a respectable North End boarding house, and had given her the name of a friend in case she had any trouble in the new city.

"Pardon me," Miss Hummel said from a step or two behind her.

Rebecca swiveled about in her chair, startled. As much as she valued the older woman's quiet efficiency, Rebecca often thought she was *too* quiet; it was unnerving the way she could suddenly appear and disappear with hardly a sound or a word. "Yes?" She forced a polite smile.

"Your gentleman friend is here."

"My what?"

"Mr. Webb. He's in the foyer."

"He is *not* my—" Never mind, thought Rebecca. Protesting would only sound like confirmation. "Thank you, Miss Hummel. I'll see him."

With a hint of a smile tugging at her wrinkled face, Miss Hummel silently swept out of the room.

Rebecca proceeded to the foyer, where she spotted Marshall Webb stealing a glance at the hallway mirror. He smoothed down his whiskers and swept a finger over both sides of his mustache.

"Good to see you again, Mr. Webb," she said. After having been embarrassed by Miss Hummel, Rebecca got a mischievous pleasure at startling Webb during his grooming.

Webb quickly gripped his derby in both hands and held it in front of his vest. "I hope I'm not intruding," he said.

"Not at all." Rebecca noticed that he was clutching the hat so tightly that the brim was facing imminent destruction. She gestured to the coatrack. "Please."

As Webb hung up his outer garments, Rebecca couldn't help but think that something was wrong. Was there bad news about the fate of Christina van der Waals? "Any progress in your search?" she asked.

"Nothing definitive. Did you speak with her cousin?"

"Yes." She took a step backward. "Shall we go to the sitting room?"

Webb nodded and followed. Rebecca still thought he seemed a bit out of sorts.

Once they were seated, she filled him in on her meeting with Liz Luck, including the fact that Gleason had beaten her and required her to "work the boxes" to earn extra money. "As far as Miss van der Waals," Rebecca said, "I believe that Miss Luck knew nothing about her coming to America, and has had no communication from her." She added, "I'm not sure that she *wants* her cousin to see the way she's living."

Webb said, "I agree. From her reaction when I first spoke to her, I was convinced that she hadn't seen Miss van der Waals. As for Warren Gleason—" Webb appeared to be censoring his thoughts before going on to say what he thought of the policeman. "I'm not convinced about him. I talked to him at a saloon near his station house. When I asked where he was on New Year's Day, he was quick to offer an alibi, as well as a witness to confirm it. A bit *too* quick, I thought, and his witness wasn't particularly convincing."

"You think Mr. Gleason did something with Miss van der Waals?"

"I don't know, but it wouldn't surprise me."

He appeared on the verge of saying something more, so Rebecca waited. It got to the point where she wanted to tell him, "Out with it already!" but she prodded more gently, asking, "There's something else?"

"Yes, actually." Webb cleared his throat. "If you have no other commitment, I was hoping I could take you to dinner this evening."

Rebecca was taken aback at the sudden switch in topics. To her profound annoyance, she felt herself beginning to blush. "I would like that," she answered.

"Wonderful." Webb's smile was full of warmth, and with the lifting of his mustache Rebecca saw that he had good teeth. "Shall I pick you up at seven?"

"Seven would be fine." *And please go now before I turn any redder,* she added silently.

Webb thought he had done a fine job with the arrangements. He had made dinner reservations at Enzio's, one of the city's finest Italian restaurants. He'd been painstaking with his wardrobe selection; besides wearing his finest cashmere suit, his collar and cuffs were new, and his boots freshly shined. For transportation, he had decided to go for something more extravagant than a hansom cab, and hired a brougham for the evening.

By the time they reached the restaurant, he realized that it was a good thing that he'd arranged everything ahead of time, because from the moment he arrived at Colden House and saw Rebecca Davies in her exquisite lace-trimmed basque and shimmering silk skirt, he was oblivious to everything but her.

After they were seated, Webb continued to be so taken with the lovely vision before him that he didn't give the menu a glance. When the waiter arrived to take their dinner orders, he could think of nothing to say but "The usual."

Barely moving his lips, the waiter whispered, "And that would be . . .?"

Webb realized that he hadn't been to Enzio's in more than a year, and had never been a regular, but the only reply he made to the waiter was a sharp look of reprimand.

"*Very* good, sir." The unfortunate waiter almost darted back to the kitchen.

Left alone again, Webb tried to shake off his schoolboy daze, and shifted to making adult conversation. "Did you see the newspapers yesterday?" he asked. "Reverend Parkhurst delivered quite a sermon Sunday. He basically accused everyone from the mayor to the police of being complicit in crime and vice."

"I heard about it soon after he spoke." Rebecca took a sip of champagne; Webb couldn't remember ordering it, but he must have. "It was almost the sole topic of conversation during family dinner. Inspector Byrnes could hardly contain his anger over the reverend's sermon."

"*Thomas* Byrnes?" Webb asked with disbelief. Chief Inspector Thomas F. Byrnes, head of New York's detective bureau, was the city's most famous and powerful police official. "You're related to Inspector Byrnes?"

"No." Rebecca laughed. "He's no relation. But he is a friend of my brother-in-law, and occasionally comes to Sunday dinner. He's usually rather charming company. But he was outraged at Reverend Parkhurst's accusations of police corruption, and called him everything from a crank to a panderer. He also said that the Reverend would be held 'accountable' for his slander, but didn't elaborate."

"I'm hoping some good might come of the sermon," said Webb. "If the newspapers investigate Parkhurst's charges, the public might learn what's really going on in this city."

"Perhaps. But I don't have high hopes. Ministers love to rail against vice, but I believe they do it for titillation as much as anything. They don't say a word against the sweatshops. Or the slumlords. Or the wife beaters. Or those who abandon their children to the streets. The clergy have an awfully narrow definition of 'sin' sometimes." Her voice had started to rise. "Sorry," she said. "I was almost about to go off on a sermon of my own."

"Quite all right."

The waiter interrupted with their dinners. He'd decided that Webb's "usual" was sole florentine. Webb didn't much care for fish, and hated spinach, but he was stuck with the selection. He almost chuckled at the waiter's unwitting luck in getting revenge on him.

When they were left alone again, Webb asked, "Your family is in the city?"

"Oh, yes. And we have been for almost two hundred years. The city was still mostly Dutch when my ancestors arrived from

England. They established a bank, and ever since then, the only thing any Davies has made is money."

"But if your family is, uh . . ."

"Wealthy." Rebecca said it as a fact, not a boast.

"Yes. Then why do you work at Colden House?"

"It's been a family charity for years—since the eighteen-twenties. Around that time, there was a Society for the Prevention of Pauperism, made up of politicians and the social elite, which took the position that charity only encouraged pauperism. They urged that all public aid to the poor be cut off. The state and local governments were quick to follow their recommendation. Mayor Cadwallader Colden was one of the few who opposed the cuts, although he was powerless to stop them. So when my family and a few others decided to privately found Colden House, it was named in his honor." She smiled. "Actually, I'm not sure if it was to honor him or because his name might be perceived as an endorsement and help bring in future contributions. Raising money to keep a charity going is always more of a challenge than getting it started."

"But you do more than merely give money to the home," said Webb. "It seems you're there all the time."

"Much to my parents' dismay." Rebecca smiled tightly. "They believe it's the duty of the affluent to be charitable, but that coming into personal contact with the needy is excessive involvement. We've come to a happy agreement, though. I go to family functions, never speak about Colden House, and pretend to be an obedient daughter. My parents, in turn, pretend to be unaware of my personal involvement in the house, and continue to provide some financial support." Rebecca paused to dab wine sauce from her lips. "It's been easier for me since my sister, Alice, married into a good family—the Updegraffs. They've been here even longer than the Davies and have much more money. Alice's husband is an investor on Wall Street and does quite well from what I understand." She smiled again, wryly. "It's a great consolation to my parents; they hardly ever remind their elder daughter that she's a spinster anymore."

Wall Street, thought Webb. That probably explained the connection to the police inspector. Byrnes was famous for having established the Fulton Street "Dead Line," below which all suspected criminals—or characters who merely didn't dress well enough—were forcibly escorted out of the financial district. It was common knowledge that in exchange for keeping Wall Street free of undesirables, the chief inspector received profitable—and illegal—stock tips. "Excuse me?" said Webb, suddenly realizing that Rebecca had asked him something.

"I said tell me about your family."

"Oh." This wasn't a topic Webb cared to discuss, but he didn't want to be rude. He poked apart his fish as he answered. "I have an older sister, married, who moved to California about five years ago. You already know my younger brother Paul—Paul Tyner. He took our stepfather's name and manages his dry goods business. Our real father was killed in the war, at Cold Harbor."

"I'm so sorry."

Webb shifted uncomfortably. "I barely remember him. My mother remarried a few years later." That reminded him: he had promised Paul that he'd go to Sunday dinner soon. Maybe this week.

Rebecca appeared to be waiting for Webb to say more, but he didn't, and the two worked on their meals silently for a few minutes. The lull in the conversation began to feel uncomfortable, and Webb knew it was his fault.

To his relief, Rebecca asked, "How did you get started writing?"

"By reading," he answered promptly. "When I was a boy, I used to love the illustrated weeklies—*Harper's* and *Frank Leslie's*—and any dime novel I could get my hands on." He smiled. "As you pointed out, I've probably read too many of them."

"I didn't mean—"

Webb waved her off. "You were quite right. I did like the sensational stories and the happy endings. I still do. Eventually, I hoped to write stories myself, so I went to Princeton to study literature. Only lasted a year, though."

"What happened?"

"It didn't work out." Webb skipped over the next several years of his life. "Later I got a position at *Harper's* as a 'contributing editor.' That means about once a month I contribute an item they find worthy of publication." He thought of the boring piece he'd just finished about Brigadier General Henry Barnum. "It's not much of a job as far as I'm concerned, but my family is happy about it.

Besides, taking the position with *Harper's* left me plenty of free time to try writing the kind of stories that really interested me. I did several, but filed them away without showing them to anyone. Finally, I sent one to Lawrence Pritchard; he bought it for his Dime Library, and I've been writing for him ever since, always as David A. Byrd."

"Has Mr. Pritchard agreed to publish your book about Christina van der Waals?"

"Yes." Webb added sadly, "That is, if there's ever going to be a book. I'm going to make some further inquiries about Warren Gleason, but after that I may have to give up. I don't know what else I can do to find her."

"You've made more of an effort than most would," said Rebecca. "A lot of these immigrant girls are considered disposable—nobody cares where they go or what happens to them." She suddenly brightened. "Oh, I do have some good news. You remember Miss Serrano, the girl from Sardinia?"

"The one who was kept in the hotel."

"Yes. She's on her way to Boston now. There's a sales clerk job waiting for her in a millinery shop, and a room in a decent boarding house."

"I'm glad to hear that," said Webb. "But I'd still like to go to that hotel and take a walking stick to the head of the manager for what he did. That would probably do more good than writing any book."

"There'd be another to take his place." Rebecca shook her head. "No, violence won't do anything to change attitudes."

"It would certainly change that particular manager's attitude," argued Webb. "He'd think twice before taking advantage of another girl. It must be hard for you to deal with the women who come to your house. Don't you ever get angry?"

"All the time," Rebecca conceded. "But I don't want the girls to see my anger. What they need is a place of peace and safety. Besides, I realize that the girls who make it to Colden House are the lucky ones. Too many never get any chance for a better life." She pushed her plate aside. "Yesterday I heard about a girl who'd been sold by her parents to work in a Patterson silk mill. She was kept a prisoner there, running a loom—until her hair got caught in a flywheel. Her head went into the machine and she was blinded. Since she was no longer profitable, she was put out on the street. She died of exposure last month."

Webb was struck silent. For the first time, he acknowledged to himself that Christina van der Waals had probably met a similar fate. The reason he couldn't find her could very well be because she was no longer alive.

CHAPTER 18

If one were to judge by the sensational headlines in Joseph Pulitzer's *New York World,* or by the lurid reports in the *Police Gazette,* it would seem that the easiest thing to do in New York City was to stumble across a corpse. But Marshall Webb soon learned that finding a body wasn't such an easy task.

He began on Chambers Street at City Hall Plaza. Passing by the Tombs—the city's massive granite prison modeled after an Egyptian mausoleum—Webb crossed Franklin Street to the imposing county courthouse on the next block. On the first floor of the Romanesque building, near the walkway that connected the courthouse to the jail, were the offices of the county coroners.

It was ten o'clock Wednesday morning, but all four of the coroners were "at lunch." The solitary male clerk who staffed the office seemed surprised that Webb had expected them to be in. It took a moment before Webb remembered that coroners were elected—and in New York, election results were determined by Tammany Hall. The corrupt political machine had most likely awarded the coroner positions to cronies who would kick back a percentage of their salaries. Reporting to work probably wasn't a requirement of their jobs.

Webb explained to the sleepy-eyed clerk, "I'm trying to find out if a girl's body was discovered in the past six weeks."

"Lots of bodies have been found—men, women, boys, and girls." The clerk leaned back in his swivel chair and put his feet up on his bare desk. He dug a pinky into his ear and yawned loudly.

"I mean a specific girl. Who could tell me if she's been found?"

The drowsy young man withdrew his finger and examined the

tip like a miner inspecting for gold nuggets. "You got a description?"

"I have a photograph." Webb took out one of the prints that Edwin Crombie had made for him.

The clerk didn't even glance at it, but he suggested, "You might try Wes Stange. He's the coroners' secretary. Whenever they have to go out to examine a body, he goes with them to take notes and such. He could probably tell you about this girl."

"Where can I find Mr. Stange?"

"He's at lunch too. But *he'll* probably be coming back, if you want to wait."

Webb did. For more than an hour, he sat on an uncomfortable bench and watched the clerk watch the ceiling. The telephone didn't ring once, and no one else entered the office until a graying, middle-aged man with a small valise shuffled in. From his pallor and his rigid facial expression, he could have passed for the subject of an inquest.

The man spoke briefly with the clerk, then came over to Webb. "I'm Stange," he said. "Something I can help you with?"

Webb handed him the photograph. "This girl came to Ellis Island from Holland on January first. She hasn't been seen since, and I was wondering if anything's happened to her. I want to know if she's . . ." He didn't have to finish the sentence; no one came to a coroner to find a living person.

Stange studied the photo. "I don't recognize her. And she's a pretty girl. I'd remember if I'd seen her."

Relieved, Webb said, "Good. So she's probably still alive at least."

Stange shifted his jaw like a cow chewing its cud. "I didn't say *that*. Only that I haven't seen her. Hell, there's dead bodies all around this town, in cellars, alleys, and of course the two rivers. We had three floaters in the East River alone last week."

"Don't you go looking for them?"

"Why would we?" Stange seemed appalled by the notion. "We got enough work to do as it is; no need to go looking for more. Somebody finds a corpse, we go examine it, hold an inquest, and do everything by the book. But we don't need any extra work."

"Doesn't *anyone* try to find missing people?"

"We don't deal with people here. Just bodies. And like I said, we don't deal with those unless we're called."

"How about unidentified bodies?" Webb asked. "Do you keep them in the morgue until they're claimed?"

Stange appeared genuinely amused by Webb's questions, but he avoided breaking into a smile. "Look, we got too damn many people living in this city, and some of them—especially the foreigners—breed like rats. Naturally, too many living people means we're gonna end up with too many dead ones. That's probably a good thing, I suppose—it thins the herd. Anyway, we can't let them stack up waiting to be identified. If bodies aren't claimed in a few days, we ferry them up to Hart's Island and dump them in Potter's Field." He shrugged. "If you ask me, anybody who doesn't get claimed when they're dead couldn't have been worth much when they were alive anyway."

"Is there anywhere else I can check about this girl?" Webb asked.

"Are you sure she's dead?"

"No."

"Then why go looking for bad news? Why don't you just let yourself believe that she's still alive?"

Webb wished he could accept that assumption. It would be far more comforting than worrying if she'd run into someone who decided to "thin the herd." But if Christina *was* alive, how had she managed to vanish so completely?

Since it was afternoon by the time Webb left the County Court Building, he waited until the next morning to go back to Cutter's Saloon.

He didn't expect to find many patrons in the bar at nine o'clock in the morning. He especially didn't *want* to find Warren Gleason there, which was why he'd chosen to make his visit at such an early hour. Whether or not the patrolman's shift had started, he was probably still at home in bed.

When he stepped inside the hushed saloon, Webb saw that there were only a few customers. Two of them were at a table, their heads resting on folded hands, probably sleeping off a long night. At the far end of the bar, standing as motionless as a statue, was a wizened old man with a half-empty schooner of beer in front of him. Gleason wasn't in the saloon, nor was the fiddle player.

The only woman in the place, wearing a stained peignoir and a red feathered boa, looked up from a table near the door when Webb walked in. "How about an early mornin' special, sweetie?" She smiled, cracking the powder that caked her hollow cheeks and revealing that there were more gaps than teeth in her mouth.

Her appearance revolted Webb, but he made the effort to decline her offer with courtesy. "Thank you, no." He gave her an apologetic smile, then went over to the bar.

The wiry saloonkeeper he'd seen before was leaning forward, his elbows on the polished bar and his chin propped on the heel of one hand. His square face was creased and mottled from years of hard living. He stood up when Webb approached and appeared to recognize him. "Rye, ain't it?"

Webb wasn't eager to drink so early, but said yes. "Cutter, right?"

"Yup. Cutter Smyth." He added in mock formality, "I am the proprietor of this establishment." He quickly poured the shot and put it down in front of Webb. "This one really is on the house." Then he poured one for himself and swallowed it in a single gulp. Judging by the gin blossoms on his pug nose, Webb suspected that he had a long history of sampling his own wares.

After a taste of the whiskey, Webb said, "Thanks. Good way to start the day."

"Sure is. But that's not what you came here for."

"What makes you think that?"

Smyth studied him through narrowed eyes. "I never forget a face. You been in here only once, and that was when you was talking to Gleason."

"You remember what I was talking to him about?"

Smyth poured himself another shot. "Something about New Year's."

"That's right. I wanted to know where he was that day. He said he was here, and you backed him up." Webb pushed his glass aside. "The thing is, you weren't very convincing."

The bartender hunched his shoulders. "If Gleason told you he was here, you oughta believe him."

"Why? Because he's a cop? We both know half the cops in New York are thieves and the others are liars."

Smyth shrugged again but said nothing.

"Look," said Webb, "whatever you tell me is not going to get back to Gleason."

Unmoved by the promise, the bartender remained silent.

Webb decided to try another tack. "You know that immigration is federal now, don't you?"

"I heard that, yeah."

"It's under the Treasury Department, and you know who their enforcement agency is?" In answer to Smyth's blank stare, Webb said ominously, "The Secret Service. You do *not* want me asking them to talk to you."

The bartender downed his whiskey and wiped his thin lips. Then he decided to talk. "I do everything I'm supposed to do to stay in business—and then some. Christ, I got my hands full keeping the city cops happy. I don't want no trouble with Uncle Sam."

"Just tell me the truth and you won't have any trouble."

"Truth is, Gleason really was here January first."

"All day?"

"Yeah. The New Year's Eve party went into the next morning. Gleason stayed up the whole night—drinking my best champagne—before going into the back room with Rosie. When they got up, he had breakfast here, then went on drinking through the day." Smyth suddenly chuckled.

"What's so funny?"

"I was just remembering his breakfast. He sent a boy out for a bucket of oysters. Rosie told me he could have used them the night before—said he wasn't worth a damn in bed."

Webb knew that closing times in New York were rarely enforced, but he asked, "How do you stay open all night? Closing time is one A.M."

"Like I said, I do everything I'm supposed to do to stay in business. I make my payments to the precinct every week."

"You also said 'and then some.' What else do you do?"

"I pay off that bastard Gleason. He takes a cut from me, too. And he takes a cut from the girls every Saturday. Look, I'm supposed to be okay by making my payoffs to the captain. And I don't mind—that's the cost of business. But Gleason ain't playin' by the rules. If he don't drink my profits, he squeezes me for them. Bastard's gonna put me out of business."

It was clear to Webb that Smyth didn't like Gleason enough to lie for him. The reason he'd appeared reluctant to back up the patrolman's story was probably because he didn't want to do him any favors.

After thanking him for the drink, Webb left the saloon. He was disappointed that he had no more leads to Christina van der Waals, but he was also strangely relieved. Webb knew that he had tried every avenue he could think of to find her, and he could now give up the search with a clear conscience. He was closing the book on her, a book that had never gotten beyond the third chapter.

CHAPTER 19

Marshall Webb certainly was a contradiction. Rebecca had puzzled over him more than once before, but the during past couple of days he'd been especially difficult to fathom. He had told her of his visits to the coroner's office and to Cutter's Saloon, and claimed that he had given up on finding Christina van der Waals. She had agreed with him that he had done all he could to find the girl, but Webb didn't appear to accept his own decision. If anything, he seemed increasingly vexed and frustrated by it.

From her own experience at Colden House, Rebecca was certainly familiar with those feelings, which were often exacerbated by uncertainty. Some girls left Colden House in the middle of the night, perhaps lonely for their homes and families no matter the misery or abuse to which they might be returning. Others, like Gia Serrano, moved on to new and better lives. But either way, few girls ever contacted Rebecca again to let her know how they were faring. As much as she would have liked to hear from them, the reality was that sometimes you never saw people again and never learned what became of them. Rebecca had come to accept that fact and had gotten used to living with uncertainty and without happy endings. Mr. Webb apparently wasn't as experienced in such matters, nor as accepting of reality.

Rebecca was glad to see that Webb was at least redirecting his energies in a positive direction. He told her that he was going to work on the book she had asked him to write, and wanted to begin immediately. He seemed determined to do something that might help others, to somehow make up for his failure to save Christina van der Waals.

So, on Saturday afternoon, under low, dark clouds that threatened snow, Rebecca led Webb on a tour through the squalid streets and impoverished neighborhoods of the East Side. They trod their way slowly along the congested sidewalks, making their way past huddles of destitute children warming themselves over steam grates, emaciated vendors hawking everything from matches to shoestrings, and filthy ragpickers scavenging through the trash that was heaped on every street and alley. The streets themselves were so jammed that traffic was almost at a standstill. Horse-drawn trucks, garment-laden men, and hundreds of pushcarts that served as miniature dry-goods stores and food markets all competed for open space. The competition was often accompanied by loud quarrels and prolonged shoving matches.

It didn't take long for Rebecca to notice another contradiction in Mr. Webb. Although his dress and manners would make him welcome company in any Fifth Avenue drawing room, he appeared totally comfortable here at the opposite end of the social scale. She noted that he didn't need any guidance through the area and appeared to know its streets.

Rebecca had wanted to show Webb the kind of lives some of her girls had led, and decided to start with one he had already met. On Ludlow Street, she pointed to a soot-stained, crumbling brick tenement. "That's where Vanessa Drobosky lived. She's the Polish girl you met at Colden House."

"I remember." Webb jotted something in his notebook. He'd been stopping periodically to write notes as they walked. "She's learning to be a telephone operator now, isn't she?"

"Yes." Rebecca was surprised he remembered that detail. She pointed toward an upper floor of the apartment building. "And that's where she used to work sewing knee-pants. Many of these tenements have sweatshops right inside. Most are for garments, but there some for making artificial flowers, rolling cigars, painting watch faces—almost any kind of industry that can be hidden indoors and operates on cheap labor."

They walked to the side of the building and took a couple of steps into an alley. The tenement's flimsy fire escapes sagged under the weight of people who were using them as dwellings. All types of bedding and clothing fluttered from the railings, making it look as if a nearby laundry had exploded. "The Dobroskys had an indoor apartment," said Rebecca, "so they didn't freeze in winter at least. But summertime must have been hell. About ten years ago, new rules prohibited the construction of windowless apartments. But landlords found a way around the law by putting in airshafts as 'open spaces.' They're used as garbage chutes, and they're part of the reason disease is rampant in the tenements—typhus, smallpox, you name it." She looked at Webb and wondered why he wasn't making note of what she'd said.

They continued walking and turned onto Hester Street. The immigrants that populated this neighborhood were predominantly Jewish and clad in traditional attire. Many of the shop signs were in Hebrew, and the pushcarts were more numerous.

"This is one of the worst areas for sweatshops," said Rebecca. "I know of children as young as six who work all day making neckties and suspenders." Farther down the block, she gestured to a narrow two-story clapboard building. "There's a saloon in there—unlicensed, of course—with a brothel on the second floor. No shortage of willing girls, I expect, especially if they've been working in sweatshops since they were young. Prostitution must seem an easy life in comparison."

"They don't always have to be willing," said Webb quietly. "That saloon is called 'The Morgue.' Women who go in for a drink are sometimes drugged and taken upstairs to be—" He quickly answered Rebecca's questioning stare. "It's a famous—infamous—dive. I've heard what goes on in there."

"It's so well known, but the police don't close it down?"

"Not as long as the owner makes his payoffs. Did you read what happened to Reverend Parkhurst?"

"Yes," answered Rebecca. "The district attorney summoned him before a grand jury and told him to prove his charges about the police department. He failed to do so, and now he may face charges himself." Rebecca didn't consider herself naive about politics, but even she was astonished at this demonstration of Tammany Hall's clout. New York's political machine could obviously silence any critic or enemy, even a minister.

"See? The police don't do much about protecting the public, but they can sure protect themselves—and their graft."

Rebecca spotted a ragged girl about eight years old with a sheaf of newspapers under her arm. Selling papers was almost the exclusive domain of boys. "Look at her," she said to Webb.

"Don't you wonder what she'll be doing ten years from now? Will she even still be alive by then?"

Webb appeared to study the girl, who was dressed in frayed calico and torn black knee stockings. He again made a couple of notes, and continued to watch the girl. "She'll survive," he said. "Look at her face, her eyes, the way she keeps glancing around her. Children that age are perceptive and they know more than you'd think. I'll bet she's a savvy one."

The girl suddenly grabbed the jacket of a younger boy who'd stepped out into the street and pulled him back on the sidewalk. "Her brother, maybe?" said Rebecca.

"Could be. Maybe she's the only one he has to take care of him." Webb wrote a couple of lines more in his notebook.

They continued walking, and Hester merged into Division Street. Although the name of the street changed, it remained one of the most poverty-stricken in New York.

Rebecca said, "There are quite a few children out on their own in this city. The Children's Aid Society puts the number at almost one hundred thousand. Another fifteen thousand live in orphan asylums and institutions." She glanced at Webb. "You're not writing this down."

"It doesn't matter if it's ten thousand or a hundred thousand—not for the book. People don't care about statistics. I need to tell the stories of individuals."

"Yes, of course." That was exactly what she wanted him to write.

On the corner of Montgomery Street, an ancient, leather-faced woman holding a bunch of red paper poppies stepped in front of Webb. "Buy a flower, sir? Only a penny." Her voice was flat, as if her sales pitch was oft-repeated and seldom successful.

"Yes, I believe I will." He gave her a smile, and the quarter he placed in her outstretched palm put a bit of a sparkle in her dark eyes. As she trudged off to find another customer, he put the well-made flower in his jacket lapel. "I wish I could have given her more," he said softly. "But she wouldn't have a chance of keeping it—and she'd likely be beaten up as well as robbed."

Rebecca was both moved by Webb's concern for the people he met and curious to learn how he knew the things that he did. "I think we've seen enough for today." She looked up at the darkening sky. "It's getting to be almost dinnertime." She hoped it would be taken more as an invitation than an observation.

In a distracted voice, Webb answered, "Yes. I suppose it is." He looked at his notebook for a few moments. "I believe I have enough for now. And I have a few ideas." He closed the book and tucked it in his pocket. "I better go home and start working on them."

Rebecca tried not to show her disappointment. He was, after all, doing what she had asked of him. It just wasn't what she wanted him to be doing this evening.

Webb worked through the night on Saturday. He only stopped writing long enough to sleep a few hours Sunday afternoon, and before he realized how quickly time had passed it was Monday evening.

He didn't produce much in that time, however. His repeated attempts to capture exactly what he had seen and heard always fell short in one respect or another. No matter how he chose his words, he couldn't portray a vivid enough image with them. Finally, he decided to write as a novelist instead of a reporter, and used his observations primarily to spur his imagination and flesh out details. Once he adopted this approach, the writing began to flow.

At one point, the flow almost became a torrent, and Webb's writing hand could barely move fast enough to record his thoughts. It was then that his telephone rang, snapping him out of his literary trance. "Yes, what is it?" he asked peevishly.

A female voice that he didn't recognize answered, "I hear you're interested in Christina van der Waals."

"Yes! I am. Who is this?"

"I'm so glad I found you. She's been sick, and I've been caring for her. I was hoping to find her relatives or somebody."

"What's wrong with her?"

"Poor girl's almost delirious with fever. Been this way for days."

"Where is she? Can I see her?"

"Yes, but please come soon. I don't know how long she'll last."

Webb was given an address and apartment number on

Houston Street. As he scribbled the information on the margin of a manuscript page, he again asked, "Who is this?"

The only answer he got was, "Please hurry."

"I'll be right there." By the time he put down the receiver, the girls he'd been writing about all weekend had evaporated from his thoughts.

CHAPTER 20

Marshall Webb had waited almost two months to see Christina van der Waals again, and had only recently resigned himself to the idea that he never would. Now, in a matter of minutes, his attitude had completely reversed and he didn't want to waste another second. He grabbed his hat and overcoat as he left his apartment and tugged them on while he hustled downstairs.

Out on the street, his first impulse was to hail a hansom cab, but after seeing the traffic snarled at Union Square he decided his long legs would probably carry him faster than any vehicle. It was only about ten blocks to Houston Street; he figured he should be face-to-face with Christina within twenty minutes.

Webb hurried down Broadway, brushing past strolling ladies and ignoring the pleas of newsboys and street vendors. Despite the chilly weather, he was soon sweating. He marked his progress by the buildings he passed: Grace Church with its gothic spires . . . the cast-iron building that had once been home to A. T. Stewart's department store . . . the six-story Carter Building, which housed John Daniell & Sons haberdashery. With each block he covered, he wondered what kind of place Christina was staying in. All he could assume was that the home must be affluent enough to have a telephone.

He turned west on Houston Street and into an eclectic neighborhood of brick warehouses, small shops, private residences, and corner saloons. There was also a small red-light district left over from the pre-Tenderloin era, when the vice trade's stronghold was south of Washington Park.

The address he was seeking was located between a photography studio and an abandoned warehouse. It was a four-story clapboard building that had once—but not in recent years—been painted yellow with black shutters. Overall, the structure looked like an old hotel that had been converted to an apartment house.

Webb went through the colonnaded entrance. The interior was lit well enough to make out the floral pattern of the faded wallpaper in the halls. The carpeting was worn so thin—all the way through in some spots—that the only color it retained was the dull brown of the dirt that had been tracked across it. After climbing to the top floor, Webb stepped around three children playing jacks in the stairwell, and found the apartment number he'd been given.

There was no answer to his knock. He rapped again, louder, and listened for movement inside. No sound came from within, and the door remained closed. Webb double-checked the address he'd written down, and looked again at the number on the door: 406. This was the place.

Two apartments down, a door opened and a woman in a calico wrapper stepped into the hallway. "Dinnertime!" she called to the playing children.

"Excuse me, ma'am," Webb said. "Do you know who lives in four-oh-six?"

She wiped her hands on a dish towel. "Nobody, as far as I know. But then I don't pay no nevermind to the neighbors. They keep to their business and I keep to mine."

"I'm looking for a girl, a Dutch girl," Webb pressed. "Her name's Christina, and she's about fourteen years old. Have you seen anyone like that?"

"Could be Chinese for all I care. As long as she keeps to herself, I wouldn't notice." Then she called to the children, "You better get in here, or I'll tan your hides!" She went back inside while the children scrambled to obey.

Webb knocked at 406 once more, then listened again. This time he thought he heard a slight rattling sound from within. When no one came to the door, he tried the knob and found it was unlocked. He debated with himself for only a moment before deciding to go inside.

The musty studio apartment was obviously uninhabited, without a stick of furniture in sight. A clothesline was strung across the room and a soiled bedsheet was hung over it as a partition. Webb heard the rattling sound again and saw that it was caused by a torn shade flapping in an open window.

Seeing that the rest of the place was barren, he went farther inside and stepped around the partition. A blonde girl, wearing the same checked gray dress that Webb had seen at Ellis Island, was lying face down on a ratty wool blanket. She was utterly motionless.

Webb's heart sank, but he tried to convince himself that she was only sick.

He gently touched her skinny arm. It was limp. Then he turned her over and her neck flopped at an unnatural angle. Christina van der Waals didn't die of any illness. Her neck had been broken.

Webb stared down at the girl's face. Her open eyes had an eerie look of surprise, and their sapphire blue sparkle appeared to have been extinguished. It wasn't the color that had made them so bright, Webb realized, but the life that had been within her.

Overcome with shock and sorrow, he slumped to a sitting position and continued to look down at Christina's lifeless face. Finally, he closed her eyelids and straightened her head, bunching one end of the blanket under her neck to support it. The effort was pointless, he knew—she could no longer feel anything—but he wanted her to rest comfortably.

Webb's mind then began to reel under an onslaught of questions: How long had Christina been here? Who had been with her? Who phoned him? How did she get a broken neck?

With no answers forthcoming, he began to ask himself what he should do next. Call a doctor? No, a doctor couldn't help her now. The police? There was no telephone in the apartment. He hated to leave Christina alone, but he had to contact the authorities.

Before he could do so, there was a cry of "Police!" at the door.

Leaning back to look past the hanging bedsheet, Webb saw two uniformed officers, one of them a sergeant, rush in. "Back here," he called to them.

With their revolvers drawn, the policemen warily came around the partition. Upon seeing Christina, the portly sergeant demanded, "What the hell did you do to her?"

"*Me?* I just closed her eyes. I found her like this—dead. And I closed her eyes."

The sergeant ordered the gawky patrolman, "Keep an eye on

him." He then holstered his own weapon and bent down to touch Christina's neck. "She's dead," he announced. "But still warm—hasn't been dead long." He rose and took a step backward. "Stand up," he said to Webb, "and keep your hands high."

Webb slowly did so; he felt dizzy with bewilderment and could barely maintain his balance.

The sergeant unfastened the nightstick hanging from his belt. "I got a daughter about the age of this girl." Without warning, he drove the end of the club sharply into Webb's stomach. "Now spill it. What happened here?"

Webb doubled over and gasped for air. Before he could get out a word, the stick came down again at his head. He raised his arm barely in time to block the blow. Pain shot all the way to his shoulder as his forearm absorbed most of the impact.

"Look at this," the sergeant said to his partner. "He's resisting arrest." He gave the junior officer a nod; in response, the younger cop holstered his gun and grabbed hold of his own nightstick.

The blows came hard and fast then. Webb protected himself as best he could, and protested that he hadn't done anything wrong. When he realized that each protest only antagonized the officers, he shut up and tried to curl his tall body into as small a target as possible.

"All right," the sergeant finally wheezed, "he's had enough—for now."

Webb looked up cautiously. The cops took a couple of steps back and conferred with each other. Both were breathing heavily from their exertion.

The younger one grumbled to his sergeant. "What about the money? Where's the money?"

"Damned if I know. I'm gonna take this bastard in to the station and get a detective. You stay here with the girl. That'll give you a chance to look for the loot." The sergeant glanced about the empty apartment. "Don't look like there's anything here, though."

Webb put up no resistance as a set of handcuffs was clapped over his throbbing wrists.

The clang of the cell door slamming shut sent a tremor through Webb that was almost as painful as if he'd been hit by another nightstick. After being beaten in the Houston Street apartment, he had been marched in handcuffs to the Mercer Street station house, where his physical description was recorded and his photograph taken for the Detective Bureau's rogues' gallery. With each step, his spirits plummeted further downward; they hit bottom when he was shoved into a zoolike cage in the station house basement.

The jail, which smelled like an open sewer, offered no amenities but plenty of company. Half a dozen men were already in the holding cell when Webb entered. One was making noisy use of the iron pail that served as a community toilet. Since there wasn't even a bench in the cell, the others sat on the dirt floor. Webb remained standing near the door; there was nothing in the cell that he wanted to come into contact with, especially not his cellmates.

Over the next hour or so, ten more men were pushed into the cell, and it became more difficult for Webb to keep his distance. Several of the men were stinking drunk, and one of them promptly collapsed to the ground, where he began vomiting. When some of it got onto the shoe of another man, the drunk was kicked until he crawled to a corner.

A short while later, police lodgers of both sexes were let in for the night. These unfortunates, who couldn't even afford the ten cents for a flophouse cot, had it little better than the prisoners. Their beds consisted of wooden planks laid on the ground next to the holding cell, and there were no facilities for washing. The lodgers proved to be as contentious as the prisoners; fights broke out over preferred spots on the floor, and a young woman whose face was scarred from smallpox was repeatedly chased off the boards whenever she tried to lie down.

Webb was only peripherally aware of what was going on around him, however. His mind was busy sorting through what had happened this evening. He thought mostly of Christina: of her limp body and lifeless face. Her death was clearly no accident, and the telephone call he'd received was no doubt an effort to set him up for the crime. It was a setup that, so far, was proving to be a success.

At the basement doorway, two uniformed officers and a third man in plain clothes spoke briefly to the jailer, then paused to light cigars before going inside. During his time in the cell, Webb had noticed that all of the cops smoked cigars when they entered, undoubtedly to fend off the foul odors that permeated the basement.

Puffing hard on their stogies, the three men approached the

holding cell. The one in the suit said to Webb, "I'm Detective O'Connor. I got some questions you're gonna answer." He nodded at the patrolmen, who let Webb out of the cell and clasped manacles on his arms and legs.

The officers led him upstairs to a small room on the first floor, where he was pushed into a straight-backed chair across a small table from O'Connor. One officer remained standing inside while the other stepped out and closed the door.

Detective O'Connor, a gray-haired, stony-faced man of about fifty, studied Webb for a few moments before speaking. "We got a fair amount of evidence against you." He dumped the contents of a brown envelope on the table; they were items that had been taken from Webb's pockets when he'd been brought in. The detective picked up a piece of foolscap. "You had the address on you, and we can check to see if it matches your handwriting."

"No need," said Webb. "I wrote it."

"Also, a neighbor woman says you were asking about a girl around the same age as the dead one."

"Yes, I did."

"What was it? A tryst?"

Webb stared back at O'Connor without answering.

"What happened? You argue about the price? Or did you get too rough?"

"Neither," Webb said emphatically. "I had been looking for Christina—"

"Christina?" interrupted O'Connor.

"Her name is—was—Christina van der Waals." As the detective wrote that down, Webb continued, "I had been looking for her for a while. This evening I got a telephone call telling me she was sick and staying at that address."

"Who called you?"

"I wish I knew. Christina was dead when I got there. No one else was around."

"Puts you in a bad position, then, doesn't it?"

Just as the caller wanted, thought Webb.

"Tell me this," said O'Connor. "Was she part of your gang? Maybe you couldn't decide how to split up the loot?"

Webb couldn't fathom why the police kept asking about money. "What gang? What loot?"

O'Connor scowled. "Fine, don't cooperate. You'll be arraigned tomorrow morning for the murder of Miss"—he looked at his notes—"Miss van der Waals. For tonight, you'll be staying in the holding cell." He began to scoop the items on the table back into the envelope, then stopped to pick up a calling card. "What's this?" He read aloud, "Marshall Webb, Harper's Weekly."

"I'm a writer. That's why I'd been looking for Miss van der Waals. She was one of the first immigrants to come in to Ellis Island, and I was planning to write about her."

"Hmm." O'Connor seemed at a loss over what to make of Webb's interest in Christina. He shook his head as if to clear it, then ordered the patrolman, "Take him back down and lock him up."

A few more men had been put into the holding cell by the time Webb returned, and it was now impossible for him to keep any distance between himself and the others.

It was also hard for him to make sense of what the police might be planning for him. What had O'Connor been talking about when he asked about a gang? And why had all the cops been asking about money? Did O'Connor believe him when he said that he'd only been writing about Christina, or would the detective go ahead and try to pin her murder on him?

Webb decided that he had to let somebody know he was here. Certainly not his family, though. Nor anyone at *Harper's*. Lawrence Pritchard, maybe? No, the poor fellow had enough trouble tolerating beer dives; he'd probably faint in a jail.

Another group of lodgers was herded into the basement and a fresh scuffle broke out over sleeping space. The woman with the smallpox scars took the brunt of it again; she was shoved about and repeatedly told to leave and "take your plague with you." She worked her way near the bars of the holding cell, where she promptly received similar abuse from the prisoners.

Webb moved as close as he could get to her. He crouched down and called, "Miss!"

The woman looked up at him, her eyes as fearful as a trapped animal's.

In a hushed, calm tone, Webb said, "I know of a place you can stay tonight. It's called Colden House, down on State Street. Think you can make it there?"

She nodded.

"Good. Tell Miss Davies there that Marshall Webb sent you. She'll be sure you get a meal and a clean bed."

The woman considered the offer a moment, probably trying to decide if it was true or another cruel joke. With nothing to lose, she stood and whispered a hoarse "Thank you."

As she turned to leave, Webb added, "And please tell Miss Davies I'm in the Mercer Street jail."

CHAPTER 21

At ten o'clock that night, Rebecca Davies, escorted by a sleepy sergeant, walked down the stairs to the basement of the Mercer Street station house.

At the bottom of the steps, a potbellied jailer greeted her with a broad leer. He tugged at his straggly black beard and eyed her up and down. "Looks to me like you can afford a better bed than in a police lodging house." He smirked at what he thought was a fine joke.

Rebecca said sharply, "I'm here to see Mr. Webb."

"Who?"

"He's one of your prisoners. Can you get him, please?"

"You can't—"

"I most certainly can."

The jailer's face colored at this affront to his authority, and the muscles in his thick neck bulged. "Listen, missy—"

The sergeant who'd accompanied Rebecca spoke up. "The captain says she can see him, Ralph."

The jailer's expression hardened even more. He apparently considered the basement to be his domain and didn't want anyone, not even a captain, telling him what to do. He couldn't disobey his superior, though. After a few moments, a sly smile twisted his lips. "Did the captain say *where* she could talk to him?"

"Not so far as I know," answered the sergeant.

"Fine." The jailer pointed to the holding cell. "You can talk to him right there."

The sergeant tried to argue with him. "Be reasonable, Ralph. She's a lady. Don't send her in there."

Ralph replied with an icy glare that silenced the other officer.

All Rebecca wanted to do was see Webb; she didn't care where. She walked right into the basement, carefully stepping over and around the sleeping lodgers on her way to the cell. To avoid giving the jailer the satisfaction of seeing her discomfort, she pretended not to notice the vile, overpowering smell. She also ignored the coarse comments from those male lodgers who were still awake and invited her to lie down with them.

It took her a moment to spot Webb in the packed cage, standing with his back to the iron bars. She stepped close to the cell and said to him, "I can't believe you're really here." When Webb turned around, she saw the ugly bruises on his jaw and forehead.

"I'm sorry," he said. "I didn't know whom else to contact. I didn't expect you'd come, though—I just wanted somebody to know where I was, in case . . ." His voice trailed off. Then he said, "I'm surprised they let you in here."

"They couldn't stop me if they tried." Rebecca noticed a small trickle of blood oozing from a purplish lump at his temple. She took off her white cotton glove and tried to dab at the wound, but Webb flinched and backed away.

"I'm all right," he said. "The cops just worked me over a little before taking me in."

"Why? What happened?" She already knew from the desk sergeant why Webb had been jailed, but she wanted to hear it from him.

"I got a telephone call telling me that Christina van der Waals was sick."

"From whom?"

Webb shook his head. "It was a woman's voice. That's all I know. She asked me to come see Christina, so I did. When I got there, she was dead, her neck broken." He shook his head again, slowly and sadly. "That poor girl. If I'd gotten there sooner, maybe I could have done something." He hesitated before continuing. "Before I could go to the police, they showed up on their own and arrested me. Tomorrow I'm being arraigned for Christina's murder." His voice sounded foggy with disbelief.

Rebecca shared the feeling. She had no doubt that Marshall Webb was innocent. He had his quirks and his mysteries, but she was certain that he was no murderer.

"I should have done something weeks ago," Webb said. "If I'd tried harder to find her, if I'd started looking for her sooner . . . maybe she'd be alive."

Almost anyone else falsely jailed would be bemoaning their own predicament, thought Rebecca. And many men would crumble simply from being in this environment and among this company. But not Webb. Not only was he holding up, he was thinking more of a dead stranger than of himself. "Don't think about what happened to her," she said softly. "Right now we have to think of helping *you*."

"Thanks, but what I want to do is find out who really killed Christina."

"You can't do that from in here. I'm going to try to get you out."

Webb said grimly, "I don't think a jailbreak is going to help matters."

There are other ways, thought Rebecca. And she was determined to find one.

Webb was dozing and enjoying a strange dream about floating over the Atlantic Ocean in a balloon with Tom Sawyer, when he was awakened by a shout of "Webb! Wake up, damn it!"

Webb opened his eyes and tried to focus through the dim, thick air and the fading vestiges of sleep. He saw the jailer approaching him, accompanied by Rebecca Davies. Webb pulled himself away from the bars he'd been leaning against and winced from the ache in his back and shoulders. The pain was alleviated by two sights: Rebecca's welcome face and the large key in the jailer's hand.

After warning the other prisoners to stand clear of the door or "get your goddamn heads busted," the jailer said, "Yer gettin' out, Webb. Come along."

Rebecca had really done it. She was getting him out of jail.

Upstairs, on the main floor of the station house, Webb was given back his belongings and warned not to leave the city. He didn't ask why he had to stay in New York, nor did he ask why he was being released. All he wanted to do was get out while he had the chance.

With Rebecca at his side, Webb walked out of the police station into the dark, quiet night. "What time is it?" he asked her.

"A little after midnight."

He looked in her eyes. "I don't know how you did it, but thank you."

Rebecca was intently studying his face and biting her lip. "You have some more cuts. The police again?" She reached into her purse and took out a lacy handkerchief.

"No. One of my cellmates decided that he wanted my coat. He became rather insistent about it." With some satisfaction, Webb burrowed his hands deeper into his coat pockets. He didn't particularly care about the garment, but if he hadn't successfully fought to keep it, other men in the cell would have wanted more from him.

Rebecca grabbed his sleeve. "Come over here." She pulled him under the light of an electric streetlamp and began blotting some of the blood with her handkerchief. This time he didn't pull away.

"Did you post bail for me?" Webb asked. He didn't think a bail amount had been set yet.

"No. You won't be needing bail. You were never arrested."

"What? I don't—"

"You remember I said my family had some connections with the police department?"

Webb nodded that he did.

"I used them. I never have before, but I couldn't think of any other way." She gently swiped the handkerchief across his forehead. "In any event, Inspector Byrnes has decided that there really wasn't sufficient evidence against you. So officially, you were never arrested; you were only held as a witness."

"I don't know how to thank you."

"I didn't do much. I never even spoke to Byrnes myself." After one more inspection of his face, Rebecca tossed the blood-soaked handkerchief into the gutter. "All I did was telephone my sister. Then she talked to her husband, and he got in touch with Byrnes. That's what took so long."

"This is sooner than I expected to be out." Webb inhaled deeply. "It feels so good to breathe again. Please thank your sister and brother-in-law for me."

"You can do that yourself. You'll be coming to family dinner on Sunday."

"Oh. Well . . ." He was a bit taken aback. "I'd be happy to." He then suggested that they walk a block over to Broadway, where they had a better chance of getting a cab.

Even on the city's busiest thoroughfare, it took a good quarter of an hour before a hansom cab pulled over for them. Webb directed the driver to Colden House; then he and Rebecca settled back in the thick leather seat.

During the ride, Webb told Rebecca more about how he had found Christina and how she had looked. As he talked, he also thought to himself, wondering if Christina had been killed because of his inquiries. His questions must have had something to do with her death, he assumed; otherwise why had he been set up to be caught with her body?

"At least it's over," Rebecca said. "You've found her."

"No, it's not over," answered Webb. "Not until I find out who killed her."

"Until *we* find out. And that can wait. For tonight, concentrate on taking care of yourself and getting some sleep."

When the cab drew up to Colden House, Rebecca instructed the driver to wait and asked Webb to come inside.

He did, and Rebecca took him into the infirmary to make a closer inspection of his wounds. She washed his face and applied salve to a few spots. Before sending him back out to the cab, she said, "There's a young woman upstairs right now getting a good night's sleep thanks to you. You go home and do the same."

Webb agreed that he would try, but doubted that he'd get much rest this night.

CHAPTER 22

Despite the fact that she'd only gotten a few hours' sleep, Rebecca was already awake by the time sunlight washed into her bedroom. She lay restless in her bed, thinking about Marshall Webb and Christina van der Waals, and imagining the questions she would undoubtedly get from her family about her efforts to have Webb released from jail.

She also thought of all that she had to do at Colden House today. There was a carpenter coming to check out one of the roof's larger leaks, and she was meeting with a retired schoolteacher to see about setting up English lessons in the house. Rebecca also wanted to talk to the girl with the smallpox scars to see if she could help her with a job and housing. What was her name again? Rebecca hated that she couldn't remember, but the girl had come so late and with the disturbing message about Webb.

Rebecca decided to allow herself a few more minutes under the warm blanket before settling on her plans for the day.

Two hours later, she knocked at the apartment of Marshall Webb. She had left Miss Hummel to take care of things at Colden House, and had told the new girl—Miss Finney, she'd finally remembered—that she could stay at least another day. Rebecca thought it more urgent to talk with Webb before he went out on his own to look for the killer of Christina van der Waals.

When Webb answered the door, Rebecca was relieved to see that not only was he still at home, but that he was looking good. At least as good as a man could with a cut cheek, a swollen jaw, and bruises on half his face. He appeared freshly washed; his chin was shaved clean—which must have been painful with his bruised skin—and his mustache and side-whiskers were carefully combed. His shirt, collar, and cravat were all impeccable.

After inviting her inside, Webb said, "I've made a pot of coffee. Would you care for some?"

"Yes, that would be very nice." Rebecca saw his bloodshot eyes; he probably had even less sleep than she.

Once they were seated over cups of coffee, Rebecca cast a sidelong glance out the window. "Things look different in the daylight," she said. "Don't they?" It wasn't a comment on the springlike weather; Rebecca wanted to know how things were looking to Webb.

Webb's gaze was directed down at his black coffee. "I suppose," he answered absently.

Rebecca waited for him to say more. When he didn't, she asked directly, "What are you planning to do about Christina van der Waals?"

"I'm not sure yet. There are some things that I don't understand at all."

"Such as?"

"The obvious questions: Where had Christina been for the last two months? Why was I called to the apartment? And *who* called me? Who wanted to put me at the scene?" Webb lifted his cup, then put it back down without bringing it to his lips. "There's also something peculiar: the police at the apartment and the detective at the station asked me about a gang and some loot. I have no idea what they were talking about—was Christina taken in by some gang? Or was she killed because I'd been asking about her?" He frowned, clearly hoping that wasn't the case. "I have to find out."

"You might want to be careful," said Rebecca. "The police could decide to take you in again. If they're put under pressure to solve her murder, they *will* convict someone, guilty or not."

"I can't worry about that. The police will do whatever they have to do, and I'll do what I have to do."

Rebecca wished she could convince him that some caution was warranted, but he clearly wasn't in the mood to be sensible. "Maybe you'll be all right," she said hopefully. "There was nothing about her in today's newspapers, so maybe the police won't feel under any pressure."

"The papers didn't get a death report?"

"It wouldn't look good for the police to have a murdered girl with no arrest, would it? They're probably withholding the information and hoping the press doesn't find out from another source."

"Damn," said Webb.

"What's the matter?"

"Liz Luck. How is she going to learn about her cousin? The police didn't even know Christina's name, so they don't know whom to notify about her death."

"I could tell her," Rebecca offered.

"No, I'll do it." Webb quickly added, "I appreciate the offer, but I feel I have to be the one to tell her what happened."

Rebecca didn't think that was wise—especially not with possibility of running into Warren Gleason—but her efforts to talk Webb out of it failed. The most he agreed to was that he would tell Rebecca before he did anything more than talk to Liz Luck.

Webb didn't know how many minutes he waited in Liz Luck's hallway. This was not a task that he wanted to perform, and he had no idea how to break the news to her. It had taken him until the afternoon before he could get himself to begin the trip to her apartment, and on the el he had composed and rejected a dozen ways to tell her that her cousin was dead. Every one of them sounded too harsh. But then, the death of a fourteen-year-old girl *was* harsh, and perhaps there was no way to make it sound otherwise.

After a deep breath, Webb took off his derby and knocked on the door.

When Liz Luck opened it enough to peer out at him, she seemed to read the news on his face. "What happened?" she asked in a small voice.

"I am so sorry, but Christina is dead."

She staggered slightly. "No-o-o." The word came out as a wail.

Webb quickly stepped inside and put out his hand to take her elbow. Closing the door with his other hand, he led her to the nearest chair.

Luck slumped onto the seat and covered her face with trembling hands. Between sobs, she said, "I knew something bad must have happened to her, but I wanted to keep hoping. Poor Christina—what happened? When?"

Webb remained standing. "I don't know everything, but she

died yesterday." He thought "died" at least sounded more peaceful than "killed." He went on, "Her neck was broken—I don't know how."

She looked up at him through wet eyes. "You mean she was still alive *yesterday?*"

"Yes."

"Where was she?"

"In an apartment on Houston Street, but I don't know for how long."

Luck began crying harder. "I should have found her. I tried. I looked everywhere. But I couldn't find her." She dropped her face into her hands again. "If I did, she'd still be alive."

Those were the same sentiments Webb had been berating himself with ever since last night. "You did all you could." He had tried to tell himself the same thing a dozen times, but never accepted it.

She sniffled and Webb gave her his pocket handkerchief. "I want to see her," Luck said. "Where is she?"

Webb assumed her cousin's body would be at the morgue, but that sounded so cold. "I'm not sure. You should probably contact the police at the Mercer Street station house. They could tell you."

A tear splashed onto the bare wood floor. "I'll need to make funeral plans. Christina is going to get a proper burial."

Webb remained a little while longer, until he was sure that there was nothing he could say or do to console her. When her crying ebbed, he said how sorry he was for her loss and offered to help if there was anything he could do. Her only answers were sobs.

By the time Webb left, he realized that whatever life had been left in Liz Luck was now extinguished almost as completely as it was in Christina.

Rebecca Davies knew exactly where to go to see Christina's body. In the past few years, she had twice been called upon to identify the bodies of girls who had once stayed at Colden House.

Wednesday afternoon, Rebecca took the el up First Avenue to East Twenty-sixth Street. There, stretching from Twenty-sixth to Twenty-eighth Streets along the bank of the East River, was the massive Bellevue Hospital complex. In addition to the hospital and medical college, the institution housed one of the city's principal morgues.

Rebecca proceeded to the hospital's dank basement, where she found the morgue attendant at a desk eating a sandwich that was almost as big as his head. "I'm sorry to trouble you," she said. "I'm here to see the body of Christina van der Waals."

The attendant, an ungainly young man with curly black hair and a thin wisp of first mustache, didn't interrupt his chewing. Crumbs fell from his open mouth when he asked, "You a relative?"

"No, I'm not."

"You gotta be a relative. Otherwise we get all kinds of curiosity seekers in here. There's some people who like to look at stiffs, you know." He bit off another chunk of black bread.

Rebecca was in no mood for petty bureaucrats. "I don't *like* to look at the bodies of dead girls. I am here because I *have* to see her. So put down your lunch and show me where she is."

The young man almost choked, but he meekly wrapped the rest of his sandwich and reached for a sheaf of documents. "What was her name again?"

Rebecca answered slowly, "Christina van der Waals."

As he scanned the papers, Rebecca braced herself for viewing the body. She wasn't particularly squeamish, but she hated to see young lives cut short.

"Number four," the attendant said. "Just came in."

That came as a surprise. Rebecca had worried that the body might already be gone, claimed by Liz Luck. Why had it taken almost two days to get to the morgue?

"I'll take you to her." The attendant got up from his desk and led Rebecca into an unheated, whitewashed brick room. "At least you picked a good day," he said. "We had that little warm spell last week, and it was pretty bad in here. I tell you, with this job, I'd just as soon winter lasted all year."

The room contained two rows of six tables each. They were all alike, all draped with white sheets, and judging by the shapes under the sheets, most of them held corpses.

Rebecca followed the attendant to a table near the back wall. A body was clearly under the white linen cloth. The young man grabbed a hold of the sheet and, with no more respect than a butcher skinning a haunch of beef, whipped it off.

Rebecca almost retched at what she saw. The naked body was that of an old man—an old man who was missing his head.

"Oops, wrong one," said the attendant with a smirk.

Rebecca was sure that it hadn't been a mistake; he'd simply wanted to shock her. It took all her restraint not to smack him across his face. As it was, the look she skewered him with had the same effect. His smirk withered and he mumbled sheepishly, "Sorry."

Silently moving to another table, the attendant drew back the sheet from a blonde girl of about fourteen. "This is her," he said.

Rebecca looked over Christina's pale naked body. The reason she had come here was because she had seen a lot of different marks and injuries during her years at Colden House, and she thought that Christina's body might reveal something about what had happened to her while she was alive. Other than the girl's slim neck being twisted, there were no other visible bruises, though. Rebecca asked the attendant, "Was the broken neck the cause of death?"

"It sure didn't make her any better." In answer to another sharp look from Rebecca, he said, "I'll check."

While he went back to his desk, Rebecca examined Christina's hands to see what kind of work she might have done. Her palms and fingers were discolored brown. Looking more closely, Rebecca saw small slivers in her fingertips. She had seen similar splinters before, in the hands of girls who worked stripping tobacco. The fingers felt callused, so Christina might have been doing that work for a while, Rebecca thought.

The attendant returned with several sheets of paper. "All the coroners say the cause of death was a broken neck."

"All? How many does it take?"

The young man nervously stammered, "It only takes one, but . . . that's not how they . . . I don't have anything to do with how the coroners operate, you understand."

"I don't understand anything," said Rebecca. "What are you trying to tell me?"

"The coroners, they get paid a fee for every corpse they examine. So sometimes they move the bodies around. Let's say a body's found in Manhattan. The coroner here will do an examination and charge his fee, then he'll have the cops move it over to Brooklyn where it's 'found' again. So the coroner there gets paid for the same body. And when he finds one in Brooklyn, he'll return the favor. Some bodies can get shipped around five or six times, New York County to King's County to Richmond County. On and on."

"They always do this?"

"No, only if they don't think the body's going to be claimed." He looked at the papers again. "There was a Liz Luck who asked for this girl's body yesterday, so they had to bring it back. Anyway, three coroners say she died of a broken neck, but none of them say how she got it."

Rebecca took one more look at Christina van der Waals. The girl appeared so young, so innocent . . . and so thoroughly lifeless. Whoever took that life away would be held accountable, Rebecca vowed.

CHAPTER 23

On Sunday afternoon, wearing a formal dress suit and white tie, Marshall Webb was seated next to Rebecca Davies in the sumptuous dining room of her parents' Fifth Avenue brownstone. Even though his clothes were of the finest material and expertly tailored, they couldn't compare with the elegance of the room's appointments. The mahogany table and carved chairs were polished to a high gloss, the silverware had a mirror finish, and the china sparkled almost as brightly as the crystal chandelier that hung from the ceiling.

Six other people dressed to the nines were also at the table. In addition to Rebecca's parents, there were her sister Alice, Alice's husband—who was introduced only as Mr. Updegraff—and two silver-haired aunts. They all sat quietly, obviously waiting for something, and Webb wondered if there was some social ritual he had neglected to perform. Then, when a clock chimed two o'clock, Mr. Davies rang a silver bell next to his finger bowl, and a liveried servant entered with a soup tureen large enough to bathe a baby.

Conversation didn't improve much once they began eating, and not much of it was directed to Webb or Rebecca. The women talked about an upcoming charity ball and mentioned the names Astor and Vanderbilt so often that Webb thought they must enjoy the taste of saying them. Rebecca's father and brother-in-law briefly discussed the latest news from the Knickerbocker and Union Clubs.

Over the fish course, Updegraff deigned to acknowledge Webb's presence. "Do you have a club, Mr. Webb?" he asked.

"No, I'm afraid I don't."

Rebecca spoke up. "But weren't you in a club on Mercer Street just a few days ago?"

Webb almost dropped his fork at her joke. He and Rebecca exchanged an amused glance. "Only as a guest. I haven't been offered permanent membership yet."

She laughed and quickly covered her mouth with her napkin.

When Webb looked away from her, he was aware that they were the recipients of appalled stares from the others at the table. He suddenly had the sense that part of the reason Rebecca invited him was to scandalize her family by bringing an accused murderer to dinner. And he was happy that he'd been able to oblige.

After a dessert of *bombe de glacé,* the ladies retired to the music room and the men to the library for cognac and cigars.

The library had only a few shelves of books, but it was plush with dark wood, rich leather, heavy drapes, and oriental rugs. The walls were adorned with English hunting prints and an eclectic collection of swords and daggers. Over the mantle was a set of antique dueling pistols.

While Updegraff poured the brandies, Rebecca's father, a short, round man with bland features and cottony hair, asked, "Do you play chess, Mr. Webb?"

"No," he lied. "I've never learned the game." After the interminable dinner, Webb had no desire to endure a chess match.

"Too bad, too bad." Mr. Davies brightened when Updegraff put a snifter in his hand and lit a cigar for him. He then sat down in a corner easy chair, where he contentedly began to smoke and drink, his attention fixed on the darting flames in the fireplace.

After Webb and Updegraff had their cigars lit and brandy in the their snifters, Updgraff imperiously gestured to a pair of leather chairs on the other side of the library.

Once the two men were seated, Updegraff leaned back and exhaled a long stream of smoke. Although his prominent chin was tilted up toward the ceiling, his dark, probing eyes were on Webb.

Webb didn't mind the scrutiny. He was enjoying his cigar—he could tell it was an especially fine one because it smelled especially bad—and the cognac was superb. Besides, Webb was also studying Updegraff, though not nearly as intently. Rebecca's brother-in-law had a strong brow and a short, thick neck; in different clothes, he could easily fit in with any street gang in the Bowery.

Updegraff finally said, "Tell me, Webb. What does your family do?"

After a deep draw on his cigar, Webb answered, "I write for *Harper's Weekly*." He didn't intend to answer about the rest of his family.

Updegraff waited for more, and sighed heavily with impatience.

The arrogant little man could wait forever, as far as Webb was concerned. Webb didn't owe him his life's story. But he did owe him something. "I want to thank you," he said, "for helping me the other night. I don't know how I would have gotten out of that pickle if you hadn't interceded with Inspector Byrnes."

Obviously pleased at Webb's gratitude, Updegraff promptly waved it off. "It was nothing. The inspector is a close personal friend, and I can always call on him. I'm sure your unfortunate detention was only the result of a misunderstanding. I've found that the police are always happy to correct their errors when a *gentleman* is involved."

Webb suspected that Updegraff himself was the gentleman to whom he referred, and wondered what "misunderstandings" he had gotten away with.

Updegraff sipped his brandy and went on, "I am of the opinion that we have the finest police force in the country. They protect those who deserve it—those of us who contribute to the city's prosperity—and maintain control of the lower classes. Any talk against them is slander if you ask me." He paused, almost daring Webb to contradict him. When no objection came, he waved his cigar. "Take that minister, Parkhurst. He's nothing but a scandalmonger trying to make a name for himself by slandering the police. In the first place, all his talk about 'vice' is overblown. Sure, there are a few dens of iniquity in the city, but what do they do except provide a little harmless recreation for red-blooded American men?"

"Hear, hear," said Webb, lifting his snifter in a toast.

Oblivious to the fact that Webb was being facetious, Updegraff continued, "And if the police accept the occasional gratuity for all their hard work, how can anyone object?"

Webb shook his head as if he were at a loss to answer.

"The police have a splendid organization," said Updegraff. "Their official duties and their unofficial, uh, *enterprises* are carried out with admirable discipline. There are some brokerage firms on Wall Street that I wish were run as well."

A grandfather clock sounded five o'clock, and Updegraff pulled out his watch to check it. He probably did it to show off his expensive timepiece, Webb thought.

Updegraff snapped shut the watch case. "Sorry you have to go so soon," he said. "I enjoyed chatting with you, Webb. Let's do it again some time."

Am I being dismissed, Webb wondered?

Updegraff noticed his puzzlement. "It's time for Miss Davies's headache," he explained. "She never stays past five o'clock."

On cue, Rebecca came to the library door. "I have a bit of a headache," she said to Webb. "Do you mind if we go?"

While the butler fetched their coats, Rebecca's family expressed their hopes that she would recover soon, and politely asked Webb to visit again. He agreed that he would, but hoped that it wouldn't be for another year or so.

Once they were outside on the broad sidewalk, Rebecca said, "What you do know? A little fresh air, and my head feels much better." She tried to glean from Webb's expression how he was feeling. She thought he'd done an admirable job facing her family, and hoped it hadn't taken a toll on him.

"I'll have to remember your remedy," he said with a smile. "I expect I may find myself with the same headache at *my* next family dinner."

Rebecca laughed. "There's one more ingredient to the prescription: a glass of medicinal wine. There's a café a few blocks from here."

Webb offered his elbow. "Then we'd better go, so you can complete your recovery."

Rebecca happily put her hand on his arm, and they strolled down to Eighteenth Street, chatting easily as they walked. When they arrived at the café, she wished she had thought of one that was much farther away.

After they'd been seated and a bottle of Montrachet uncorked,

Rebecca said, "Tell me honestly. What did you think of my family?"

Webb hesitated a bit too long before answering, "They seemed nice enough." After another moment, he added, "Your brother-in-law is certainly full of himself, though."

She laughed. "That he is. But my sister loves him, so he must have some good points. That's what I keep telling myself, anyway."

"I noticed that no one mentioned Colden House during dinner. They never ask about your work there?"

"Oh, no. They prefer to pretend that I don't do anything so unladylike as to perform useful labor."

"Like they pretend to believe your five o'clock headaches every Sunday?"

Rebecca laughed again. "Exactly! Now don't get me wrong. I love my family, but their lives and mine have become very different. Sometimes it's hard to find anything to talk about with them."

The two of them continued to talk until the bottle was almost empty. Then Webb became quieter and Rebecca wondered if she'd said something wrong. "What are you thinking?" she asked.

"I have a confession to make."

"About?"

"What I've been doing the past couple of days." He toyed with the stem of his wineglass. "I've been looking for someone who might have seen Christina van der Waals."

Rebecca was a bit irked. "You promised me you wouldn't do anything without telling me first."

"I know. And I'm sorry. But I had to do something, so I went to the apartment building where I found her. I knocked on every door and showed her photograph to everyone who would look at it. No one remembered seeing her. I went back the next day in case I'd missed anyone who was out the first time. I also stopped in at the shops near the apartment. Still no luck."

"So she probably wasn't living there for any length of time."

"That's what I figure. Especially since the apartment didn't look inhabitable."

"I have an idea of where she was." Rebecca then told him about her visit to the morgue and said she was certain that Christina had been working as a tobacco stripper.

"Where would she do that?" Webb asked.

"That's what we need to find out." She hoped Webb noted the "we." "I've asked around, and I think the place to start is at the Barge Office."

CHAPTER 24

Rebecca's reasoning made sense, Webb thought. They knew that Christina van der Waals had been ferried to the Barge Office after being processed at Ellis Island, and that she didn't make it from there to Liz Luck. Since new immigrants were often taken from the Barge Office to work in sweatshops, and Rebecca believed that Christina had been stripping tobacco for some time, it was possible that she'd been abducted there.

As Webb and Rebecca walked the short distance from Colden House to the Barge Office, he was conscious that this Monday was February 29; tomorrow would mark two months since Christina's arrival in America. And it was one week since he'd found her dead, broken body.

The noisy scene outside the Barge Office was as chaotic as Webb remembered from his previous visit. A group of immigrants from the transfer boat *J. H. Brinkerhoff* had just landed and were milling about with children and baggage in tow, seeking relatives or directions. A small army of newsboys hawked the city's major papers—the *World, Herald, Sun,* and *Tribune,* as well as foreign language newspapers such as *Il Progresso Italo-Americano* and *Yidisher Tageblatt*—to the newcomers. Money changers shouted offers to convert foreign currency to dollars, and railroad agents sold tickets to "anyplace in America." Numerous other fast-talking "agents" offered jobs and rooms—probably of the kind that the Droboskys had been lured into, Webb thought.

Rebecca pointed to one such agent, who was loudly offering trips to "the beautiful hills of Pennsylvania." "I've heard about him," she said. "The 'beautiful hills' are outside Pittsburgh, and the immigrants who go there are put to work mining coal. They have to work a long time to pay off their train fare, room, and board. Some never get out of the mines." Rebecca looked as if she wanted to shout a warning to everyone within earshot. She shook her head slightly, apparently realizing how futile that would be. "All right," she said. "We have to find which of these swindlers takes girls for tobacco stripping. Do you have Christina's photograph?"

"Yes." Webb always carried it with him. "But what good is it going to do? Even if we find the man who took Christina, he isn't going to admit it. They don't even say what the jobs really are."

Rebecca bit her lip. "You're right. But maybe somebody else saw her."

"And they'd remember her face from two months ago? I was here two weeks after she arrived, and didn't get anywhere."

"All right. Let me think."

It sounded to Webb as though Rebecca had taken it upon herself to decide on a plan. "While you're thinking," he said, "I'll go find out who might have taken her."

Before she could say anything, he walked off toward the building's main entrance, where several newsboys were aggressively pushing their papers. In the past, he'd found newsboys to be rich sources of information. They often had the perception of children combined with the street smarts of the Bowery Boys, and were aware of everything that transpired on their turf.

One tow-headed boy stood on the fringe of the group, a bundle of newspapers under his arm and a copy of the *Sun* held up in his hand. He was coatless, and his frayed trousers were held up by a single suspender. The boy's wide eyes darted about looking for potential customers. On Webb's approach, he tried to force the paper on him.

Webb didn't accept it. "You sure have a lot of competition out here," he commented.

"Yeah, I know," the boy said sourly.

"Almost as much as those fellows trying to recruit immigrants to work for them."

"You want a paper, mister? It's a penny." The boy already started looking past Webb for a new customer.

"How long have you been working this place?"

"Since last summer. It's a penny for a paper, mister."

"You must know a lot about what goes on here, then."

Like most boys, this one fell for the flattery and turned his attention back to Webb. "You bet I do."

"So maybe you can help me." Webb took a quarter from his pocket. "There's a lot of men out here, taking people to all kinds of jobs."

The boy's eyes were riveted on the shiny coin. "You lookin' to hire somebody, mister?"

"No. What I want is to know who offers jobs in tobacco stripping."

"Well . . . nobody would *offer* that." The boy smiled slyly. "Of course, they might call it something else—'farm work,' maybe."

Webb returned the smile. "Who'd offer that kind of farm work then?"

"Most likely Joe McQuaid." He nodded in the direction of a peanut cart. "That's him, with the big hat."

"Thanks." Webb dropped the coin in the boy's palm. "Keep the paper."

When Webb returned to Rebecca, he asked teasingly, "Have you finished thinking?"

"Yes." Her reply was curt. "Have you found out who's involved in tobacco stripping?"

Webb couldn't conceal his satisfaction. "Yes. His name's Joe McQuaid. He's the one in the planter hat by the cart over there."

"Good work." Rebecca promptly began walking toward the man, and Webb had to hurry to keep up with her.

McQuaid, who held a bag of peanuts and stood amid a litter of shells, was a fashion disaster. Besides the broad-brimmed straw hat—a ridiculous thing to wear in New York in winter—he combined a striped brown suit with a checked green vest and a bright red bow tie. The awful outfit at least drew attention away from his face; McQuaid's loose skin looked like melted wax and he had a sleepy left eye that was like a permanent wink.

Rebecca gave the man a smile so charming that Webb felt a minor pang of jealousy. "Mr. McQuaid?" she asked.

He doffed his hat and bowed, revealing a bald scalp. "Josiah Daniel McQuaid, at your service, ma'am."

"I believe we may be of *mutual* service," she said.

As he put his hat back on, McQuaid looked Rebecca up and down so directly that he should have been slapped. "In what way, Miss . . . ?"

Webb was curious to hear the answer to that question himself. He wished Rebecca had told him what she had in my mind before approaching McQuaid.

"Miss Davies," she said. With a wave of her hand at Webb, she added, "And this is Mr. Byrd."

McQuaid eyed Webb more warily than he had Rebecca.

"Mr. Byrd is my associate," Rebecca explained. "In my business, a strong man can come in handy sometimes." From that statement, Webb deduced that his job was to remain quiet and look tough.

"And what business is that?" asked McQuaid.

"Girls."

McQuaid's sleepy eye almost snapped open, and he grinned broadly.

"I run a home for young women," Rebecca continued. "But there are far more women coming to me than I can accommodate."

"Ah, so you're looking for somebody who can use the surplus." McQuaid winked with his good eye. "I'm sure I can help you with that. You see, it's a matter of supply and demand. *My* business is to make sure them that has a demand gets supplied. Right now, the demand for girls is higher than I've ever seen it. Especially for the pretty ones. You got those kind of girls?"

"Don't misunderstand me," said Rebecca. "These are decent girls. I'm looking to find honest work for them."

McQuaid's droopy face betrayed his disappointment.

"But it doesn't have to be easy work," she quickly added. "Too many of them think I should simply feed and house them forever, and that's expensive."

McQuaid nodded.

"Now, if you should know of anyone who needs laborers, I can supply them. Of course, I'd like to recoup some of what I've spent to board these women."

"Quite understandable," said McQuaid. "And it just so happens that I think I know someone who can put those girls to work."

"Doing what?"

"Don't worry. It's respectable."

"I would prefer to see that for myself. Can you arrange for me to visit their workplace?"

McQuaid hesitated. "I don't expect I can do that. It's no place for a lady such as yourself."

Rebecca pressed. "We might be able to do a lot of business together, Mr. McQuaid—for quite some time. But I do feel a responsibility for these girls and would like to see what they will be doing."

The promise of business did the trick, and Webb admired the way Rebecca had handled this man.

"I'll see what I can do," said McQuaid. "You understand, though, that I have my expenses, too.

"Of course. This is a situation where we can all profit."

McQuaid decided to press a little further himself. "We can profit more," he said, "if you weren't too particular about what the girls do."

"I don't mind how hard the work is or if the conditions are less than ideal. Most of them are used to a hard life."

"That's not what I mean," said McQuaid. "I mean pretty girls can get jobs working in very nice conditions."

"And those who want to employ such girls would pay more to whomever supplies them?" Rebecca sounded tempted.

"Of course."

She thought a moment and appeared agreeable. "Then let's leave that as a option for the future. For now, let me see what you can offer the homely girls."

McQuaid laughed and suggested that Rebecca return the next day.

CHAPTER 25

The 11:50 passenger train of the New York, New Haven & Hartford Railroad pulled out on time from Grand Central Depot Thursday morning. As the locomotive wheezed its way up Fourth Avenue, the train's wheels scraped loudly on the rails and the car rocked and rumbled, making conversation difficult. That had its advantages, Webb soon found, because it meant that he and Rebecca had to lean close to each other in order to be heard.

Webb slid a little closer across the hard wooden bench they shared, and turned to speak in Rebecca's ear. He caught the faint scent of perfume—jasmine, he thought—and noticed that her fair skin had been lightly powdered. Soft wisps of blond hair curled over her ear. It took some effort for Webb to avoid getting lost in the pleasant distraction of Rebecca's face being mere inches from his. "Did McQuaid tell you anything else?" he asked. He had had to miss Rebecca's second meeting with Joe McQuaid because he'd been called into the *Harper's* office to work on an article about the upcoming Chicago Exposition.

"No," Rebecca answered, tilting her head to speak into his ear. "Only the names of the inn and the men we're supposed to meet."

Webb enjoyed the feel of her breath on his neck, and wished she would say more. "I didn't expect we'd have to go all the way to Windsor, Connecticut," he said. The trip meant that Webb was violating the police order he'd been given not to leave New York City, but it didn't deter him from going.

"Neither did I," said Rebecca. "I know that tobacco stripping is an established industry in Manhattan, but it's usually on a small scale, with people working in their own apartments. Connecticut is where they grow the tobacco, though, so I suppose it makes sense to have workers at the source."

An obnoxious train boy who'd been aggressively working his way down the aisle arrived at their seat. In a voice that was a cross between a dog's bark and a duck's quack, he rattled off the list of items that he had for sale. His full tray contained everything from yesterday's newspapers and dog-eared dime novels to bruised apples and soggy pickles, all at exorbitant prices. Webb gave him a dime for a bag of gumdrops; he didn't want them, but he knew the boy would pester them for the rest of the trip until they bought something. Train boys were more extortionists than vendors, and Webb suspected that only the police department had a better-organized shakedown racket.

Rebecca and Webb each attempted to chew a piece of the stale candy and gave up talking for a while. After crossing the Harlem River, the train picked up speed and rolled along more smoothly. Although they could now hear each other easily, neither Rebecca nor Webb made any attempt to move apart.

Webb decided to ask Rebecca something he'd wondered about ever since he'd seen the privileged lifestyle of her family. "I'm curious," he said. "With your background and social connections, how did you become so committed to your work at Colden House? You could easily be living a life of leisure."

"I wasn't always so committed," she answered. "Especially when I was younger. But my family pushed me into overseeing the operation of Colden House as a charitable duty." She smiled tightly. "I think they regret that now. Then, once I got to know the girls there, I didn't see any important difference between them and me. Except that they'd had fewer opportunities and more hardships—and often they'd had to endure tragedies that I had never even imagined, much less experienced." After a thoughtful pause, she continued, "Now I probably devote too much of my life to Colden House, but I believe I can do more good there in one day than I could ever do on Fifth Avenue." She turned to look Webb in the eyes. "What about you? You must have come from a well-to-do family—you're educated, you dress well, and your manners are those of a gentleman. So why do you have such sympathy for the poor? I've seen how you looked at some of the people we've met. Your concern is genuine."

Webb answered less readily than Rebecca had. "I grew up in Five Points," he said. "There was no tougher—or poorer—neighborhood in New York." When the city later began cleaning up the notorious slum district and razed the tenement building in which he'd grown up, Webb shed no tears over the loss of his childhood home. "My father worked in a glue factory on Elizabeth Street, grinding up bones and hooves." He drew a deep breath before continuing. "Then the war came, and when they started drafting men to fight for the Union, the wealthy were allowed to pay their way out of service. For three hundred dollars, a rich man could hire a substitute to fight for him. That was a fortune to people like us, so my father hired himself out in the spring of 'sixty-four. Two months after going to war, he was killed."

"How awful. I'm sorry."

Webb went on in a quiet voice, "We had the three hundred dollars, so we were able to survive. My mother blamed my father's death on the fact that we'd been poor, though, and she set out to remarry—and to marry well. She succeeded; within three years, she was Mrs. Tyner, and my brother and I had a wealthy stepfather."

"What surprises me," Rebecca said, "is that most people who go from poverty to riches try to put on airs and avoid contact with anyone who might remind them of their own humble beginnings. You still have a concern for the underprivileged. And you seem comfortable in poor neighborhoods. Most people in your situation would never go back."

"I went back some time ago," Webb said softly.

"What do you mean?"

It was something Webb never spoke of, but he felt comfortable talking with Rebecca, and she seemed to be someone he could risk telling about his past. Besides, once she knew the worst about him, he'd have nothing more to hide. "I think I mentioned that I had a year of college," he said.

"Yes. Princeton, wasn't it?"

Webb nodded. "My mother coaxed her husband into paying my tuition. She was determined that my brother and I get off to a good start in life and meet the 'right' people." He slouched a little in the seat. "I thought I did meet the right people. My roommate came from a family that owned several shipping lines; he and I soon became fast friends. And I met a girl whose father was a congressman from New Jersey. By the end of my freshman year, we were engaged."

He paused for so long, recalling events that he'd tried hard to erase from his memory, that Rebecca had to ask, "What happened?"

"She eloped with my friend. I took it like it was the end of the world—it was certainly the end of *my* world. I started drinking . . . and worse." He turned to look Rebecca in the face. "I am not proud of the way I behaved back then, but I can't change what's past." She nodded that she understood, and he went on, "I was a regular in some of the worst dives in New York. If I didn't drink what money I had, I gambled it away. Then one night, drunk as usual, I had a lucky streak in a poker game. But I barely made it out to the street before I was mugged. I was beaten, stabbed, and left to die in the gutter. I hate to admit it, but I actually hoped that I *would* die. Came close to doing just that, I learned later, but eventually I dragged myself out of the gutter and made it to my brother's house. He got me a doctor and then he helped me get my life straightened out. My *Harper's* job came as a favor to my family." He looked at Rebecca again. "I've led a decent life ever since. And, ever since I got back on my feet, I've had the notion that I'd like to see everyone else end up all right, too. I guess I do want happy endings."

Rebecca didn't reply for a moment. Then she laid her hand over his, and they rode for a while in silence.

Rebecca had thoroughly enjoyed Webb's company during the journey to Hartford. It was no reflection on him that, after they'd switched to a slow-moving local train for the remaining miles to Windsor, her attention was largely focused out the window. She was simply captivated by the scenery, and enjoying the fact that it was such a different world from the crowded, callous streets of lower Manhattan.

The idyllic Connecticut River Valley was beginning to show unmistakable signs of the coming spring. The river flowed smoothly, its crystal water free of ice. Along its banks, the ground looked rich and fertile, ready for this year's tobacco crops. The occasional patches of forest that they passed appeared as if leaves were about to bud at any moment, and Rebecca found herself craning her neck to keep them in view so that she wouldn't miss the blossoming.

Not until a two-horse omnibus carried them to their final destination, the Warham Inn on a dirt road north of downtown Windsor, did she bring her attention back to the reason for their visit.

The rustic three-story inn had the appearance and atmosphere of a fine country house, with a wraparound porch, an indoor bathroom, a spacious dining room, and a comfortable parlor with a view of the river. Rebecca and Webb checked into their respective rooms and returned downstairs in plenty of time for their appointed meeting. They sat and chatted in the parlor while they waited for the others to join them.

At a few minutes to four, a pair of slender, somber-looking men, each about fifty years old, ventured timidly into the parlor. Except for a half-foot difference in their heights, they could have almost been twins; both were clean-shaven, with sharp features and thin dark hair combed carefully over balding crowns. The similarity in appearance extended to their severe black suits and high, stiff collars. From their clothes and rigid bearing, they gave the impression of a couple of straitlaced ministers. Addressing Webb, the taller of the two men asked, "Mr. Byrd?"

"Yes." Webb stood and offered his hand.

The man pumped it enthusiastically. "Pleased to meet you. I'm Henry Ballard, and this is my partner, Mr. Frist."

Frist also shook Webb's hand, but when introductions were made to Rebecca the two men barely acknowledged her presence.

Ballard looked around the parlor. No one else was in the room, but his voice was hushed when he said, "This appears to be sufficiently private. Shall we talk here?"

"Yes, certainly," said Webb.

The men dragged over a couple of wicker chairs, placed them across from Rebecca and Webb, and primly sat down.

"It's good of you to come all this way," said Ballard. "I think you'll see that this is a most rewarding place to do business. The Connecticut Valley is growing more prosperous every day."

Rebecca asked, "Did Mr. McQuaid make it clear what kind of business we're interested in?"

Ballard's only reply was a surprised stare. His thin face appeared as astonished as if he had just been addressed by one of the potted plants that adorned the parlor.

Rebecca sensed the problem: Ballard did not intend to discuss business matters with a woman. She resisted the temptation to force the issue, and instead gave Webb a look intended to say, "He's all yours."

Webb took the cue and promptly asked Ballard the same question.

"Yes," he answered. "Mr. McQuaid mentioned that you might be able to help with the staffing needs of one of our enterprises."

"You have many enterprises?" Webb asked.

Puffing himself up, Ballard said, "We have several interests. Mine are primarily brickyards; in fact, I happen to own the two largest brick-making factories in Connecticut." He paused until Webb cocked his eyebrows to indicate how impressed he was by this. Ballard went on: "Mr. Frist's main business is farming tobacco. He's brought his expertise from Kentucky, and now he owns half the tobacco fields in the Valley."

"Almost half," corrected the soft-spoken Frist. It was clear to Rebecca that he was the subordinate partner.

Ballard cleared his throat. "Yes, well, it will be *more* than half soon enough." Addressing Webb again, he said, "We also have a joint business venture. As you may know, the market for tobacco products is booming, especially with all the machine-made cigarettes they're churning out now. Tobacco products need tobacco leaf, and tobacco leaves need to be stripped from the stalks. So we've established a little facility for stripping tobacco; some of the leaf is grown by Mr. Frist, but a good deal of it is from other farmers as well."

"And for that," said Webb, "you need workers."

"Exactly. As I said, business is booming, and we've had trouble finding suitable labor in this area. Mr. McQuaid has been a godsend to us; he's supplied almost all of the workers currently in our employ." Ballard frowned slightly. "Recently, however, he has been unable to fill our growing needs. He's even taken some girls away from us, bringing them back to New York to fill some positions there. So we are quite shorthanded at the moment."

"What do they do in New York?" Webb asked.

Ballard pursed his lips distastefully. "I have my suspicions," he said, "but I prefer not to know for certain. All that concerns me is the fact that we are short of help here."

Rebecca could remain silent no longer. "That's where I can help. I have a number of girls who need work. And I am sure you will find them suitable—most are without families and are accustomed to hard work."

Ballard nodded appreciatively but continued to address Webb, "How many can you supply?"

"That depends," Webb answered. "There are several matters to be resolved first. For one thing, Miss Davies has spent a great deal of money caring for these girls. She would need to recoup some of those costs."

"I'm sure you will find us to be very generous," answered Ballard. "But we would prefer to handle the payments through Mr. McQuaid. My understanding is that you will supply the girls to him, he will pay you directly, and then he will make the transportation arrangements."

"That won't be a problem," said Rebecca. "But, as I've told Mr. McQuaid, before entering into any agreement, I want to see the facility where these girls will be working."

"I'm afraid that's impossible," said Ballard.

Frist shook his head and drawled, "It's no place for a gentlelady such as yourself."

"I must insist," Rebecca said firmly. "I feel somewhat responsible for these girls, and I do not intend to send them to you until I see their workplace."

The two men continued to shake their heads.

With a resigned sigh, Rebecca turned to Webb. "Well, at least we had a pleasant day in the country, even if we couldn't transact any business. Would you be so good as to get my bags?"

Ballard pleaded with Webb. "Can't you talk some sense into her, Mr. Byrd?"

Webb held up his hands as if to answer that it would be hopeless even to attempt to reason with her.

Rebecca felt especially pleased when it was Ballard who surrendered. "It's rather late to go there today, but we can send a carriage for you in the morning. Shall we say, eight o'clock?"

Eight would have been fine with Rebecca, but she answered, "Make it nine."

Webb again held up his hands, indicating that her answer was the final one.

CHAPTER 26

It was a relief to Webb when the soft-spoken Frist arrived alone the next morning. He had the feeling that if Rebecca was subjected to any more of Henry Ballard's condescension, the arrogant fellow would have ended up with a sock in the eye—administered not by Webb, but by Rebecca.

Frist, dressed like a gentleman farmer in a light linen suit and a Panama hat, apologized for his partner, saying that Ballard had to meet with his banker on other business. He offered to take them out on his own, and the offer was promptly accepted.

Webb helped Rebecca into the rear seat of Frist's canopy-top surrey, then eased himself next to her. The Kentuckian slid into the front seat, picked up the reins, and gave them a snap to spur his horse forward.

From its pace and gait, Webb suspected that the old roan was arthritic. But they were in no hurry anyway, and the slow progress kept down the amount of dust that was stirred up, so he and Rebecca settled back to enjoy the fresh country air and unseasonably warm sunshine.

After they crossed over to the east side of the Connecticut River, Frist turned onto a rutted dirt path that aspired to be a road. It cut through a vast, barren field. Over his shoulder, Frist said, "This is one of my farms."

Rebecca leaned forward so that he could hear her over the clopping of the horse and the creaking of the wheels. "But there's nobody out here."

"No, ma'am. It's not the season yet. We won't be planting the seedlings until late May or early June."

"If there's no work, why do you need workers?"

"To strip last year's crop. That goes on year round."

"Where do you do that?"

"We'll be there soon enough, ma'am." He gave Rebecca a quick backward glance. "If I may say so, ma'am, there's still time for you to reconsider."

"Why should I do that?"

"As I mentioned yesterday, it's no place for a lady."

"Aren't your workers ladies?"

"No, ma'am, they're just girls. They don't have the sensibilities a lady such as yourself has."

Rebecca laughed. "I'm usually accused of having too *few* sensibilities. Don't worry, Mr. Frist. I'm sure you can't show me any worse than some of the things I've seen in the city." She breathed deeply. "And I'm certain my girls will enjoy working for you out here in the fresh air. So please drive on."

He touched the brim of his hat in surrender. "As you wish, ma'am."

They continued through the empty fields for almost half an hour, then turned onto a narrower path through a densely wooded area. Low branches and thick underbrush scraped the sides of the surrey.

They arrived at a small clearing in the middle of which was a large, ramshackle barn. Its bare wood didn't yet show the gray of long-term weathering, so Webb thought it was of fairly recent construction. The only other vehicle in sight was an unhitched farm wagon at the side of the barn, with a chestnut workhorse tethered to a nearby sapling.

Frist eased to a stop next to the wagon and hopped out. "Here we are," he announced. As Webb helped Rebecca down from her seat, Frist tied up the horse.

One of the barn's double doors was open, and the three of them walked toward it. Frist suggested to Rebecca, "You may want to hold a handkerchief over your face, ma'am. The dust can be a bit overwhelming if you're not used to it."

She said, "Thank you," but made no move to take his advice. Frist muttered, "As you wish," and led them inside.

Webb almost gagged on the first breath of air that he tried to inhale. Tobacco dust filled the barn in a thick haze. It was slightly sweet and totally nauseating, and every lungful was like taking in a large pinch of snuff.

Visibility inside the barn was poor. Not only was it cloudy with tobacco dust, but the only illumination was the meager sunlight that squeezed its way through knotholes and gaps in the boards. It took a few moments before Webb's eyes could adjust to the darkness. Once they did, he saw that the barn's rafters were packed with bundles of tobacco leaf, and thousands of stalks with leaves still on them were stacked around the walls. In the middle of the barn were several long, crude tables—nothing more than planks supported by sawhorses—around which twenty to twenty-five girls worked, passing stalks from one to another and removing the leaves with their bare hands.

Some of the girls must have looked up at them when they entered, because a gruff voice barked, "Get yer eyes back on yer work!"

Webb searched through the fog of dust and spotted a man in bib overalls and a slouch hat seated on a tall stool near the wall. A small opening had been broken through the wall near his seat, providing him the freshest air in the place.

Frist called to the man, "How are we doing today, Barney?"

Barney, who appeared to be some kind of overseer, replied, "We'd be doin' a damn sight better if we had girls who was willin' to work, Mr. Frist."

"Watch your language, sir! We have a lady present."

"Sorry, Mr. Frist." Barney looked at Rebecca and tugged at his cap. "My apologies, ma'am."

Frist said to him, "We won't disturb your work. I'm just going to show these good people our operation."

"Yes, sir."

Webb didn't see how it could be possible to disturb Barney's "work," since his sole job appeared to consist of sitting and yelling.

Frist waved toward the forest of leafy tobacco stalks piled against one of the walls. "We usually harvest the tobacco crop in late summer and bring the stalks in here to cure for a couple of months. Then we strip the leaves. We've already stripped my crops; these are from a couple of other farmers. The leaf is inferior, but the money we get for stripping them is good." He led Webb and Rebecca to one of the tables, where a half-dozen girls were hard at work. "In Kentucky," he went on, "we would wait until the tobacco was 'in case'—that's when it's moist and pliable—to do the stripping. These New England winters are too dry to permit that, though, so the tobacco in here is pretty brittle. It makes for more dust, and the girls get a few splinters, but the procedure is basically the same."

At the table, an older, rawboned girl, whose plain frock was stained brown from handling tobacco, picked up a fully-leafed stalk and began the stripping process. She pulled off a few leaves, then passed the stalk to the next girl, who did the same and passed it on to the next worker in line. Webb estimated that the girls ranged in age from about twelve to twenty, but they all appeared tired and frail and aged beyond their years.

Frist explained the process as the stalks made their way down the table. "The most experienced girl starts off," he said. "She removes the trash leaves. Then each girl down the line strips off a specific grade of leaf, with the most valuable ones taken off first. By the time the stalk gets to the end, all that's left are the tips and greens. That's where we put the newest girls until they learn to judge the grades." He pointed to the rafter. "Each grade is tied into hands and stored until we either take them to market, or the farmers who contract with us pick them up."

A tiny, doll-like girl standing at the end of a nearby table raised her hand and called to Barney. "I need to use the privy, sir!"

"Get back to work! You went an hour ago."

"But I—" She suddenly turned to the side and vomited onto the floor.

While the overseer went into a tirade over her messing up a few leaves, Frist said to Webb and Rebecca, "She's one of the new ones. Some of them take a while to get accustomed to the smell of tobacco."

Webb was feeling queasy himself. He knew that even if he stayed in the barn for a year, he would never get used to the foul, dust-laden air.

Rebecca asked, "Where are the girls housed?"

"They have sleeping quarters behind the barn," Frist answered. "Perfectly adequate accommodations. They're quite comfortable there."

"And their meals?"

"We provide those, too. I can assure you, Miss Davies, we provide for all the needs of these girls. We feed them, house them, and give them a place where they can do honest labor. If you ask me, they have it mighty good." Frist nodded benevolently. "If they pay off their room and board, they can even leave whenever they choose."

"I can't imagine many would want to leave such a comfortable situation," said Rebecca.

Webb caught the edge of sarcasm in her voice. Frist was oblivious to it. "Not many do," he said.

"Well," said Rebecca. "Thank you so much for the tour. I believe my girls would do very well here. Shall I get in touch with Mr. McQuaid to make the arrangements?"

Clearly happy with her decision, Frist said, "Please do. And the sooner the better. We could use at least ten more girls right away."

"Before we go," Rebecca whispered. "I could use a privy myself."

Frist stammered before admitting, "There is no actual facility. The girls use the bushes out back."

"That will do," she said.

Rebecca went outside, and Frist excused himself to discuss a few things with Barney.

While he waited, Webb watched the girls laboring at the tables. Either the work or the conditions had taken a toll on them. Almost all of them had sallow skin, and they moved lethargically—not from lack of effort, as far as Webb could tell, but like decrepit old women with bad joints. It was hard for him to see their downturned eyes, but Webb got enough glimpses to tell that they appeared dull and resigned. There was more life in the celluloid film strip that he had seen in the Edison laboratory than there was at these tables.

When Rebecca returned, Frist was still huddled with the overseer. That gave Webb a chance to speak with her. "We know that Joe McQuaid has been supplying girls to this place," he said. "But we still don't have proof that Christina was one of them."

"I know," Rebecca said. "I'd like to show her photograph to these girls, but not while they're being watched."

"I have the feeling they're always watched."

"Maybe not at night."

Frist returned to them, and they quickly switched from their conversation to uttering compliments about his stripping operation.

* * *

Rebecca was certainly glad that she had Marshall Webb with her. Neither of them had any idea what might await them behind the stripping barn, but having Webb along gave her a feeling of security. It wasn't that she felt he could protect her—she knew he could be of little help if they were confronted by an armed guard or a pack of dogs. What comforted her was the fact that he'd willingly gone along with her plan, even taking it upon himself to hire a horse and buggy from a livery stable near the inn.

Their journey back to the tobacco barn had been a slow one, traveling in the dark of night with only a single driving lantern to illuminate the same route they had taken that morning. The light was so feeble that Webb had to keep their horse reined in to avoid outrunning its glow. Once they reached the woods, he stopped the buggy and tied up far from the barn. Driving through the woods was too treacherous at night, and they wanted to make their approach more quietly than they could with a horse.

That morning, when Rebecca had claimed to need the outhouse, she had actually taken the opportunity to look for the girls' living quarters. Now, leaving Webb outside to keep watch, Rebecca made her way for the rickety shack that was their home. She was relieved to find no guards or dogs in sight.

Balancing a bundle of food that she'd bought in town, and a policeman's lantern that Webb had thought to purchase, she tried the door. It was unlocked and creaked open at her touch. Once inside, she crouched down, lit the whale-oil lamp, and opened its lens to produce a small, focused beam of light that stabbed through the murky shadows.

What Frist had described as "perfectly adequate accommodations" might have been suitable for livestock, but not for human beings. There was a table similar to the one in the stripping barn, and a few canvas camp stools, but no other furnishings. The "beds," which ran along two walls, were nothing more than piles of straw with coarse blankets thrown over them.

Despite the lack of decent bedding, all of the girls appeared to be asleep. Their sleep couldn't have been very sound, however, since they were all wheezing or coughing. No surprise, thought Rebecca, since the tobacco dust they'd been breathing all day also permeated the air of their living quarters.

She took the photograph of Christina van der Waals from her skirt pocket, and quietly approached the girl nearest the door. She gently shook her awake, keeping the beam of light off her face. The girl awoke, only slightly startled.

"Sshhh, it's all right," Rebecca whispered. When the girl seemed acclimated to her presence, Rebecca held up the photo and directed the light at it. "Have you seen her?"

The girl shook her head, said something in a Slavic language, and turned over to go back to sleep.

Rebecca fared little better with the next girl, who at least studied the photograph for a minute before shrugging noncommittally and uttering a few words of German. The image in the photograph wasn't very clear, Rebecca knew, and the viewing conditions were far from optimal. She worried that she might get no definitive answer in these circumstances.

She continued down the row of makeshift beds, trying several more girls without success, before a dark-featured young woman with matted hair took a long look at the photograph. "Christina?" she said in a hoarse voice.

"You've seen her!" Rebecca spoke louder than she'd intended, and several girls stirred in their sleep.

"Yes," the girl replied. "I liked her. She was Dutch, but spoke English. She used to tell me stories about Holland." A sudden cough racked her body and she gasped for air.

"Christina worked here?"

The girl nodded.

"For how long?"

"I can't say exactly. The days are all the same in this place, and it's hard to tell time."

"Do your best," Rebecca coaxed.

The girl propped herself up on her elbows and furrowed her brow. "Christina came a little after New Year's, I think. I remember we had some turkey that day. And she left about two weeks ago, with the others."

"What others?"

"The pretty girls. A man came from New York. He took all the pretty girls away."

"Do you know his name?"

"No, I don't think I ever heard it. He had a funny eye, though, like it was always winking."

Rebecca waited until the girl finished a brief coughing fit before asking, "Why did he take the girls?"

"Nobody would say." The girl nodded to herself. "But I know. Some of the girls were working here because they refused to work in the bawdy houses. Sometimes one of them would change her mind and be taken back to New York. I suppose a lot of them wanted to go back two weeks ago."

"They all went willingly?"

"Well, now that you mention it, maybe not. Some of the girls argued, including Christina. But they were all put onto a wagon. All the pretty ones." She sighed wistfully and ran her fingers through her thick hair.

"What's your name, dear?"

"Sarah."

"How did you come to work here, Sarah?"

"My family needs the money."

"You get paid regularly?"

"Yes, ma'am. Well . . . not cash in hand. Mr. Barney is saving my money for me, and when it's up to fifty dollars, he'll give it to me and I can go home to my parents."

Rebecca waited until Sarah caught her breath again after another coughing spell. "How long have you been here?"

"About a year."

"How much do you have saved?"

"Thirty-seven dollars." She smiled with pride. "I'm more than halfway there."

Rebecca doubted that the total would ever reach fifty. "Don't any of the girls try to run away from here?"

Sarah shook her head, as if the thought had never crossed her mind. "We're in the middle of nowhere; where would we go? Besides, we all need the work."

This was the kind of situation that infuriated Rebecca the most. Not only were these girls exploited, they were grateful for the work. "Sarah," she said, "if you ever do leave and you need a place to stay, come see me at Colden House in New York."

"I'm not leaving without my fifty dollars."

"I hope you get it soon." Rebecca opened the bundle of foodstuffs. "Meanwhile, take these things and share them with the rest of the girls. There's some sausages, cheese, and bread. You should probably hide them so Barney or Mr. Frist don't wonder where they came from."

"Yes, ma'am." She coughed. "Thank you, ma'am."

"I wish I could have brought you more. One thing: *please* don't tell anyone I was here or that anyone was asking about Christina."

"I won't, ma'am."

When Rebecca left, she paused before going outside and looked back at the girls. She wished that she could take them all with her.

CHAPTER 27

Marshall Webb was exhausted by the time they pulled into Grand Central Depot on Saturday. After the late-night excursion to the tobacco farm, he had gotten only a couple of hours' sleep before he and Rebecca left the inn to catch the first train they could out of Windsor. During the train ride back to New York, Rebecca had managed to sleep, but Webb was too preoccupied. He was busy thinking of how he could portray what he had seen in words. At first, he made written notes, but after Rebecca's head listed over onto his shoulder he tried to avoid waking her; he then kept his arm still and settled for composing descriptions mentally instead.

When the two of them stepped out from the depot onto the streets of Manhattan shortly after noon, it was clear that not only was their country outing over, so was the first blush of spring. A slashing, icy drizzle, pushed sideways by gusting winds, rained upon them like a fusillade of arrows. It stung their faces and chilled their feet.

Webb hailed a hansom cab, which sheltered them from the weather until they reached Colden House.

While the driver waited, Webb walked Rebecca to the front door.

"I have an extra umbrella," she said. "Why don't you borrow it?"

Webb didn't care whether he had an umbrella or not, but he followed her into the foyer so they could have a more private good-bye than they could at her doorstep.

They had just closed the door behind them when Rebecca's assistant Miss Hummel, came running into the hallway. "Miss Davies! Thank goodness you're here!"

"Why?" Rebecca asked. "What's the matter?"

"We're being flooded!" The woman was almost hysterical. "I was starting to prepare lunches when all of a sudden the ceiling came crashing in. There's water everywhere!"

"Let's see." Rebecca hurried to the back of the house, with Webb and Miss Hummel following close behind. When they got to the kitchen, they all drew up short; the entire floor had turned into a pond with fallen plaster making a soggy island near the pantry.

Miss Hummel pointed to a ragged hole, almost two feet in diameter, in the ceiling. "I tried to plug it." She had used a blanket, which sagged under the weight of more water.

"That's no good," said Webb. "If you block the flow, the water will build up in the ceiling and come through someplace else. Do you have a bucket? I'll pull the blanket out."

Rebecca sighed. "What we need is a new roof." She asked Miss Hummel, "How is it upstairs?"

"There are some leaks in the bedrooms. I have a couple of the girls plugging them."

"I better go see," said Rebecca.

"You go ahead." Webb took off his overcoat. "I'll see what I can do down here."

As the two women headed upstairs, Webb remembered the waiting hackman. He dashed outside to dismiss the driver, then went back to the kitchen, where he located a small zinc washtub. After positioning the tub under the hole in the ceiling, he reached up and pulled out the sodden blanket. A torrent of water poured down, splashing Webb and nearly filling the tub. Just in time, he thought; with that amount of water, its weight could have taken down most of the remaining ceiling. He hoisted the tub and carried it to the back door. After dumping its contents in the yard, he put it back under the hole in the ceiling. The water coming through was now only a small stream.

His next step was to begin bailing the kitchen floor. While he was looking for an implement to do that, Miss Hummel came back downstairs. "Something I can get for you, sir?"

"I was looking for something to get up this water."

She quietly went into the closet and came out with a couple of mops and a tin pail with an attached wringer.

The two of them fell to work; every time the pail was full, Webb dumped it outside. His clothes were soon soaked, but it wasn't long before the water level of the floor was down to a few small puddles.

When Rebecca returned, she surveyed the kitchen and said, "I can't believe how much you've done!"

"How are the bedrooms?" Webb asked.

"Only small leaks. We put chamberpots under them, and the girls will watch for any more."

Miss Hummel glanced out the window. "It looks like the rain's slowing down."

"Maybe we'll survive until the next rainstorm," said Rebecca grimly. "This time of year, that should be a few days at the most." She took the mop from the older woman. "I'll finish up here. Thank you, Miss Hummel."

Rebecca mopped the remaining water, and Webb shoveled up the fallen plaster. By the time the floor was clean, there was only a slow drip falling into the tub. "What a homecoming," she said to Webb. "And your clothes are ruined. I'm so sorry."

"It's nothing," he replied. "Just water."

Their work done, the two of them slumped into chairs at the kitchen table.

Rebecca said, "Some trip, and some homecoming."

"I thought the trip was a good one," said Webb.

"It was." She nodded thoughtfully. "It was. But tiring—and discouraging to see those girls out there."

"Isn't there someone we can tell about that place? Some authority?"

"Not that I know of. And what saddens me most is that the girls there aren't treated any worse than thousands of girls right here in the city. If the authorities don't want to do anything about what's happening here, why would they go all the way out to Connecticut to help anyone? Besides, what could they really do? There probably aren't any laws being broken. What's going on in Windsor is standard practice."

Miss Hummel had quietly come to the table and put mugs of hot cider in front of them. Webb hadn't even noticed her heating the drinks. Then, just as silently, she was gone.

"There was a crime committed *here,*" Webb said. "Christina van der Waals was killed." He wrapped his cold, wet fingers around the warm mug. "We know that she'd been at the tobacco farm for most of her time in this country. Now we have to find out what happened to her when she got back to New York."

"Do you have any ideas?"

"We have to start with Joe McQuaid. He's the one who took Christina to Windsor, and he's the one who brought her back."

Rebecca frowned slightly. "We know he brought her back, but nobody said that he's the one who took her to Windsor in the first place."

"Ballard did. Or was it Frist?" Webb couldn't remember. "One of them said McQuaid supplied their workers, so he must have brought them Christina." There was something wrong about that, Webb thought, but he couldn't put his finger on what was bothering him.

"Mr. McQuaid is quite the entrepreneur," said Rebecca. "Supplying girls for both tobacco stripping and prostitution."

"Odd combination."

"The tobacco stripping is probably so that prostitution will look more appealing in comparison. And either way, he gets paid. More from the brothels, I'm sure; that's why he was telling me how much we could make from 'pretty girls.' "

"What I want to know," said Webb, "is whether McQuaid is the one who killed her; it wasn't long after he brought her back to New York that her neck was broken." He paused. "Or did he deliver her to a brothel, and somebody there killed her?"

Rebecca suggested, "Perhaps the next thing to do is to find out what brothels he's been supplying with girls."

Webb nodded. That sounded sensible. But before going on to do anything else, he needed to go home and get some sleep and dry clothes.

Back at his apartment, Webb found that he had to settle for one out of two.

After a long, hot bath, he slipped into a clean muslin nightshirt and then into bed. But he couldn't slip into sleep. Thoughts and images kept flitting through his mind, everything from Christina van der Waals's pale, lifeless face to the nearly dead eyes of the girls working in the tobacco barn.

When he realized that continuing to lie in bed wouldn't accomplish anything, Webb decided to get up and try to put those images on paper.

Still in his nightshirt, he sat down at his desk, pulled out a stack of fresh paper, and began writing. It was a halting effort, and ultimately proved to be no more successful than his attempts to sleep. He simply could not find the right combinations of words to convey the hopelessness in the weary eyes of the girls he'd seen, nor could he adequately describe the way they moved so slowly and painfully during their labors.

Webb got up from the desk and began to pace the parlor floor. This was one of the few times when he wanted to describe harsh reality rather than pen a fanciful rags-to-riches tale, but his writing skills fell short.

He paused to look at one of the framed Civil War woodcuts on his wall: Thomas Nast's *Reveille in Camp,* which showed a group of earnest drummer boys rousing Union troops from their rest. Then he briefly studied the next picture, an 1863 *Harper's* cover illustration of General George Stoneman; the major general was astride a beautiful black steed, brandishing his sword to lead his troops into battle.

When he was a boy, Webb had loved the engravings that appeared in *Harper's* and *Frank Leslie's* illustrated weeklies. They had portrayed the war in which his father died to be a noble, glorious campaign, and that's what Webb had wanted to believe. Mathew Brady's photographs, on the other hand, were stark and harsh, and Webb never liked to look at them. He didn't want to see a picture of those drummer boys lying dead on the field of battle, nor did he want to see that general missing a leg from a Confederate mortar shell.

After he began writing novels, Webb still had a preference for the glorified over the grim, and wrote hopeful stories that ended as he thought they should—with success for the righteous and punishment for the corrupt. But he couldn't script the outcome of the events he was involved with now. He needed something more powerful than pen and paper to aid him. Thinking again of the difference between Brady's photographs and Frank Leslie's woodcuts, Webb suddenly realized exactly the kind of tool he needed.

CHAPTER 28

Edwin Crombie couldn't believe that his otherwise-intelligent partner could be so dense when it came to matters of business. "We need to bring in some money, Gus. And to do that, we have to offer pictures that people will want to see."

"But *baseball?*" Gus Sehlinger shook his head, causing his white beard to sweep back and forth across his knitted vest. "Why would anybody pay to see such nonsense?"

"They do, Gus. Every day during the season, thousands of them shell out fifty cents for a seat in the ballpark."

"Then let them continue to go to the ballpark." He peered over his spectacles. "We have spoken of such big plans. Me, I want to use our moving pictures to educate. And your idea to take pictures of important events, like the Columbian Exposition, is very smart. But we have so little film stock. Why should we waste it on baseball?"

"Because, damn it, I'm running out of money!" Crombie took a moment to compose himself—and to reprimand himself for revealing his financial situation to Sehlinger. He leaned forward and went on with forced calm, "We need some surefire attractions, Gus. Next month is opening day of baseball season, and I want to film a few minutes of the action. My idea is that, even though thousands of people fill the ballparks, there are tens of thousands more who can't get to the games and may pay to see our film." Sehlinger opened his mouth to speak, but Crombie cut him off. "That's not the only attraction I want to capture. When summer comes, I want to take the camera to Coney Island to take some pictures there—Coney Island postcards sell like hotcakes, so moving pictures can't miss." To reassure Sehlinger, he added, "I still want to film the other things we talked about: important events, notable people, and your educational subjects. But to do that we need to remain in business, and that means starting off with material that's proven to attract customers."

Sehlinger was impervious to Crombie's appeal. "I would rather five doctors learn to perform surgery than five thousand people pay us money to see girls in bathing costumes at the beach."

Crombie wasn't going to win this argument today, he could tell, so he decided to change course. "About your educational films, Gus: Let's say somebody does want to teach a medical procedure. They usually teach a whole classroom of students at once, don't they?" He didn't share Sehlinger's desire to educate people—raking in their money was Crombie's only goal—but it was a chance to raise a new idea with his partner.

Sehlinger shifted uneasily; Crombie wasn't sure if it was because of the conversation or because of the hardness of the milk can on which the old man was seated. "I suppose that is true," he finally allowed. "Why?"

"Then we need to *project* these films—like a magic-lantern show." Crombie thought back to his tent show days, when customers flocked to see his programs. "That way a whole roomful of people can see the picture at the same time."

Sehlinger hesitated. Crombie knew that, as usual, his irascible partner was seeking a reason to reject his suggestion. "I do not know if that is such a good idea," Sehlinger finally said. "Edison considered using a projection system, but decided instead to make a device that allows only one person at a time to view his picture strips. He intends to charge a penny per viewing. You cannot make as much money if you show the picture to a lot of people at once."

Crombie promptly argued back, "Sure we can. Charge them a *nickel* apiece to see *several* films. Of course, it would only work if you can figure out a way to project this film large enough for them to see it. Maybe that's not even possible."

Sehlinger began tapping the stem of his pipe on his lower teeth. "I will give it some thought."

His partner could never pass up a challenge, Crombie knew. If only to prove that it could be done, Sehlinger would soon come up with a projection device. Feeling successful on that score, Crombie opened his mouth to suggest again that Sehlinger "borrow" some film from the Edison laboratory. He cut himself off when Emily poked her head into the carriage house.

"Mama says there's a man for you at the front door," his daughter said.

"Did he give his name?"

Distracted by the mewing kitten in her arms, Emily absently answered, "Yes."

Crombie couldn't help but smile. "What is it?"

"I forget. I think he's a sheriff."

What would a sheriff want, Crombie wondered. And what was a *sheriff* doing in Brooklyn anyway? They had a police force here.

Emily called into the house, "Mama! What's the man's name?" A moment later, she turned back to address her father. "Mamma says his name is Marshall Webb."

"Who?" *Oh, yes,* he remembered. *That writer.* What could he want? "I'll be right there." When Emily went back in the house, Crombie said to his partner, "He's the fellow you made those prints for. The one who was looking for that Dutch girl from Ellis Island."

Sehlinger sputtered nervously. "He was at the laboratory, too. He knows I work for Edison. You can't let him see me here."

"Don't worry. I'll get rid of him." As he said the words, Crombie remembered that Webb was a persistent kind of fellow and might not be dismissed easily. Before he reached the door, he also remembered that Webb suggested he might be willing to help publicize their American Kinemascope Company in *Harper's.* For that reason alone, he merited some courtesy.

Crombie put on a friendly manner when he greeted Webb. "I'm sorry to keep you waiting."

"Quite all right. I'm sorry to disturb your Sunday."

Crombie saw that even for a Sunday Webb was dressed too formally. His pearl gray suit was something that might be worn to a society ball, and his hair and whiskers were as carefully groomed as if he'd come directly from a barber shop. There was a haggard look to the man's eyes, though. "Please come in." He would only allow him into the parlor, so that Sehlinger would remain safely out of view.

Webb removed his high-crowned derby and stepped inside.

Crombie offered a seat, which was declined, and something to drink, which was also politely turned down. *Good,* Crombie thought; *he doesn't intend to stay long.*

After again apologizing for the intrusion, Webb said, "I've come about your moving-picture camera."

"We're still not ready for the public to know about it," Crombie said. "Perhaps by fall."

Webb shook his head. "I don't intend to write about the machine, at least not until you give me the go-ahead. I came here in the hope that you might be agreeable to using it. I think there's a way you can do a lot of good with the camera and do well for yourself in the process."

Crombie's interest was piqued—especially by the part about doing well for himself. "What do you have in mind?" He again gestured to a chair, and this time Webb sat down. Crombie settled onto the sofa.

Webb asked, "You're familiar with the Jacob Riis book, *How The Other Half Lives*?"

"I've heard of it."

"I believe you could accomplish what Riis tried to, and that your *moving* pictures would do it far more powerfully."

"You want me to film *poor people?"* Crombie failed to see how there could be any profit in that.

"I want you to show what really happens to the girls who come to this country trying to make a decent life for themselves." Webb then went on to relate horrific accounts of a Polish family who'd been taken to a tenement sweatshop, and a slave-labor camp in Connecticut where girls stripped tobacco.

Crombie tried to listen politely, but when Webb began to tell him of girls being forced into prostitution, he snapped, "I don't even want to *hear* about such things. What makes you think people will want to *see* them?"

"They may not want to," Webb answered thoughtfully. "But I believe they will, the same way they bought Riis's book. And when they see what I've seen, they will be outraged. Outraged enough, I hope, to insist that things change."

Crombie saw no commercial appeal in such pictures, and had no desire to be involved in a public crusade. He didn't want to come right out and admit that to Webb, however. "Even if I wanted to," he said, "it isn't possible. We have almost no film stock left, and it's extremely difficult to obtain."

"Why?"

"Flexible film was only invented a few years ago. Eastman is the sole manufacturer, and he supplies Edison. If we tried to order some, Edison would know that he had competition."

"What if I could get you some film? Would you do it then?"

"Where would you—" Never mind, thought Crombie. He wasn't going to get involved in something like this. "We can't," he said, holding up his hands. "We have too many other commitments."

From the hallway came Gus Sehlinger's voice. "We will do this."

Crombie was as astonished by his partner's words as he was by his unexpected appearance. "Gus, what the hell—"

The older man walked over to Webb and held out his hand. "Mr. Webb, we have met before, in the laboratory of Thomas Edison, but we were never introduced. My name is August Sehlinger." After the two men shook hands, Sehlinger sat down and said to Crombie, "I told you, Edwin, I want to use our machine to educate. And Mr. Webb is talking about things that people need to learn." He pushed up his spectacles. "I learned them myself when I came to this country, and I know that many of my friends have had to endure the sweatshops and the tenements." His voice dropped. "I also know what befalls far too many girls in this city. There is not an immigrant in New York who does not know some family who has lost a daughter."

Sehlinger must have lost his mind, Crombie thought. "Isn't there something you've forgotten?" he asked. "Now Mr. Webb knows that you're working for both me and Edison."

"I work *with* you, not *for* you," the older man corrected. He looked to Webb. "I ask that you keep my secret. And I offer you my assistance."

After assuring Sehlinger that his secret was safe, Webb told them that he wanted to begin by investigating a man named Josiah McQuaid, who picked up immigrant girls at the Barge Office.

"You want us to be detectives, too?" Crombie asked derisively.

The writer answered calmly, "McQuaid supplies girls for the tobacco-stripping operation as well as putting them in brothels. That much I'm sure of. He might have also been involved in a murder. You remember that photograph you made for me?"

Crombie and Sehlinger both said that they did.

"The girl in that picture, Christina van der Waals, is dead. Her neck was broken a few days after McQuaid brought her to New York. I'd like to find out what he's involved with, and exactly who's getting girls from him. He's seen me, though, so I can't talk to him myself."

Crombie couldn't contain himself. "This is madness! All I want to do is put on a show. I have no intention of investigating murder or white slavery!"

Sehlinger gave him a long look of disappointment, but said nothing in reply. He turned to Webb. "I will see what I can learn about Mr. McQuaid for you."

Crombie then stalked out of the room, leaving the other men to talk about dead girls and tobacco farmers. He had a business to run, and it appeared that he would have to run it alone.

CHAPTER 29

Webb didn't want to risk taking out his watch to check the time—not with a dozen men in The Hole who'd be happy to relieve him of the possession—but he was certain that Lawrence Pritchard was at least ten minutes late.

The bartender again asked, "What'll it be?" and for the second time Webb answered that he'd wait for his friend before ordering. The reply earned him a stern look and a warning that "We don't allow no squatters here. If you don't buy a drink soon, you're out on your ass."

At that moment, the dime-novel publisher walked into the seedy saloon. He was flaunting an elegant silver-headed walking stick that Webb didn't remember seeing before.

Pritchard joined Webb at his table. "So sorry for the delay." He surveyed the barroom with obvious distaste. "Knowing what kind of a place this is, I decided to come prepared." He held up the cane.

"Is that real silver?" asked Webb.

"Of course. And the stick is ebony."

"If you wanted protection, a blackjack would have been a better option."

Pritchard frowned, causing his pince-nez to slip. "Why?"

"Because the men in here already have blackjacks, so they won't want to steal yours. A fine cane with a chunk of silver, on the other hand . . ."

Webb didn't think it was possible, but his editor's pale skin blanched a shade whiter. He hissed at Webb, "There are hundreds of places we could meet and not be seen together. I swear you insist on coming to dives like this because you *like* them."

Webb thought about that. He honestly didn't know *why* he wanted to come to hellholes like this one, but it was strangely true that he sometimes felt more alive in such places, among people who were teetering on the line between life and death. Perhaps it had something to do with the fact that it was in a place such as this that he had been nearly killed years before. Ever since then, he'd kept himself too sheltered, too reserved. His meetings with Pritchard provided him a chance to step out of his protected lifestyle for a while, and into the city's underworld. Whatever the reason, after all he'd experienced the past couple of months, Webb no longer felt a need for any additional thrills. And he didn't care anymore if he was spotted with the dime-novel editor. "You're right," he said to Pritchard. "I apologize."

The bartender bellowed again, "Now, what's it gonna be?"

"A change of venue," answered Webb. To the surprised editor he said, "Shall we?"

Pritchard nodded and the two of them left the saloon.

Outside on Broome Street, with the curses of the bartender still audible, Pritchard said, "You know, we really didn't have to leave on my account." He began swinging his walking stick. "I can take care of myself."

"I know," said Webb. "I was in the mood for some fresh air." Not that there was such a thing in the Bowery, where the streets were thick with horse excrement, decomposing garbage littered the curbs, and clouds of stove ash blew from overflowing trash barrels.

Pritchard inhaled noisily. "Ah, yes. Like a day in the country," he said facetiously.

Webb chuckled. "I'll walk with you back to your office."

As they headed to Park Row, Pritchard said, "I brought you a copy of your new book."

"Keep it," said Webb. "I already know what happens."

"Yes, I know, you wrote it." Pritchard then added rather sharply, "In fact, you wrote it twice. *Shady Sam, the Scourge of Snake Canyon* is almost the same story as one you did for me a year ago—the one about the bandit of the Black Hills. I was very disappointed."

Webb had always liked his editor, and he felt bad about letting him down. "I'm sorry. I know it was one of my lesser efforts. I've been rather preoccupied lately."

"It's not the story itself that was so disappointing," Pritchard said. "For a Western, it's adequate, and will probably sell well enough. But you had my hopes up about your story of the Dutch girl. I was really hoping we could get that one into publication soon."

"I had trouble finding her," Webb said quietly.

Pritchard pulled up short outside the entrance to Ferrell's Dime Museum, a shabby brick structure that had once housed a pawnshop. He swung up the tip of his walking stick and pointed it at a bright-yellow handbill. The sign advertised that the museum was currently displaying the bullet that had killed President Garfield. "Do you think it could be genuine?"

Webb answered, "I'm sure it's every bit as authentic as the one that killed Lincoln. That bullet's on display over on Grand Street." Dime museums were almost as numerous as burlesque houses in the Bowery. Many specialized in exhibiting the jarred remains of malformed embryos, two-headed calves, four-legged chickens, and other accidents of nature. Some museums, like Ferrell's, offered "artifacts," which were much easier to obtain and equally successful in attracting the gullible. Three different dime museums had the club that killed Captain Cook, many displayed locks of Marie Antoinette's hair—of every shade from blond to brunette—and there were enough pieces of the True Cross in the Bowery to build a "True Ark."

Clearly disappointed, the editor resisted the temptation to go inside, and they resumed their walk. "I had an idea about the Katie book," he said. "Why don't we issue it in monthly parts, the way Dickens did? That makes it cheaper to publish, and we can drag out the story if it sells. Also, you don't need to have a finished manuscript for us to start publishing. You don't even have to know how it ends yet."

"I do know how it ends," Webb said sadly. "The girl is dead." He went on to tell Pritchard about finding Christina's body, and related what he and Rebecca had learned in Connecticut.

"You think she was brought back to the city for prostitution?" Pritchard asked.

"That's probably what McQuaid had in mind for her. He supplies girls to the brothels. I can't believe she went with him willingly, though."

Pritchard was silent for half a block. After clearing his throat he said, "I am about to break a confidence, which I don't like to do. But it may explain why McQuaid took the girl."

"Tell me."

"I had a visit from a private detective, a rather obnoxious fellow named Charles Gardner. He's been hired by Reverend Parkhurst. You know how the good Reverend has been pilloried in the newspapers for attacking the police department?"

"Yes. And it appears to have silenced him."

"Only for the time being. Parkhurst felt humiliated at being dragged before the grand jury and threatened with a slander suit. So now he's intent on getting evidence to prove his claims. Gardner is acting as his guide, taking him to the worst brothels and gambling dens in the city."

"So why did he visit you?"

"Gardner wants to write a little book about his involvement with the minister. He says they've seen some incredible—and appalling—activities, and thinks the public might want to read about them."

"Are you going to publish it?"

"No. The fellow didn't impress me. But he did tell me something interesting: After the minister's sermon, business at the brothels picked up tremendously. He said he'd been told by several of the madams that the sermon was the best advertising they could have had—every politician and businessman in New York wants to 'investigate' the vice trade personally. They also told him that because of the increased business, their houses have been desperately short of girls to accommodate all the additional customers." Pritchard coughed again. "As I said, I don't like breaking Gardner's confidence—he made me promise to tell no one what he and Parkhurst are doing—but I hope this might help."

"Thanks, Lawrence. I appreciate it." Pritchard's revelation could certainly explain why Joe McQuaid brought all the "pretty girls" back from the tobacco farm.

The question that had been bothering Webb lately, however, wasn't why Christina van der Waals had been brought back. It was why she had gone to the tobacco farm in the first place. Had McQuaid met her when she arrived at the Barge Office? And if he had, why had she gone with him when she was expecting to meet her cousin? Pritchard wasn't the one to discuss those questions with, though. Webb wanted to talk with Rebecca.

* * *

Rebecca left the eggbeater in the bowl, wiped her hands on her apron, and hurried out to the hallway for the telephone. She picked up on the sixth ring, silently warning whoever was calling that they had better still be on the line.

Her attitude brightened considerably when she heard Marshall Webb's voice. Even with a poor connection, it sounded warm and strong.

She answered his question: "No, it's no interruption. I was in the kitchen."

"Any more floods?"

She laughed. "No. But then, it hasn't rained. The good news is that we should have the roof patched within a few days." Rebecca didn't add that she'd only gotten the money for repairs after enduring a lecture on prudent fiscal management from her father.

"I have some news," Webb said. He then told her about a couple of men with a moving-picture machine, who would try to get some information about Josiah McQuaid. "I gave them your name, too. Hope you don't mind."

"Not at all." She hesitated. "I also have some news: Mr. McQuaid was here."

"At Colden House?"

"Yes, he showed up last night. I was *not* happy about that, and I told him so in no uncertain terms."

"How did he know where to find you?"

"I'd given him my real name at the Barge Office. I thought I had to, in case he wanted to check to see if I was legitimate." She still wasn't sure if she'd done the smart thing or not, but she certainly regretted that he now knew where her girls lived. "Mr. McQuaid said he heard that it went well in Connecticut, and wanted to know when I could provide him with some 'farm hands.' I put him off, and I think I convinced him that he should never come to the house again. I told him it was a business precaution: if anyone learned that he and I were working together, girls wouldn't come to the house and then I wouldn't be able to supply him with any."

"I hope he bought it."

"Me too," she sighed.

Webb next told her that he'd learned from his publisher about a recent boom in the vice business, which explained why Mc-

Quaid had been so eager for a supply of fresh girls. She and Webb then both puzzled over the question of why Christina had been in McQuaid's company in the first place.

"Maybe I'll ask Liz Luck," Rebecca said. "I've been meaning to visit her and see how she's faring. I think I might also tell her that her cousin was out of state, so it wasn't her fault that she couldn't find her." Rebecca hoped Webb would realize that he wasn't at fault for failing to locate the girl, either. "I can't see Miss Luck for a couple of days, though. Miss Hummel is visiting her sister. She's been holding down the fort here for me lately, so I'm taking on her chores while she's gone."

When Webb told her that he'd be busy for a couple of days, too, Rebecca didn't think to ask what he'd be doing. What she thought at the moment was that it appeared the two of them wouldn't see each other again until the weekend, and that would make it a full week apart. Too long, in Rebecca's view.

CHAPTER 30

Webb walked into Tyner's Dry Goods Emporium with even greater reluctance than usual. He already owed Paul for his last favor, and now he was here to ask another.

He found his brother in the store's lace department, supervising two male assistants who were taking inventory. While the blue-clad clerks busily measured lengths of various rolls and ribbons, a haggard Paul Tyner recorded the information in a duck-bound ledger. The bags under his eyes, Webb noticed, sagged more than he remembered, and the strands of brown hair that Paul usually combed over his balding head hung limply down to his high collar.

When he spotted Webb, Paul tightened his lips, causing his stiff beard to tilt up slightly.

"Hello, Paul," Webb said. "You're looking well."

His brother ignored the greeting and the lie. "I don't want to see you here," he said. Before Webb could respond, Paul continued, "I don't want to see you anywhere except in mother's dining room. You promised to come for dinner, yet week after week you disappoint us."

"You're right. I'm very sorry. I'll—"

"You don't have any *sorrys* left to use," Paul snapped.

Webb knew that Paul was never going to let him forget his mistakes of the past; it seemed that Paul kept a ledger of personal grievances, and Webb would never be able to clear his account. Webb's initial impulse was to walk out of the store, but he found himself feeling more sad than angry about his brother's attitude. In a measured voice, he replied, "I should have given you an explanation before now, but the fact is, I've been spending quite a bit of time with a young woman. In fact, I've gone to Sunday dinner with her family."

Paul struggled to decide on a response. "A nice girl?"

Webb disregarded the allusion to his earlier preferences in female companionship. "Very," he answered calmly. "You've spoken with her: Miss Rebecca Davies."

"At . . . that house."

"Colden House. By the way, she's most grateful for the blankets and towels you—"

"Shh." Paul jerked his head toward the clerks. "No one needs to hear about that." He then told his assistants, "Check the storeroom and see if there's any stock we've missed. Be back here in ten minutes." After they left, he sighed heavily and leaned back to counterbalance his huge belly. "Last week we sold a lady some Spanish lace that was labeled Chantilly—charged her double what it was really worth. She came back the next day and made quite a row over it with Father. He passed the complaint on to me, adding some choice words of his own. Now I have to do a complete inventory and make sure every last ribbon and thread in the shop is labeled correctly."

For the first time, Webb wondered if his brother actually enjoyed his position at the store. "I see I've come at a bad time for you, but I was hoping I could impose for a favor."

"Favor?"

"Not a donation this time," Webb quickly assured him. "I'd like you to order some material for me."

Paul brightened a bit. "That's no problem at all. What kind of material do you need? There isn't a fabric made that we can't get."

"It's not fabric. It's photographic film—for moving pictures."

"*Moving* pictures?" Paul gave him a quizzical look, as if waiting for the punch line.

"Yes. Some inventors, including Thomas Edison, are developing cameras to take photographs that reproduce movement. I know a man who has such a camera, but he can't order the film stock himself. It's only manufactured by George Eastman, and this fellow worries that Edison will learn of his invention from Eastman if he orders it directly. But if *you* order the film for the store, you can simply say that some local photographers have asked about it."

Paul appeared reluctant. "Are you certain that your friend will purchase this material? I don't want to be stuck with it. We're already carrying too much inventory."

"I'll be paying the bill," Webb said. "And I don't expect a discount—add your usual markup."

The last sentence clinched the deal. "Just let me know the particulars," Paul said, "and I'll place the order."

"Thank you."

The clerks returned, and one of them asked Paul what they should do next. Before answering them, he said to Webb, "Mother will be very pleased to hear that you have a lady friend. And she'll be even more pleased when you bring Miss Davies to dinner with you."

It was clearly a surcharge for the film order. "I'll do that," Webb said. He thought to himself that he might even enjoy showing up for dinner with Rebecca on his arm.

The last time Webb had walked into the Mercer Street station house, his hands had been manacled and he'd been prodded along by a patrolman's nightstick. Wednesday afternoon he went in alone, voluntarily, and with his head held high.

Upon telling the desk sergeant the reason for his visit, Webb was pointed to the waiting area and told to have a seat. He didn't have to wait long before Detective Tom O'Connor came out to see him. The detective's shapeless brown suit was so old and rumpled that it could have been discarded by one of the basement lodgers, and the mangled cigar stub clamped between his teeth had been reduced to little more than a plug of chewing tobacco.

O'Connor's expression was as hard as granite; in fact, his face and short-cropped hair might have all been hewn from the same coarse, gray rock. "I'll be damned," he said when he spotted Webb. "Usually when we release a prisoner, they try to stay released. Not many of 'em come back willingly. What the hell do you want?"

"To speak with you," Webb answered. "About Christina van der Waals."

The detective gnawed at the cigar stub for a few seconds. "Come back to my office."

Webb followed him to a drearily appointed room that had DETECTIVES painted on the door. Although the office was spacious enough, there was little in the way of furnishings. Four plain pine desks, a few filing cabinets, and a small conference table were the only furniture. The walls, which had been painted a bland shade of green many years before, were decorated with a street map of the city, some photographs from the rogues' gallery, a couple of "wanted" notices, and a large color print of boxer John L. Sullivan.

O'Connor shared the office with three other detectives, but they were occupied in a card game and barely gave them a glance when they entered. Webb and O'Connor had relative privacy when they sat down at his desk.

The detective spoke first. "You decide to confess?"

Webb couldn't tell if he was kidding or serious, but he gave him a look that, either way, should have been a sufficiently negative answer. "I'm here to find out if you've learned anything," he said.

O'Connor worked his jaw, shifting his cigar stub to the other corner of his mouth. "You got things a little backwards, Mr. Webb. We don't answer to you. You answer to us."

"I gave you answers the last time I was here. This time I have questions."

The detective's face remained rigid, but there was a hint of amusement in his deep-set eyes. "Such as?"

"What did you mean about loot and a gang? You and the patrolmen both said something about money."

"Did we? I don't remember."

One of the detectives at the table called, "We're startin' a new hand. You in, Tom?"

O'Connor briefly chewed his cigar while he made up his mind. "Not this one," he answered.

Webb tried again. "Would you tell me this: Why did the police happen to come to the apartment when they did?" That was one question that had been bothering him ever since his arrest.

The detective leaned back in his chair, all trace of amusement vanishing from his eyes. He'd apparently decided that he didn't like being on the other end of an interrogation. "Like I said, we don't answer to you. And if you insist on poking your nose in police business, there's a good chance you'll get it cut off. You really want to continue?"

"Do you really want me to stop?" asked Webb. "All I'm doing is asking a couple of simple questions. If you answer them, I won't have to go to the newspapers with other questions—such as, why are there *three* coroner's reports?" He was glad that Rebecca had told him that bit of information.

A slight fissure cracked O'Connor's stony expression. "We don't have nothin' to do with the coroner's office."

"Of course you do. You notify the coroners whenever you have a body. And maybe you get a little percentage of their fees when you 'relocate' one for them." Webb was guessing about the payoffs, but he doubted that the police performed that service for free. "Look, I don't care about how much you or the coroners skim from the public trough. Just tell me why the cops came to the apartment that day."

"Aw, what the hell," grumbled O'Connor. "I didn't come into it until they found there was a dead girl, anyway." He tossed his cigar into a cuspidor, causing tobacco juice to splash onto the bare wood floor. "The station got a report that a team of bunko artists were in the apartment splittin' up loot from a big score."

"Who made the report?"

"Dunno. I didn't take the call. We just tried to get some patrolmen there fast."

Probably to make sure they got some of the cash for themselves, Webb figured. "And you never found any money, or the con men, I take it?"

"Not that I know of."

Okay, back to the murder. "Do you have *any* leads to Christina van der Waals's killer?"

"Besides yourself?" O'Connor's flat voice again concealed whether he was joking or serious.

Webb again ignored the detective's question. He thought it must be obvious to anyone that he'd been set up: first a phone call to Webb to tell him where Christina was; then a call to the police to make sure he was discovered with her body. He demanded, "Haven't you been investigating? Haven't you found anything?"

O'Connor shifted uncomfortably. "The case is open."

"A girl has been murdered and you're doing nothing about it?" Webb couldn't veil his anger or his contempt.

"There hasn't been a real push to get it solved. Besides, we got limited manpower, and new cases every day."

No "real push" probably meant that no big reward had been

offered for solving the crime. Webb muttered, more to himself than to O'Connor, "What about justice?"

The same detective who'd interrupted before yelled again, "Tom! You gonna play or what?"

O'Connor gave Webb a cold, hard look. "If you really insist that we pin the girl's murder on somebody, we will. But be careful what you wish for."

"I want you to find who *really* killed her."

The detective continued to give Webb an icy stare. Then he ended the discussion by calling to the others, "Deal me in."

Webb left the station house knowing for certain that if Christina's killer was to be found, it wasn't going to be by the New York City Police Department.

As Rebecca Davies laced her long kid gloves, she wondered how much she should reveal to Liz Luck about her cousin's brief life in America. She wanted to comfort the woman by providing some knowledge of where Christina had been, but she didn't want to disturb her with the awful details. Perhaps she should say that Christina had been working on a tobacco farm in Connecticut, and leave it at that. There was no need to tell her about the stripping barn, or about Joe McQuaid's plans for Christina back in the city.

She was almost ready to leave Colden House when Miss Hummel came to her room. "Excuse me, Miss Davies."

Rebecca smiled at the sight of her. It was good to have Miss Hummel back at the house; running the place without her for the past two days had given Rebecca a much greater appreciation for just how much work the quiet woman did. "Yes, Miss Hummel?"

"Santa Claus is here."

"Pardon me?"

There was a rare look of humor in Miss Hummel's eyes, and the creases around them were lifted in a smile. "There's an old gentleman asking for you at the door. He's the spitting image of St. Nick."

"Let's hope he's brought us a bag of presents, then." Rebecca took the pins out of her hat and placed it back on the dresser. "I'll be right down."

When Rebecca saw the man in the foyer, she had to struggle to keep from laughing. Miss Hummel's description had been perfectly accurate: the elderly gentleman had a long, white beard and a round, red nose on which were perched tiny gold spectacles. He must have left his red suit at the North Pole, however, for he was dressed in heavy tweed.

"Is there something I can do for you?" she asked.

"Miss Rebecca Davies?" His accent was German.

"Yes."

He made a stiff bow. "My name is August Sehlinger. I hope I am not intruding."

Rebecca couldn't make that determination until she knew why he was here, but she answered politely, "Not at all."

"I was given your name and address by Mr. Marshall Webb. I went to see Mr. Webb first, but he is not at home and I must be getting back to New Jersey. He told me that I could speak as freely to you as I could to him, so I came here. I have some information about a Josiah McQuaid."

"Oh, yes, come in." Rebecca was pleased that Webb had spoken of her that way, and curious to find out what the information was.

She led Sehlinger into the sitting room. Within moments of his taking a chair, Miss Hummel came in with a tea tray and held it before their guest.

"You are very kind," he said as he took a cup from her. "Thank you so much."

Rebecca thought she detected a blush in Miss Hummel's cheeks, and she mentally filed it away as something she could tease her about later.

The older woman silently whisked out of the room, and Sehlinger tasted the tea. With a contented sigh, he said, "Just what I needed." Settling more comfortably onto the seat cushion, he withdrew a briar pipe from his breast pocket. He didn't light up, but caressed the bowl with his thumb as he said, "Mr. Webb has told me that this fellow McQuaid is preying on young immigrant girls. As you can probably tell from my accent, I am an immigrant myself." He paused and looked at Rebecca expectantly.

She took the cue. "I didn't notice an accent. You must have been here for some time."

He smiled, obviously pleased. "Almost fifteen years." Then his expression darkened. "I have many friends who also came here from the old country, and I know very well the abuses they have experienced. The worst ones have been to their wives and daughters. So when Mr. Webb told me about McQuaid, I was happy to offer my assistance." He paused again.

"That was very good of you." Rebecca wondered if he was going to tell her the information or continue to seek pats on the back.

"I have learned that McQuaid supplies many of the girls to a"—his voice dropped to a whisper—"house of ill repute."

Did this man think she'd never heard of a whorehouse? Rebecca wondered. "Do you know which one?" she asked.

He nodded, causing ripples in his fluffy beard. Still speaking low, he said, "The house is on Water Street. It is called the Roost."

Rebecca hadn't heard of that particular establishment, but then there were more brothels in New York than there were streets. "Do you know anything about the place?"

"Such places are largely the same, aren't they?"

No, many of them catered to particular tastes, Rebecca knew. "Do you know how he gets the girls? Does he pay them? Kidnap them?"

"All I know is that many girls are taken there directly. Others go to a tobacco farm first and are later brought back to the Roost. McQuaid makes money from them no matter where they go." He paused to sip his tea.

"Is there anything else you can tell me?"

"Not yet."

"Thank you for the information, Mr. Sehlinger."

"Ach, it is nothing. I will learn some more, and I have a partner who will help." He frowned slightly. "I simply have to convince him. He is a young man, and his head is busy with ideas for getting rich. I believe I can convince him that some things are more important, however." He looked at Rebecca earnestly. "Please believe me, I want to stop this man McQuaid."

She did believe him, and thanked him again for his efforts.

CHAPTER 31

Gus Sehlinger had a great knack for making no sense. Exasperated by his partner's badgering, Crombie finally said, "What are you doing here, anyway? Isn't Edison going to miss you?" Sehlinger should have been toiling away in room five of the Thomas Edison laboratories, not sitting comfortably on a sofa in Edwin Crombie's parlor.

The old man took the pipe from his mouth. "So he will dock me a day's pay—so what? You have not heard a word I said, Edwin. I keep telling you that some things are more important than money or a job."

"Yeah, as long as you *have* money."

"You will, Edwin, you will." Sehlinger nodded confidently. "You are smart and you work hard. But it isn't everything. And I believe you know that. I have seen you with your wife and daughter. *Family.* There is nothing more important than the people you love."

Through the hallway, Crombie could hear Helen and Emily laughing in the kitchen, where they were baking cookies. He loved the sound, and he hated to admit that once again, Sehlinger was right. "Yeah, I know," he grumbled.

Sehlinger went on. "The people who come to America, they come to make life better for *their* families. And people like Josiah McQuaid and the sweatshop owners and the slumlords, they destroy those families." He punctuated his argument by wagging his pipe like a forefinger. "So please, let us do something to stop this McQuaid, and see if we can help find out what happened to the Dutch girl."

Crombie sighed, not for the first time. "Gus, there are two reasons why I'm not going to do what Webb wants. One is that I have *my* family to take care of, and the way for me to do that is to make American Kinemascope a success. That's what I have to concentrate on. I can't afford to waste the time or the film doing favors for Marshall Webb."

Sehlinger persisted. "Didn't Mr. Webb say that he might be able to supply us with some film stock?"

Crombie shifted in his easy chair and briefly debated whether he should try to sneak a beer past Helen. Sehlinger's company had him craving one badly. After deciding to wait until lunchtime, he answered, "Webb telephoned yesterday. He told me the film's been ordered, but I'm not confident that Eastman will fill the order—he might be shipping all of his material to Edison. Even if he does send some to Webb, it won't arrive for some time. I want to get pictures of the St. Patrick's Day parade next week, and then there's opening day at the Polo Grounds coming up." Before Sehlinger could argue about the baseball game again, Crombie continued, "The other reason I'm not interested in doing what Webb wants is because it won't do any good. Nobody wants to see a moving picture of girls stripping tobacco or sewing kneepants. I've been a showman for years. I know what the public wants, and it's not the kind of subjects that Webb was talking about. Webb himself said that he wants people to become outraged by what they see, and demand changes. But if they don't go to see the pictures, then there's no outrage, no change." He shrugged. "Nothing will be achieved."

"You make some sense," Sehlinger conceded.

At last, the old man was catching on. "It would be a lot of effort," said Crombie, "and accomplish nothing."

Sehlinger tapped the stem of his pipe against his teeth. "Tell me, Edwin. Since you know what attracts an audience, what *would* make a picture appealing to them?"

"Exactly what I told you about the Ellis Island pictures and the Columbian Exposition: they need to portray events or scenes that the audience might never otherwise see. People are curious about things that are outside of their everyday experience."

Still tapping, Sehlinger asked, "How else could you draw a crowd?"

Crombie thought back to his tent-show experience. Besides his magic-lantern presentations, the attractions usually included a variety of dwarves, strong men, and bearded or tattooed ladies, all wearing little clothing. "Give them something lurid or titillating," he answered.

"Well, then, I should think that film of a brothel would fit the bill on both counts." Sehlinger idly fingered his beard. "Why not forget about sweatshops, and start with the Roost, the place McQuaid is supplying with girls?"

Crombie wasn't sure, but he felt like Sehlinger had steered the course to that conclusion. There was a very good reason why filming at the Roost—or any other brothel—was out of the question. Sehlinger should have realized it himself, since he'd built the camera, but Crombie was more than happy to point it out to him. "The camera is difficult enough to move around outside; how do you propose that we smuggle it into a whorehouse without anyone noticing?"

The old man coughed and answered quietly, "I do not know."

"And if we did get the camera inside, how could we film? There wouldn't be enough light to film indoors."

Sehlinger muttered a few words of German. Then he said, "It would not do to show up at such a place with a camera anyway. You would have to make them *want* you to take pictures." He thought a bit more. "We do not need the pictures themselves so much at this point. The important thing is to find out about McQuaid and the people who run the brothel."

"You already did, didn't you?"

"I only learned that he is the one who brings them the girls. I never went inside; I do not know how the business operates. That is what we must learn if they are to be stopped."

"Why not simply go in as a customer? Wouldn't that be easier?"

"Easier, perhaps, but not effective. They would not confide in a customer. It must be somebody they could view as a business partner." He rattled his teeth with the pipe again. "There must be some way."

Crombie didn't have to think very long to realize that there *was* a way. The question was whether he would give in to Webb and Sehlinger, and assist in a hopeless cause.

CHAPTER 32

Webb didn't appreciate how long a week it had been until he saw Rebecca Davies again. He was well aware that he enjoyed her company, but he had never before realized just how much he missed her when they were apart. The feeling that he had when he saw Rebecca's smile again, though, reminded him that he wanted to see her more often.

Fortunately, they had agreed to spend this Saturday evening with each other, and their plans did not include touring East Side tenements or sneaking into sweatshops. First they would have a quiet dinner, and then it would be off to the Grand Theatre, which proudly billed itself as "the only fireproof theatre in New York," to see Lillian Russell in *La Cigale.*

At Enzio's restaurant, they were attended by the same courteous waiter who had served them during their previous visit. When the waiter asked if he wanted "the usual," Webb quickly opted for the shrimp scampi instead, which proved to be an excellent choice.

For a while, Rebecca and Webb talked easily about the same topics that any other couple in the restaurant might have been discussing. They commented favorably on the food and on the music provided by a strolling violinist, and exchanged reviews that they had heard about Miss Russell's performance in the comic opera that they would be seeing later.

Then, working on a plate of linguini and clams, Rebecca said seriously, "I finally had a chance to speak with Liz Luck."

"How is she?"

"Not well, I'm afraid. Not only is she devastated by her

cousin's death, but I think she's had a terrible time with her husband."

"Merely living with him must be terrible," said Webb.

Rebecca pursed her lips and nodded. "No doubt. But lately it's been even worse. I'm worried about her."

"What happened?"

"He didn't want to pay for Christina's funeral, so she scraped together enough of her own money to bury her cousin. According to Gleason, though, she didn't have any money of her own—every cent she earned was rightfully his. So he gave her a beating for 'stealing' from him."

Webb felt his color rise and his muscles tense. He wished he could give Officer Warren Gleason a bit of his own—with interest. Forcing himself to remain calm, he said, "Gleason seems to have an overpowering hunger for money. He already gets a policeman's salary, plus a share of the graft that goes with being a cop. But he's not satisfied." Webb shook his head. "He wants more, so he forces his wife to sell herself, and extorts money from a local saloon. I'd like to know what he does with all the money. What does he spend it on?"

"Certainly not on housing," Rebecca answered. "They're going to be moving again because they haven't paid the rent." She paused for a sip of water before continuing. "I told Miss Luck about Christina working at the tobacco fields. I tried to make it sound like she was farming, and didn't mention what the conditions were really like. She said she wished Christina had stayed there, far away from this city, and asked me why her cousin had come back. I didn't want to tell her it was probably to work in a brothel, so I said I didn't know. Then I asked her why Christina would have gone there in the first place."

"And?"

"She said she had no idea. The question certainly bothered her, though. I think Miss Luck might have been blaming herself again, believing that her cousin had first gone to the Baylor Opera House and then left when she saw what kind of place it was."

After Rebecca finished telling him about Liz Luck, Webb proceeded to report on his meeting with Detective O'Connor. "The police are doing nothing," he concluded. "Even if there was a reward offered for solving Christina's murder, I don't believe the detectives would conduct an honest investigation. At most, they might pin the crime on some convenient 'suspect' in order to collect the reward money."

"I agree," Rebecca said. "I wouldn't trust the police to begin a legitimate investigation at this point."

Webb said thoughtfully, "If Christina's killer is going to be found, it's going to be up to us to find him." He hesitated, not wanting to say anything to put a damper on the evening. Then he admitted, "I actually feel a bit guilty that I'm not working toward that end at this moment. To be honest, though, I'm not even sure *what* to do next."

"Right now," Rebecca said, "I think all we can do is wait. Joe McQuaid has seen us, so we can't go following him ourselves. I'm convinced Mr. Sehlinger will do all he can to help, so let's see what he comes up with." She raised her wineglass. "I propose that we not discuss it for the rest of the evening."

Webb promptly agreed and they clinked their glasses to seal the deal.

As they resumed eating, Webb moved to a new topic. "I saw my brother this week. We've been invited to Sunday dinner." As he spoke the words, Webb realized that it sounded as if the invitation had come solely from his brother. "I mean, I would be very happy if you could accompany me. Of course, if you have to be with your own family . . ."

Rebecca smiled. "I believe they would be most understanding—and probably relieved. I would be happy to join you. Tomorrow?"

"Tomorrow . . ." Webb repeated. No, he decided; the prospect of facing his family tomorrow would cast a shadow on this evening for him. "It's an open invitation," he said. "I thought perhaps next week." For tonight, he wanted to do as Rebecca suggested and have a good time.

Edwin Crombie figured that a busy night would be the best time to try the sales pitch he had in mind. So, shortly after dark on Saturday, he took a cable car from Brooklyn to lower Manhattan and made his way to Water Street, a short block away from the piers of the East River. Crombie could hear the clanging bell of the Hunters Point Ferry as it pulled out of Catharine Slip.

As he approached the neighborhood of the Roost, he saw that the area was even busier than he had imagined. Streetwalkers lounged in doorways, smoking cigarettes and brazenly offering their services in the most vulgar terms. Their prospective customers ranged from sailors and dockhands who worked the nearby waterfront to well-dressed businessmen seeking a little short-term companionship before returning to their affluent homes uptown.

Crombie found the Roost near the corner of Jefferson Street. There was no sign on the building's brick front, but the address matched what Gus Sehlinger had given him, and the traditional red light in the window proclaimed that the residence was a brothel. If any further confirmation was needed, it came from a woman in a sheer purple gown who was leaning against the door jamb. "How about it, sweetie?" she said to Crombie. "I need to get off my feet and on my back. Come on inside with me."

He brushed past her and reached for the door knocker. "No, thanks. I'm looking for someone inside."

"Suit yourself, sweetie, but you won't find any better than me."

The door was opened by a small mountain of a man whose muscles bulged under an ill-fitting serge suit. "Welcome to the Roost," he said blandly. "There's a bit of a wait tonight, but you'll find our girls to be well worth it." His breath whistled through a crooked nose that had once been broken and never properly set.

Crombie stepped inside a small foyer. Clods of earth scattered over the worn wood floor were evidence that dozens, perhaps hundreds, of pairs of boots had recently traipsed through. "I don't mind waiting, but I'm only here to see the proprietor."

"Why?" The doorman looked puzzled. Judging by his dull-witted face, Crombie assumed it wasn't an unusual condition for him.

"I hear you have a shortage of girls," Crombie said. "I can help fill that need."

The man lifted a meaty paw to Crombie's chest and shoved him back toward the door. "This is a respectable place. We don't hire no Nancy boys here. You go over to Greene Street if you're looking for that kind of work."

Crombie blanched. "*That's* not what I mean!"

The pressure against his chest eased. "You got some real girls?"

"Let me talk to the owner."

The doorman endured the agony of thought for a few seconds before agreeing. "I'll get Miss Sherrie. You wait in the parlor." He pointed out the brothel's waiting room, a few feet down the hallway.

Crombie ventured only a foot or so into the parlor, which was decorated in the cheap, gaudy, titillating style that was customary for houses of this type. The thick carpeting, striped wallpaper, and plush sofas ran the color palette from crimson to scarlet. Painted nudes in chipped gilded frames hung on every wall. Gaslight glittered from a glass chandelier, and a cracked mirror on one wall made the room appear twice its size.

He was pleased to see the number of men crowded into the room, some of whom were obviously impatient to get upstairs. They filled every chair in the parlor, while two scantily clad young women tried to entertain them with lewd dances and flashes of bare skin. Musical accompaniment was provided by a Negro piano player who wore a formal black suit and a blindfold of the same color. Two uniformed policemen sat at a small bar, swigging from bottles of wine; they appeared to be as much a part of the establishment as the prostitutes and the bartender.

After a fifteen-minute wait, a slender woman of about fifty came into the parlor, accompanied by the doorman. From her appearance, Crombie thought that she'd probably been quite attractive in her youth. But her efforts to remain young fell sadly short. Her unnaturally black hair was obviously a wig; she appeared to be wearing a layer of face powder for every year of her life; and her pink chiffon gown would have been more appropriately worn by a ten-year-old. "I'm Miss Sherrie," she said brusquely. "What can I do for you?"

"It's what I can do for *you,*" Crombie said. "What we can do for each other, really."

"I don't have time for games tonight. If you have girls, I can use them. And I'll pay you a finder's fee. Otherwise . . ." She nodded toward the door.

"I have photographs, not girls."

Miss Sherrie pointed a long, red fingernail at the men sitting in the parlor. "These gentlemen aren't looking for pictures. We already have some rather exotic photographs smuggled in from Cuba and France. They're not the same as a warm, soft woman." She eyed him sharply. "I hope you know that."

"I do; I'm married." Crombie quickly went on, "You haven't seen pictures like these, though, and"—he nodded toward the men on the sofas—"neither have they."

She smiled slightly. "They can't show anything more than the ones we got from France."

"These are *moving* pictures."

Her smile changed to a frown. "What are you talking about, 'moving' pictures?"

Crombie took a step into the foyer, out of view of the men in the parlor, and reached into his coat pocket. When, after a brief hesitation, Miss Sherrie joined him, he showed her a booklet that Gus Sehlinger had put together. It was made from the Ellis Island prints, which had been bound together on one side.

"What's this?" she asked.

Crombie ran his thumb across the free edge of the prints, causing the picture frames to flip quickly. The impression of motion was unmistakable. The ferry steamed up to Ellis Island, and immigrants stepped onto the wharf, the same as they had on New Year's day when he captured their images on celluloid.

"That's very clever!" The madam laughed brightly. "But I don't think my customers would be sufficiently entertained by pictures of people walking off a boat."

"This is merely a crude sample to demonstrate the idea. I can take moving pictures of anything—including anything you might want your girls to do. You can charge your customers for looking at them, or you can just use the pictures to maintain their interest while they're waiting. Some of the men in your parlor appear rather impatient; you wouldn't want them to give up the wait and leave before a girl becomes available for them, would you?"

"No, I wouldn't." She took the booklet and worked it once herself. "I don't know if this will do the trick, though, so to speak."

Crombie ignored the pun. "These moving pictures are best seen through a viewing box. I didn't want to bring one here until I knew if you were interested, but I certainly could. It reproduces motion perfectly."

She nodded. "All right, I'm interested." Then she looked up at him. "Why did you come to me? Why not some other house?"

"I've heard that yours is one of the best, and that you're a shrewd proprietor. I'm looking for someone who's smart enough to try something new." Crombie gave her his most ingratiating smile.

The madam appeared pleased at the answer. "What's your name?"

"Edwin."

She didn't ask for a last name; Crombie knew that in her business names didn't mean much anyway. "All right, Edwin. Bring the viewing box. I'd like to see more."

Crombie said, "I do have a concern."

"What's that?"

"I haven't yet made any moving pictures of the kind I hope to make here. I've been worried about what the police might do if they discovered such material. I expect I'd be violating all sorts of Comstock laws."

Miss Sherrie laughed. "The police would probably want copies to show at the station house." She laid a clawlike hand on Crombie's forearm. "Don't you worry about the police. We don't have any trouble with them—the patrolmen enjoy our wine and girls, and the captain enjoys his protection fees. The worst they might do is raise our weekly payments to the precinct; you and I can work out who's going to cover that cost if and when we make a final deal." She turned toward the parlor again. "Feel free to make yourself comfortable. I'm sorry we don't have any girls to offer you at the moment, but have a drink on the house." To the doorman she said, "Victor, see that Edwin gets whatever he wants from the bar." With that, she headed for the staircase.

Victor led the way through the crowded parlor, taking Crombie to the bar in the rear of the room. He remained at his side while Crombie ordered a beer and took a long swallow of cheap lager. The doorman then asked in a hushed voice, "Could I see that picture book again?"

Crombie was a bit hesitant to display the bound film prints in front of people, but seeing that no one was paying attention to them, he handed the booklet over to the man.

Victor flipped through the pages again and again, running his thumb at different rates to vary the speed of motion. He laughed like a child at each sequence of fluttering images.

While the doorman happily played with the photographic book, Crombie surveyed the room. He saw nothing attractive or enticing. The two half-naked girls trying valiantly to entertain the crowd rarely smiled; they looked increasingly harried at having to maintain the interest of so many men, and annoyed at having to fend off their incessant groping. The restless men appeared irritated by the long wait, and frustrated that the dancing girls repeatedly refused to service them right there in the parlor. The only individuals in the room who appeared content were the drunken patrolmen and the Negro piano player, whose blindfold kept him from having to see the others.

Curious about that, Crombie asked Victor, "Why is he wearing a blindfold? To show off that he can play without seeing the keys?"

The doorman's eyes remained on the photographs. "Nah, it's so he don't see the girls. Can't have a colored boy seeing white girls in the altogether." He flipped through the book again. "I like the boats."

Crombie had decided earlier not to press Miss Sherrie for information during this visit, since it might raise suspicions. But Victor was probably less wary than his boss. "Why do you have a shortage of girls?" he asked the doorman. "When I took these pictures at Ellis Island, I saw lots of immigrant girls coming in. Why don't you hire some of those?"

"We do." Victor flipped through the pictures again. "We have an agent there who gets them for us. But not all of them are willing to do this kind of work. We try 'em for a while anyway, but if they never take to the business we get rid of them."

"How?"

"Put 'em out on the street."

Just then a haggard young blonde wearing a lacy chemise and tight stockings came into the parlor for her next customer. She was forcing her lips to smile, but the result was more like a painful grimace, and her heavily painted eyes looked as if they were about to burst into tears. Crombie noticed that although she wore women's lingerie, they weren't worn comfortably; she looked like a child playing dress-up in her mother's clothes. He took a closer look at her face and was sure that she couldn't have been more than thirteen years old.

The image of his daughter, Emily, wearing her Annie Oakley costume, suddenly came to Crombie's mind. The world-weary girl in the chemise was only a few years older than Emily.

CHAPTER 33

Sunday dinner had been so excruciating that Rebecca had decided to come down with her five-o'clock headache at four-fifteen.

She wasn't sure why this particular visit to her parents' home had been so difficult for her. True, conversation with her family had been scant and stilted, but in recent years that had become the norm. What little had been said to her tended to be either unwanted advice or unsubtle inquiries about her social life; this, too, was nothing unusual, and she had developed a knack for affably parrying their suggestions and questions. Perhaps what made this dinner different was that she missed having Marshall with her. She was actually mildly annoyed that he hadn't been seated at her side—never mind that she hadn't invited him. *Well, next weekend,* she thought. Then they would be together with his family.

When Rebecca returned to Colden House, she'd barely closed the door behind her before Miss Hummel came racing down the stairs. The older woman usually moved so silently, that the clatter of her rapid footsteps was startling.

"What happened?" Rebecca asked. She could tell there must be a more serious problem than a leaky roof.

Worry creased her assistant's usually placid expression. "There's a lady here to see you. Her name is Liz Luck."

Rebecca was sure it wasn't a social call. "What does—"

"Miss Luck is injured," interrupted Miss Hummel. "I think she needs to see a doctor."

"What happened to her?"

"She's been badly beaten, and I think her arm is broken." Miss

Hummel shook her head. "The poor woman wouldn't give me any details, though; she says she'll only speak to you, Miss Davies. She's very scared. I hope we can help her."

"Thank you, Miss Hummel." Rebecca quickly slipped out of her coat and hurried upstairs to the infirmary.

Converted from a small bedroom, the infirmary didn't contain any real medical equipment. A couple of cabinets were stocked with basic supplies: bandages, headache powders, and miscellaneous salves and ointments. There were two narrow beds, a ladder-back chair, and a washstand with a large enamel basin. The chair, cabinets, and iron rails of the bed were painted the same antiseptic white as the walls.

Liz Luck, lying on her back in one of the beds, was the room's sole occupant. She was fully clothed in a faded tartan-plaid dress, with her forearm draped over her eyes. Her blond hair, looking limp and damp, cascaded over the pillow.

"How are you, Miss Luck?" Rebecca asked quietly.

Liz slowly removed her arm from her face. One eye, bruised so purple that it looked like a wine stain, was swollen shut, and her blood-caked lip was split. "I can't stay with Warren any more," she said in a hoarse whisper that was slurred from difficulty in moving her mouth. "I had to leave him." Her breathing was ragged, and she flinched in obvious pain every time she inhaled.

"You did the right thing, and you came to the right place." Rebecca tried discreetly to look for injuries without appearing to stare. She noticed the way Liz kept one arm motionless at her side—probably broken, as Miss Hummel had said. And her painful breathing might be due to broken ribs. "When did he do this to you?"

"Last night."

"Did you leave him then?"

"No, ma'am. I couldn't leave the house until he did, around noon today." She paused to gasp a lungful of air. "I hope you don't mind me coming. You said I could."

"Yes, of course. You're most welcome here." Rebecca only wished that Liz had been able to get to Colden House earlier. It must have been an agonizing night for the woman, suffering with these injuries and facing the possibility of additional ones.

"I brought my things."

Rebecca spotted a worn canvas satchel on the floor next to the bed. "That yours?"

"Yes. It's everything I own." Liz again struggled to take in a breath of air. "I'm never going back to him. I have to find someplace else to live."

"Let's take care of first things first," Rebecca said. "We need to have a doctor examine you."

Liz attempted to sit up. "I can't pay for a doctor."

Rebecca decided a small lie was in order. "There's no charge. This doctor donates his services to Colden House." Rebecca didn't think Liz would accept the treatment otherwise.

Liz began to protest; then she winced with pain, fell back on the mattress, and agreed to receive medical care.

Before Liz could change her mind, Rebecca left her briefly alone and went downstairs. She first telephoned a trusted doctor who had treated a number of Colden House's residents over the years, and coaxed him into coming to the house within the hour. She then stopped in the kitchen to pour a glass of orange juice for her new guest; the woman needed some nutrition, and from the look of her mouth she probably couldn't comfortably eat solid food.

Rebecca returned to the infirmary with the orange juice and a straw. "The doctor will be here soon."

Liz nodded and sat up enough to accept the drink. She took a few sips, but her bruised lips couldn't close tightly enough around the straw, and juice trickled down her chin.

"Why don't you just rest until the doctor comes?" Rebecca said, as she gently wiped away the orange juice.

Liz promptly slumped back on the mattress, and Rebecca sat down in the chair. Since speaking and breathing were clearly painful for the woman, Rebecca decided to wait until she had been treated before talking with her any more.

After about five minutes, Liz Luck broke the silence. "I thought he was going to kill me," she said weakly.

He came close, thought Rebecca. "You're away from him now. And you never have to go back. We can help you go someplace else."

"Where? Where would I be safe from him? Warren is a cop; he can track me down anywhere." She inhaled too hard, and moaned with pain. "And he doesn't even *want* me. All he wants is money."

Rebecca assumed that Liz must have been short in earnings again this week, but she didn't ask. She could get the details later.

Liz went on without prompting, though. "He's still angry with me about paying for Christina's funeral." She made a whimpering sound. "And he said some horrid things about her."

"Such as?" The words were out before Rebecca could remind herself not to ask questions yet.

"He called her 'a worthless tramp.' And when I told him not to talk about her that way, he went into a rage. He said Christina was only worth twenty dollars alive, and that I was a fool to spend twenty-five on her funeral." She paused for breath. "Then *I* got angry and demanded to know what he was talking about. Warren was drunk and raving mad. He started saying worse things, and I thought it was just to hurt me. But then he told me he had Christina's letters—he got the mail she'd sent and kept it from me."

It wasn't unusual, Rebecca knew, for men like Gleason to cut their wives off from their families; it was a way for them to keep control. "So he knew Christina was coming to America?" she asked.

"Yes. He said he did, anyway. And he said he was damned if he was going to support her, so he made sure she wasn't ever going to make it to our apartment."

"Do you think he . . ." Rebecca couldn't complete the question.

Liz Luck knew what she was asking, though. "I don't know. After Warren calmed down a little, he tried to take back some of the things he said. Maybe he was worried he said too much; I don't know." Along with soft moans from the pain, she began to sob quietly. "He said all he did was introduce her to a friend of his so that she wouldn't come to us." She paused for a few moments. "I don't think Warren could have killed Christina. He's really not a bad man; he's just had a bad break in life. When he joined the police force, his family couldn't afford to buy him a rank higher than patrolman—every position on the force has to be bought from Tammany Hall, you know."

Rebecca nodded that she was aware of that illicit system.

Liz went on, "It's only three hundred dollars to be a patrolman, but fifteen hundred to buy a promotion to sergeant. Warren is still waiting to save that much, and while he waits he keeps talking about how life has cheated him."

Rebecca found herself both furious at Warren Gleason's conduct and exasperated at Liz Luck's statement that "he's really not a bad man." It was a relief to her when Miss Hummel brought the doctor into the room.

Although Rebecca remained in the infirmary during the examination, her thoughts were more of Christina than of Liz. She wondered if Josiah McQuaid was the 'friend' Gleason had mentioned. And she tried to figure out what Gleason had meant by the comment that Christina was worth only twenty dollars alive.

CHAPTER 34

Marshall Webb could provide no answers to Rebecca's questions. "What we don't have," he said, "is a solid link between Warren Gleason and Joe McQuaid. Of course, there *could* be a connection between them, but we'd only be guessing to assume one."

"It seems to fit the circumstances," said Rebecca. "Gleason admitted to Liz that he knew her cousin was coming to New York. He also admitted that he introduced Christina to a friend of his so she wouldn't come to stay with them." She nodded thoughtfully. "We know that Christina was taken to Connecticut by McQuaid, which kept her conveniently out of the city and away from Liz Luck—exactly as Gleason wanted. So it makes sense that McQuaid was the friend Geason mentioned."

Webb didn't disagree with Rebecca's theory; he simply thought they needed more information before they could draw conclusions. "How would Gleason and McQuaid know each other?" he asked. "Gleason seems to stay in the Tenderloin; that's where he lives, works, and plays. McQuaid operates down at the Barge Office and supplies girls to Connecticut and that brothel on the East Side. As far as we know, their paths would never cross." He thought a moment. "And *when* would Gleason have introduced Christina to McQuaid? He was in Cutter's saloon all day New Year's."

Rebecca pursed her lips. "I don't know."

"Also, if McQuaid took Christina out of the city as a favor to Gleason, why did he bring her back?"

Rebecca didn't have an answer to that, either.

Miss Hummel came to the open doorway of the sitting room.

"Miss Luck is sleeping peacefully now," she said. "I'm going to retire myself if there's nothing else."

"Thank you," Rebecca said. "You've done enough for one night. I'll check in on her later."

When the older woman left, Webb said to Rebecca, "I'm glad you called me. I only wish there was something I could do to help."

"There's nothing more any of us can do for Liz tonight. The doctor set her broken arm, examined the rest of her injuries, and gave her some laudanum to help her sleep. He was worried about her difficult breathing, but it's probably due to broken ribs—nothing can be done for those except keep her from moving too much and hope that they heal with time."

Webb wondered if that was really all that could be done. Sleep and time might eventually mend Liz Luck's latest physical injuries, but what could ever relieve the sense of terror that she must have lived with these past years. And, of more immediate concern, what could be done to prevent Warren Gleason from committing more violence against her in the future? When Webb realized that Liz Luck must have asked herself that latter question many times, he found himself getting as angry as he had when Rebecca first told him what Gleason had done to Liz. He felt frustrated, too, not knowing how to keep such a thing from happening again. Struggling to suppress his anger, he asked, "Did she say what set Gleason off this time?"

"Money again. At least that was part of it." Rebecca shook her head. "But men like him don't really need a reason. They just find some excuse so they can claim their brutality is justified. Some of them even convince themselves that they're right to do what they do." Rebecca's own anger and frustration were visible in her taut face and burning eyes.

Webb asked with forced calm, "What *can* we do to help her? And to stop Gleason from hurting her again?"

Rebecca answered promptly, "Get her far away from him—someplace where he can't find her."

"Is that all?" It didn't seem right to Webb that the only solution was to move Liz Luck out of range of her husband's fist. "Gleason is the one who should be put away—in a jail cell."

"I agree. But it's never going to happen."

"Why not?"

Rebecca explained, "For one thing, Liz refuses to report the beating. And I can't blame her. Because even if she did, the police won't do anything about a husband 'disciplining' his wife—especially not when the husband is one of their own. No, Warren Gleason has nothing to fear from either his wife or the authorities."

Webb remained silent for a while, contemplating the utter unfairness of it all. Gleason not only had gotten away with forcing his wife into prostitution to provide him with extra income, but he basically had a license to batter her whenever he had the whim. And Joe McQuaid was free, still working at the Barge Office, where he could lure more girls like Christina van der Waals into slave labor at the tobacco farm or oblige them to sell themselves in a brothel. Yet Liz Luck was the one who had to go into hiding.

"What are you thinking?" Rebecca asked.

"Pardon me for being blunt," he said. "But as far as I'm concerned, Gleason and McQuaid should both burn in hell, and the sooner the better." He considered how they might be pushed along in that direction, and came up with an idea. "You know, instead of waiting to see if we can find a connection between them, let's force the issue and see what happens."

"Force it how?"

"Set one of them against the other. If they don't know each other, no harm done—except perhaps to them, and I won't lose any sleep over that. If they *are* friends, maybe we can turn them into enemies." He thought to himself, but didn't say aloud, that he'd be perfectly content if they ended up killing each other.

Josiah McQuaid's droopy jowls pulled up into a grin when Rebecca approached him outside the bustling Barge Office Monday afternoon. He tugged the wide brim of his straw hat in greeting and held out an open bag of peanuts. "It's a pleasure to see you again, Miss Davies," he said. "Where's Mr. Byrd today?"

She didn't find the sight of McQuaid to be a pleasure at all. In both appearance and manner, she found him thoroughly repulsive. But it was his occupation that Rebecca really hated. After declining the offered nuts, she answered, "I gave Mr. Byrd the afternoon off."

With only a slight adjustment of his facial muscles, McQuaid's sleepy eye turned into an intentional wink, and his smile became a leer. "It'll be a pleasure to conduct business just between the two of us," he said. As if a brilliant thought had just occurred to him, he added, "Say, why don't we get away from all this noise, so's we can talk in private. I know a little place on Pearl Street where we can get a bite to eat, maybe a drink or two. . . ."

Rebecca had already had lunch and now had to struggle to keep it down. "That's a kind offer," she said sweetly, "and I wish we *could* do business. But I'm afraid it's out of the question."

McQuaid's lower lip sagged and his features twisted in a frown. "Why? I thought you was interested."

"Oh, I am. But something has come up."

"Whazzat?"

"I was visited at Colden House by a couple of police officers." Rebecca paused for effect. "They informed me that there's somebody here preying on immigrant girls, and they wanted to know if any of my residents had encountered such a person."

McQuaid was indignant. "I don't prey on nobody. I provide employment opportunities."

"Yes, I understand that. And of course I told the police that I hadn't heard about any of my girls running into problems here."

Relief softened his face. "I appreciate that, ma'am." Then he frowned again and asked, "But if you got rid of the coppers, then why can't we do business? I really need—"

Rebecca cut him off. "Because they informed me that they will be continuing to look for an agent working the area of the Barge Office. They said that a young Dutch girl had been taken from here, and was later killed."

McQuaid was visibly shaken. "And they're investigatin'?"

Rebecca had the sense that McQuaid was both disturbed by the mention of the Dutch girl and puzzled by the notion that the police would bother to investigate the death of an immigrant girl. "Yes," she said. "They mentioned something about the Immigration Bureau pushing them to find the girl's killer. Apparently, with Ellis Island having just opened, they don't want any negative publicity." She hoped the embellishment about the Immigration Bureau would lend plausibility to her claim that the police were actually doing their jobs.

McQuaid glanced about nervously, then folded up his bag of peanuts as if he were packing to leave. He stammered, "I sure hope it wasn't one of my girls who got herself killed. But you know how it is in this city." He shrugged. "I can't be expected to protect them once they're on their own."

"I understand," said Rebecca. "And I hope *you* understand that I won't be able to enter into a business arrangement until that matter has been resolved—or at least until the police abandon their investigation."

When McQuaid said that he understood perfectly, Rebecca excused herself and returned home. For now, she had learned all she needed to from Josiah McQuaid.

While Rebecca was at the Barge Office, Marshall Webb was preparing to carry out his part of their plan. Most of the preparation consisted of telling himself again and again that he would have to restrain his overwhelming urge to give Warren Gleason the same kind of beating that the patrolman had inflicted on Liz Luck.

Since Gleason's beat appeared to be restricted to the barroom of Cutter's Saloon, that's where Webb went to speak with the officer. After taking the el to the Tenderloin, he walked through a brief sun shower to the corner of Seventh and Twenty-ninth.

As soon as he stepped inside the saloon, Webb noticed that the atmosphere was quite different from what it had been on either of his previous visits. There were as many customers as he had seen the first time, but no sense of relaxation or revelry. The tension in the place was so palpable that even the smoky air seemed immobilized with fear. There was no conversation, no click of poker chips at the tables, and the fiddle player's bow was tucked under his arm.

Few eyes glanced at Webb when he entered. Most kept a wary watch on Warren Gleason, who was standing at the bar. The patrolman was in the midst of a profanity-laced tirade that targeted everything from women to foreigners to the police department. Gleason's slurred speech and unsteady stance were evidence that he was thoroughly drunk. His ranting didn't appear to be for the benefit of any particular audience; the way his head bobbed and listed, he sometimes seemed to be addressing the moose head on the wall, while at other times he looked at his helmet on the bar. The patrolman's face was so florid that even his bushy mustache appeared to be a brighter shade of red.

Rosie was the person nearest him, but she stood at a cautious distance; Webb could see fear through the paint and powder that masked her face, and thought she might spring away at any moment. Behind the bar, a scowling Cutter Smyth twisted a towel so hard that Webb could hear the occasional snap of broken threads.

When Webb had first met Gleason, he thought the hulking, thick-necked police officer resembled a bull. The resemblance was even stronger now that he was snorting with anger. It wouldn't take much to make him charge, and Webb was about to wave a red flag in front of him.

As Webb approached the ranting officer, Smyth caught his eye and gave his head a small shake, trying to warn him away. Rosie appeared relieved at the sight of Webb, perhaps hoping that he would keep Gleason's attention directed away from her. From the corner of his eye, Webb noticed that a few of the other customers had a different kind of hope in their expressions, probably anticipating some entertainment.

Remaining a few feet from the officer—just far enough to step away if he swung at him—Webb said, "Mr. Gleason."

The big patrolman turned slowly, revealing that the front of his blue tunic was wet with spilled beer. He staggered slightly and supported himself with one hand on the bar. In his drunken condition, it took a moment for him to recognize Webb. "You seen my Lizzie?" he demanded.

"No, I haven't." At the mention of "my Lizzie," Webb found himself tempted to goad Gleason into a fistfight. No matter how strong the patrolman was, his reflexes would be sluggish from booze, and Webb was sure that if he could stay out of the big man's grasp he could box him senseless. He forced himself to resist the temptation. For one thing, it wouldn't achieve what Webb needed to accomplish today. Second, there was a revolver in Gleason's belt, and a right jab was no match for a loaded pistol.

"She's gone!" Gleason bellowed. "Just packed up and left." He squinted at Webb through red eyes that looked incapable of focusing clearly. "You *sure* you ain't seen her? You sure as hell been nosin' around enough."

"Yes, I'm sure. And as to my 'nosing around,' I have to confess that I haven't been entirely honest with you."

"Watcha mean?" The officer clumsily reached for his schooner of beer; his meaty hand knocked it, splashing foam onto the polished bar. He ordered Smyth, "Put another head on it, Cutter."

The bartender immediately moved to comply.

Webb continued, "I'm not really with the Immigration Bureau. I'm actually a writer—for *Harper's Weekly*. And I've been assigned to write a story on the exploitation of immigrant girls."

"What the hell does that have to do with me? All I want is my goddamn wife back." He lifted the fresh beer to his lips.

"It appears to have quite a lot to do with you—regarding one particular immigrant girl, at least."

"You don't know what the hell you're—"

"I *do* know," said Webb. "We've made some inquiries at the Barge Office. There's a fellow there named Josiah McQuaid who gave us your name. He claims you contacted him about Christina van der Waals."

Gleason took a long swallow of beer. "He does, does he?"

"Yes. And of course, with Christina being killed, we have to investigate that for our article." Webb then decided to add an embellishment that he hoped would press Gleason to talk. "My editor has already contacted Inspector Byrnes, who assures us that the police department will cooperate with us fully. I thought perhaps you'd like to tell me your side of the story first."

Foam dripped from Gleason's wide mouth as he roared, "I don't give a goddamn about Byrnes, or McQuaid, or your goddamn story! You can all go to hell! I want my Lizzie back, and anybody who tries to keep her from me is gonna be dead meat."

Webb took a step backwards. He could tell he would be getting nowhere with Warren Gleason today. "This obviously is a bad time to talk," he said. "If you ever want to—"

"Get the hell out of here!"

Webb did so, backing away so that he could keep an eye on the raging patrolman.

Out on the street, he considered Gleason's reaction to what he'd said. Webb knew that it was difficult to determine what a drunk might be thinking, and he couldn't be sure that he had accomplished much.

He continued to think as he traveled back to Union Square. He found himself troubled that Gleason's sole concern was getting Liz Luck back. Remembering the "dead meat" threat, he suddenly wasn't so sure if his idea to set Gleason and McQuaid against each other was such a smart one. If the two of them did know each other, they were sure to compare notes on their meetings with Rebecca and Webb today, and they might figure out that Liz Luck was at Colden House.

The moment Webb got into his apartment, he telephoned Rebecca. After warning her that she should probably get Liz Luck somewhere else where she'd be safe, he added, "It was peculiar how Gleason kept insisting that wanted 'his Lizzie' back, as if he truly missed her."

"I'm sure he does miss her," said Rebecca. "He thinks of her as his property. He's lost something that he believes is rightfully his, and he wants it back."

That could be, thought Webb. Or Gleason might have another reason for finding his wife: he might have realized that he had admitted too much to her, and wanted to make sure that she never revealed it.

CHAPTER 35

Marshall Webb got little sleep that night. He kept reviewing his encounter with Warren Gleason, as well as Rebecca's account of her meeting with Josiah McQuaid, trying to determine what information they had gained and at what possible cost.

He felt certain, as did Rebecca, that Gleason and McQuaid knew each other. Confirming a link between the two men had been one of their objectives, so they had at least accomplished that goal. Rebecca might have accomplished even more—she had the impression that McQuaid might be scared enough to cease his operation for a while.

It was harder for Webb to predict what might come of his talk with Warren Gleason. The policeman had appeared totally unconcerned about being exposed in the pages of *Harper's* or investigated by higher-ups in the police department. Nor did he seem bothered by the lie that McQuaid had named Gleason in connection with Christina van der Waals. Was Gleason untroubled by what Webb had said because he had nothing to fear? Or was he too drunk for Webb's words to register? If the latter was the case, Webb knew from his own experience that Gleason would probably remember them later.

Most likely, thought Webb, Gleason had simply been too obsessed with finding Liz Luck to care about what Webb had said to him. As Webb recalled Gleason's rage over his missing wife, he found himself increasingly worried about Rebecca. If Gleason learned that Luck was at Colden House, he might not be satisfied with getting her back. The patrolman might be intent on carrying through with his threat to turn anyone who harbored her into "dead meat." That could especially be the case if he thought his wife had told others anything that could incriminate him.

Shortly after dawn, having gotten less than two hours of rest, Webb placed a telephone call to Edwin Crombie.

Helen Crombie answered; she said that she had already been awake but that her husband was still asleep.

"It's rather urgent," said Webb. "Could you wake him, please?"

It was five minutes before Crombie's grumpy voice came through the receiver. "This better be important."

"It is."

"My film stock come in?"

"Not yet, but it shouldn't be much longer." Webb thought to himself that he should check with Paul to see when the film could be expected.

"Then what do you want?"

"Can we talk?" Webb asked.

"Yeah. Go ahead. Talk."

"In person."

"I suppose. Where?"

Webb wanted to meet outside Manhattan. "Your house. And could you have Gus Sehlinger there, too?"

"All right. How about tonight?"

"Perfect. Thank you."

After they got off the phone, Webb resumed thinking about Rebecca and Liz Luck, and began to get angry with himself. His idea to put pressure under McQuaid and Gleason had seemed smart at the time, but now he thought the potential payoff could have too high a price tag.

Although he was seated on a crate in his own carriage house, the conversation was so bizarre that Edwin Crombie found himself looking around to reassure himself that he was indeed at home. His gaze lingered on the brass sign near the door:

American Kinemascope Company
Edwin D. Crombie, President

This workshop was supposed to be a place of business, a place where he and Sehlinger could develop the technology and plan the sales campaign to launch an entire new industry. So why did their company headquarters suddenly seem like the hideout for a street gang?

Marshall Webb had taken upon himself the role of ringleader. He kept talking about the need to "do something" to prevent Josiah McQuaid and a policeman named Gleason from harming anyone at Colden House. It was clear to Crombie that the "any-one" Webb was most worried about was his lady friend, Rebecca Davies. Gus Sehlinger proved to be as bad as Webb; the old fellow talked eagerly about "punishing" the two men for what had happened to the immigrant girl, Christina van der Waals.

Worse than all their reckless talk of how to stop Gleason and McQuaid, in Crombie's view, was that they paid little attention to what he had been trying to say. After all the badgering that Webb and Sehlinger had done to prod him into helping expose the vice trade, they continually interrupted his attempts to tell them about his visit to the Roost.

Crombie finally thought to himself, *this is* my *home, it's* my *business, and they're damn well going to hear what I have to say.* "Damn it," he said. "Would you two listen to me? There's no sense talking about what to do until you've got all the information you can get—and I have some." He paused until they'd given him their full attention.

Sehlinger took the pipe from his mouth and stroked his white beard with the stem. "What is it, Edwin?"

As payback for their refusal to listen to him earlier, Crombie kept them waiting a bit longer before relating what he had learned at the Water Street brothel, including the fact that it had police protection. He concluded by telling them that there was an "agent" at the Barge Office who supplied the place with immigrant girls to work as prostitutes.

Webb immediately asked, "Is it Joe McQuaid?"

"I don't know. I didn't want to ask too many questions on the first visit; it might have made them suspicious." Crombie stood and walked over to the oak viewing box that Sehlinger had recently completed; it ran the developed film perfectly and did a marvelous job of reproducing motion. "Next time, I'll be bringing this with me." He put his hand on the crank. "It should convince them that I'm on the square, and then maybe they'll tell me more." He turned back to face Webb and Sehlinger. "Anything in particular I should be asking?"

"I'd like to know about the police," said Webb. "Who were the officers you saw there, and who takes the payoffs? I doubt that Warren Gleason has anything to do with the Roost since it's not even close to his precinct, but it's worth checking." He ran a finger along his side-whiskers. "Also find out if McQuaid brings them girls after they've worked in the tobacco farm for a while. If so, he might have brought Christina van der Waals there."

"I'll try," Crombie said. "It might take a while to build their trust, but I'll keep going back if I have to."

Sehlinger cleared his throat. "You seem to have had quite a change of heart, Edwin. I am very proud of you."

"Yeah, well, anything to get this over with," Crombie grumbled. "Then maybe we can get back to the moving-picture business." He didn't mention that part of the reason for his change of heart was seeing the girl who reminded him of Emily at the brothel.

Webb spoke up. "The problem is that time is short. Don't get me wrong—I'm very grateful that you're involved, and learning whatever you can at the Roost will be a big help. But right now, there is an angry—and probably drunk—cop who intends to get his wife back come hell or high water. I don't think there's any limit to what Gleason might do: He's already given his wife broken bones, he could be involved in the death of her cousin, and he vows to turn anyone who protects his wife into 'dead meat.' " His voice rose. "I want to make sure that the women at Colden House are protected from him."

We know, we know, thought Crombie. Webb had already expressed that concern a dozen times. "How do you propose to accomplish that?" he asked the writer.

"I'm not sure," Webb answered. "I first thought that turning Gleason and McQuaid against each other was the best approach. Then it seemed like that was only going to make things worse—certainly more dangerous. Now, I'm again thinking that it's our best chance to end things quickly." He leaned forward, his elbows on his knees. "Gleason is tough, and he's a cop. I don't know how to stop him directly. But Joe McQuaid could be the weak link in their little chain. I'd like to put more pressure on him and see if he cracks." Webb scowled and murmured, "What I'd *really* like to do is send him off to the tobacco barn for a while. Give him a taste of what those girls go through, and then he'll be eager to tell us what he knows about Gleason and Christina van der Waals."

Crombie didn't respond. In his view, Webb's comments about taking McQuaid to the tobacco barn didn't merit any more serious consideration than a drunken idler's scheme hatched in some bar.

Gus Sehlinger squinted behind his spectacles and asked simply, "Why not?" Crombie and Webb both shot looks at the old man.

Proving that he hadn't taken his own words seriously, Webb asked, "What do you mean, 'why not?' "

Sehlinger sounded completely serious when he answered, "I mean put Mr. McQuaid in a place where he will be extremely uncomfortable. Not the tobacco farm, of course. I have a friend who owns a glassworks factory in Jersey City. The furnaces in his place are hotter than Hades. I am certain that Mr. McQuaid would find it sufficiently unbearable that he would readily tell us anything we want to know."

"Are you *mad?*" Crombie couldn't help but yell. "You want to *kidnap* a man and put him into forced labor in order to get him to talk?" He had often questioned his partner's sense, but never his sanity. Now he had serious doubts.

Sehlinger answered calmly, "We are not playing by rules here, Edwin. We are trying to save lives. I would be happy to go to the police if they would do their jobs. But when the police are criminals, where does one go?"

Crombie looked to Webb, hoping he would tell the old man that his notion was crazy. He was startled to see that the writer appeared to be considering the idea.

Webb said, "I don't think there's time to wear McQuaid down that way. Gleason could do something at any moment."

"It will only take one work shift," said Sehlinger.

"Why not longer?" Webb asked.

"Because the shock and fear are worst at the beginning—a fresh blister that breaks is always more painful than a callus. I assure you, Mr. McQuaid will think he has been in hell—and of course, he will not know that it is only to be for a short time."

"I'm having nothing to do with this," Crombie said. "I don't even want you talking about it in my home. This is *criminal.*"

Neither of the other men paid him any attention; he had been relegated to the role of bystander.

Although Webb didn't appear all that comfortable with the scheme, he asked Sehlinger, "How do you propose we do this?"

The old man absently tapped his pipe. "As I said, the owner is a friend of mine. He immigrated here from Bavaria, did very well for himself, and now employs other immigrants." An edge of anger came into Sehlinger's voice when he continued, "Probably every one of his employees at the glass factory has had a daughter or a niece or a sister who has been treated like the van der Waals girl. You leave me to manage this; I will have plenty of volunteers to help with Mr. McQuaid."

From the old man's tone, Crombie realized that even though Sehlinger had never known the Dutch girl, this had become a personal matter for him.

CHAPTER 36

Rebecca Davies said a mental thank-you to her sister, Alice. As far as the rest of their family knew, Alice Updegraff was merely a dutiful daughter and obedient wife, who maintained a respectable household and attended all the proper social functions. But she also had a good heart and shared Rebecca's concern about the girls at Colden House. In her own way, Alice even helped fund the home; of course, as a woman, she had no money of her own, but she would routinely alert Rebecca when their father was in a generous mood and might be agreeable to making a donation. Now Alice had helped in another way: She had found a safe place where Liz Luck could recuperate.

Rebecca carried Liz's satchel as the two of them walked upstairs to her new temporary quarters, in a small apartment on East Fifty-second Street. Rebecca hadn't wanted to risk taking Liz to any of the established shelters because it would have been too easy for Warren Gleason to search them for her. But he would never be able to track her to this place. It was the home of the Kimballs, relatives of Alice's parlor maid.

Before knocking on the door, Rebecca told Liz for the third time, "You're going to be fine here."

"But I trust *you,*" the battered woman said quietly. "Why can't I stay with you?" Some of her bruises had started to heal, but her spirit remained fragile.

"Because Warren might find you at Colden House. It wouldn't be safe for you there. Don't worry, I'll come by to check on you from time to time, and the Kimballs are very nice people."

The door was opened by Martha Kimball, a short, well-fed woman with a cheerful round face. One young girl clung to her gingham skirt, while another tried unsuccessfully to hide behind her. "You must be Miss Luck," the woman said warmly. "It's so good to have you." Mrs. Kimball appeared on the verge of giving Liz a hug, but wisely lowered her arms; Rebecca doubted that Liz's broken arm and ribs could have withstood the embrace.

Liz's eyes were directed down at the braided rug. "Thank you for taking me in," she said.

"No need for thanks. I'm happy to have some adult company—my husband works all day and night."

After exchanging greetings with Rebecca, Mrs. Kimball led them to the small bedroom that would be Liz's. The room's one window overlooked the solid-brick wall of the building next door. Lace curtains softened the view, though, and there were some colorful prints on the walls to brighten the room.

"It's not much," Mrs. Kimball said, "but I think you'll be comfortable. The towels by the washbasin are clean, I cleared a drawer for you in the dresser, and I put fresh sheets on the bed this morning."

"The room is splendid," answered Rebecca.

Liz nodded in agreement. "You're very kind. Thank you." Then she looked up, struggling to focus her swollen eye. "But what will I do?"

"Rest," said Rebecca. "You need it."

Mrs. Kimball said, "I'll keep the girls from disturbing you. I'll try to, at least—they can be a bit noisy sometimes."

"That's all right," said Liz. "I like children."

"Well, if they bother you, just let me know. And tell me if you can think of anything you need."

Liz said that she would, and Mrs. Kimball left them alone to unpack.

Rebecca opened the satchel and began neatly placing the contents on a dressing table. "This will be a good place for you to recover. After you're feeling better, we'll get you a new job and a new home."

"Maybe I should just go back to Warren," Liz said. "That's where I should be living. It's where I belong."

"No," Rebecca said emphatically. "You're still young. You have a lot of life left, and you shouldn't be spending it with someone as cruel as Warren Gleason." While she continued unpacking, she thought to herself that she had better find something for Liz fast, before she decided to go back to her husband. Rebecca had no doubt that if Liz were to make such a tragic decision, she would never live to regret it.

Josiah McQuaid was pathetic, Webb thought. The heartless "agent" had performed what was probably the first honest day's labor in his life, and he looked as whipped as if he had spent an eternity in the flames of hell. The loose skin on McQuaid's face seemed to sag almost to his chest, and his eyes were clouded with despair. He wore no hat, and his awful suit was gone, replaced by a ragged flannel shirt and faded denim pants with holes in both knees.

Exactly one week ago, Webb had spent the evening at the theater with Rebecca Davies. This Saturday night, he was seated on an overturned wine barrel in the empty back room of a waterfront warehouse in Jersey City. The dirt floor vibrated as trains rumbled through the nearby railroad yards, and horns and whistles from boat traffic on the Hudson River periodically split the air. The air needed cleaning more than splitting, for odors from the slaughterhouse and stockyards a few blocks away made the warehouse smell like a cross between a latrine and a morgue.

Besides Webb and McQuaid, there were three other men in the dusty room. Gus Sehlinger, who had made all the arrangements, sat on a packing crate next to Webb. Two broad-shouldered young men in coarse work clothes stood on either side of McQuaid; they had forcibly escorted the agent into the place, and made sure that he didn't attempt to leave.

Rebecca Davies wasn't present; Webb had enough misgivings about the method by which McQuaid was being convinced to cooperate that he hadn't told her what he was doing. Edwin Crombie was also absent; he had told Sehlinger in no uncertain terms that he would have no part in the plan and didn't even want to know what was going on.

What was going on was an interrogation, with Marshall Webb doing the questioning. "You know why you're here?" he asked McQuaid.

The agent answered glumly, "They said you wanted to talk to me." He cocked his head, indicating the men standing next to him.

"And you know what we want to talk to you about."

McQuaid squirmed uncomfortably. "I can guess." He held out his red, blistered hands. "And I'll tell you whatever you want. I'd rather be in prison than go back into that damn factory."

"Good," said Webb. "Then tell us about Warren Gleason."

McQuaid's willingness to talk suddenly faltered. "I thought you wanted to know about the girls."

"You don't get to choose the questions," said Webb. "You either answer them or you go back to molding glass."

"At least I'd be alive. If Gleason finds out I talked . . ." McQuaid shook his head.

"Gleason can't do anything to you if he's put away in prison. On the other hand, if you don't talk, and Gleason is led to believe that you did anyway . . ." Webb shook his own head with mock sadness. "Well, I sure wouldn't want to be in your shoes."

McQuaid turned his sleepy eye on Webb and snapped, "You don't play fair, Mr. Byrd."

"The name is Webb. Marshall Webb. And I'm not playing at all."

"So *you're* Webb." McQuaid's entire body slumped. "Damn."

"Tell us about Gleason," Webb pressed.

"All right, all right," McQuaid sighed. "Can I have some water first? Them furnaces boiled every drop out of my body."

Sehlinger spoke up. "We do not have any water." He dug into the pocket of his tweed jacket and pulled out a small silver flask. "I do have some brandy, however."

McQuaid licked his dry lips and eyed the flask like a starving dog eyeing a piece of meat. "Can I have some? Just a sip."

"Perhaps later," said the old man. "First you answer Mr. Webb's questions." He slowly opened the flask and sipped its contents. "Ahh, good cognac." Looking back up at McQuaid, he reminded him, "You were about to tell us about Warren Gleason."

"Yeah, yeah. I'll tell you." McQuaid licked his lips again. "I never met Gleason before December. He was looking for somebody who might be in the market for an immigrant girl, and he wanted it to be somebody outside his own neighborhood. He asked around and heard about me." A look of pride momentarily crossed McQuaid's face, as if he was pleased at his notoriety. "Anyway, one day Gleason came up to me outside the Barge Office. He told me that his wife's cousin was coming to New York, and he didn't want her staying with them. He gave me a letter that said when this Christina girl's ship was coming in, and a photograph that came with it." He hesitated. "She was an awfully pretty girl."

"Yes, she was," said Webb. "So what happened to her?"

McQuaid went on, "Gleason wanted a finder's fee for the girl. Usually, I don't pay more then ten dollars, but she was a real looker and Gleason was a good negotiator, so I ended up giving him twenty."

"Did Gleason say what he wanted you to do with her?"

"Nah, he didn't care as long as he got his money and she was kept out of the Tenderloin."

"How did you get her to go with you?"

"When she came into the Barge Office on New Year's Day, I showed her the letter and photograph and said that her cousin asked me to pick her up and take her home. The girl got right in the wagon. Then I took her and a few other girls up to Connecticut. After a month or so of stripping tobacco, they're generally willing to work the brothels instead—that's where I make my real money."

It took all the self-control Webb could muster to keep asking questions instead of raging at this man. "Was Christina willing to work the brothels? Is that why you brought her back to New York?"

"No. What happened was, after that crazy minister started preaching about all the vice in the city, the demand for girls got to be more than I could supply. So I brought a truckload of girls back from the farm before they were really ready." McQuaid's words were coming slower and more reluctantly. "That Dutch girl wouldn't cooperate at all. I contacted Gleason—found him at a saloon in the Tenderloin—and told him I wanted my twenty bucks back. Said I'd take the girl to her cousin otherwise." McQuaid's tale stalled completely while he lightly wiped a handkerchief over his face and neck. "My skin's still burning from that damn furnace."

Webb was in no mood to listen to complaints. "Go on."

Dropping his gaze from Webb to the floor, McQuaid said, "That's when I found out what a nasty son of a bitch Warren Gleason really is. He told me if the girl ever made it to his apartment alive, *I'd* end up in the East River." He shook his head. "But he said there *was* a way to get my twenty back: All I had to do was get rid of the girl permanently."

"You mean kill her."

McQuaid nodded. "And I was supposed to set you up for it. Gleason said you were asking a lot of questions about the girl, and it was starting to make him nervous." He looked up at Webb, his eyes beseeching him to understand. "I'm no killer. I've never killed anyone in my life."

"But you agreed to kill Christina van der Waals?"

"No, I never agreed. I told Gleason to keep the money; I didn't want it badly enough to kill for. Then he said that either the girl or me was gonna end up dead. It was my choice, he said." He looked down again. "I decided it wasn't going to be me."

"What did you do to Christina?"

"Took her to an apartment on Houston Street. I slipped her a Mickey Finn, by the way, so she was already knocked out. Then I had a girl I know make that call to you from a hotel on Broadway—never told her why. When I figured you'd be on your way to the apartment, I broke the girl's neck and left down the fire escape. I never saw you go into the place, so I didn't know until tonight that you were Webb." He passed the sweaty bandana over his lips. "Then I joined the girl who called you back at the hotel. She told me you were coming, so I made a call of my own—to the police. Told them there were a couple of con men in the apartment splitting up some loot."

"Why did you tell them that? Why not say a girl had been killed?"

"Because I wanted them to show up fast. And the way to get a cop's attention is to make him think there's easy money in it for him."

"What if I hadn't been home when your accomplice phoned me?"

"I didn't care if you got pinned with the murder or not. Hell, I didn't want any part of killing the girl at all. I only did it to keep Gleason from killing *me*. I figured as long as the girl was dead, that would satisfy him, whether or not you took the fall for it."

Webb thought for a few moments before saying, "Gleason will still be coming after you—unless you go to the police first and tell them what you've told us."

McQuaid looked as if he'd been handed a death sentence. "You think they'll believe me over one of their own?"

"It won't be only you. I'll tell them what I know, and Gleason's wife can confirm some of what you've said."

"I don't have a choice?"

"Not if you want to stay alive."

McQuaid nodded slowly. "I do." Then he said, "All right, I'll talk to the cops."

Gus Sehlinger spoke up, addressing Webb. "You can go home if you like. We will see that Mr. McQuaid makes it to the police station safely."

Webb was happy to leave that responsibility to Sehlinger and his young friends. He didn't want to remain in Joe McQuaid's presence a moment longer.

CHAPTER 37

Webb took a long, hot bath as soon as he woke up Sunday morning. But no matter how much he scrubbed, it didn't make him feel any cleaner than had the one he'd taken when he got home the night before.

Everything about the meeting with Joe McQuaid troubled Webb. Even though Gus Sehlinger had made the arrangements, Webb knew that he was at least an accessory to kidnapping, and that McQuaid's confession had been coerced. Webb tried to convince himself that their actions had been necessary, and that McQuaid didn't merit any sympathy, but he still didn't feel any better about what he had done. Perhaps what bothered him most was the feeling that he had acted no differently than McQuaid would have.

After dressing in a lightweight wool suit and putting a pot of coffee on the stove, Webb began to pace the parlor restlessly. Gus Sehlinger had promised to telephone as soon as McQuaid had turned himself in to the police. All that was left for Webb to do now was wait.

He was working on his second cup of coffee, still pacing, when he stopped to stare at the framed Civil War woodcuts on his wall. It occurred to him that last night's scene had been more like a grim Mathew Brady photograph than one of these romantic engravings. But reality, especially the reality of a young life meeting a violent end, *was* grim. Joe McQuaid had taken such a life—that of an innocent fourteen-year-old girl—and had ruined many others. If he wasn't stopped, he would no doubt go on to harm other young girls. Webb slowly came to accept that even though he didn't feel any victory or satisfaction about last night, he had done the right thing. McQuaid and Warren Gleason should both be safely behind bars soon.

Bored with the pacing, and still restless, Webb decided to take his telephone receiver off the hook and run out for the morning newspapers. He returned minutes later and stretched out in his easy chair to read the papers and resume waiting for Sehlinger's call.

Webb first scanned the headlines to see if perhaps McQuaid had already gone to the police. He found nothing about McQuaid or Gleason. All of the papers did, however, provide extensive coverage of Reverend Charles Parkhurst. The crusading minister had just gone public with the results of his private investigation. The news articles described in lurid detail Parkhurst's accounts of his visits to brothels and gambling dens. And the editorial pages praised the minister for his courage, while at the same time taking Tammany Hall and the police department to task for their corrupt system of payoffs and patronage.

Webb was in the middle of a *New York World* account of Parkhurst's visit to a Cherry Street dance hall when the telephone startled him.

He sprang for the receiver. "Hello?"

Sehlinger's accent was immediately recognizable. "We have lost him," he said.

"You *what*?"

"Josiah McQuaid. I am sorry, but we do not know where he is."

Webb wanted throw the receiver against the wall. "What the hell happened?"

Sehlinger cleared his throat. "It would not do for us to have dragged McQuaid into the police station. He had to go in on his own in order for the police to believe him. So we kept some distance from him." The old man hesitated before saying, "It was too much distance. McQuaid slipped into a crowd and got away."

All Webb could say was, "Damn."

Rebecca enjoyed Marshall's company enormously, but she was somewhat disconcerted by the amount of time he'd been spending at Colden House the past couple of days. At first she was flattered, believing that he simply enjoyed her company, too. It didn't take long for her to realize, however, that he had a different motive for being at the house. Although he tried to be subtle about it,

Marshall obviously had the notion that he was there to provide protection. The intent was sweet, but Rebecca was also mildly annoyed that he would assume she needed someone to protect her.

By the time Marshall showed up again early Wednesday morning, Rebecca had come to accept his intentions as gallant, and had made a list of tasks that he could perform while he protected the residents of Colden House.

Throughout the morning, Marshall worked tirelessly on the staircase, nailing down some loose steps and shoring up the banister. His efforts made a vast improvement to the staircase, but a stray nail had taken a toll on his trousers, leaving a tear of several inches at the knee. After lunch, Rebecca asked him to replace some of the kitchen tiles that had come loose during the flooding a couple of weeks ago. Coincidentally, she found enough chores to keep herself busy in the same room.

Shortly before dinner preparations were to begin, Miss Hummel came to the kitchen doorway. "There's a telephone call for you, Miss Davies."

Rebecca had hoped to enjoy a few more minutes alone with Marshall before others joined them in the kitchen. "Who is it?"

"That handsome gentleman with the white beard—Mr. Sehlinger."

When Sehlinger had visited Colden House, Miss Hummel referred to him as "Santa Claus." Rebecca was amused to hear that he'd risen to "handsome gentleman" in her estimation. "I'll be there in a second," she said.

Rebecca dawdled for a moment to watch Marshall put one more tile into place before going out to the hallway telephone. When she heard the agitation in Sehlinger's voice, she wished she hadn't hesitated at all.

"I am so sorry to trouble you," he said. "I have been trying to reach Mr. Webb for more than an hour, but there is no answer. I have some urgent news, and thought perhaps I should tell you."

Rebecca wanted to hear what he had to say, but since Sehlinger preferred to talk to Webb, she replied, "Mr. Webb is here. I'll get him."

She did so, then stood by his side as he picked up the receiver.

"What's happened, Gus?" Marshall asked.

The chattering from the earpiece wasn't clear enough for Rebecca to make out Sehlinger's words.

"Oh, damn!" said Marshall. "How did it happen?" He then listened for another minute before saying, "All right, thanks for letting me know."

He hung up the phone and faced Rebecca. She could tell that Marshall was shaken by Sehlinger's news. "Joe McQuaid was beaten to death," he said. "His body was found in Bryant Park."

Rebecca was somewhat ashamed of herself, but she didn't feel at all sad to hear of McQuaid's death. Her first thought was that he was now permanently out of business; not one more girl would have to suffer because of Josiah McQuaid. Marshall seemed upset, however, so she asked, "What is it that you're not telling me?"

He answered glumly, "McQuaid was going to turn himself in to the police and confess."

"Confess to what?"

"He killed Christina van der Waals. Warren Gleason put him up to it. McQuaid was going to tell the cops about Gleason, too."

"Why didn't—how do—" Rebecca didn't know what to say. She was astonished at the news and furious that Marshall had been keeping this a secret from her.

Rebecca wasn't any happier when Marshall took her into the sitting room and told her the outrageous account of how McQuaid had been kidnapped and pressured into confessing.

By the time Edwin Crombie reached the second-floor landing of the quaint Hoboken apartment house, he was wishing that he had paid the cab driver to lug his heavy package upstairs. Manual labor wasn't Crombie's strong suit; he was an entrepreneur, not a longshoreman. Shifting the weight of the cardboard box, he proceeded up one more steep flight of steps, then dropped the package outside Gus Sehlinger's door.

Crombie paused to catch his breath, then rapped on the door.

When Sehlinger answered, he peered up at his partner with surprise. "Edwin! I wasn't expecting you. Please, come in."

"I brought you something." Crombie shoved the box into the apartment just far enough so the door could close.

"What is that?"

Crombie brushed his hands on his khaki jacket and looked around the parlor. He'd only been here a few times, and it always looked exactly as Sehlinger's late wife had left it. The cushions of the overstuffed furniture were covered with lace doilies, and there was decorative china everywhere: in a glassfront cabinet, on dozens of wall shelves, and on the fireplace mantle. "This is the film negative that Webb got for us," he said. "It was delivered this afternoon."

"But why bring it here? Why not leave it in the workshop?" Sehlinger appeared utterly bewildered.

"Because I don't want it. I don't want anything to do with Marshall Webb. You can give this back to him."

"Come, Edwin, sit down." Sehlinger waved his meerschaum pipe at a sofa. "Let us talk."

"Good idea." Crombie had some things to say to his partner.

"I have some beer in the icebox. Would you like some?"

Crombie thought his labor carrying the film should earn him at least two. "Yes, please."

Sehlinger left him alone for a couple of minutes and returned with a tall glass of dark beer. After giving it to Crombie, he sat down in an oversized chair. "So tell me, Edwin: What is the matter?"

Crombie took a long swallow of beer before answering. "Kidnapping is the matter. Conspiracy is the matter."

"You did none of that."

"No, but I'm connected to it." Crombie wasn't angry; he was actually more disappointed than anything. "I'm not a callous man, Gus. I hate what Joe McQuaid is doing, and I'm sorry for those girls in the tobacco barns and the brothels. And I was willing to help stop him. I don't mind deceiving those people at the Roost, but I'm *not* willing to do anything criminal."

"You didn't—"

Crombie cut him off. "You and Webb were in my home when you planned to kidnap Joe McQuaid. My *home,* where my wife and daughter are. What if McQuaid goes to the police? What if the police come to see me? I knew what you were planning; that makes me an accessory. What does my family do if I go to prison?" He shook his head. "I want no more contact with Marshall Webb. And I will not be going back to the Roost."

Gus Sehlinger dug a tobacco pouch from his sweater pocket and slowly filled the bowl of his pipe. Crombie watched as his partner lit up and began puffing; he knew that Sehlinger only smoked when he was upset. Through a cloud of smoke, Sehlinger said, "There is no need for you to go back to the Roost. Josiah McQuaid is dead."

"What?"

"He was killed—beaten to death."

"By one of your friends?"

Sehlinger flushed and his woolly beard quivered. "No. How could you even ask such a thing?"

"How should I know how far you'd go to stop him? You and Webb were talking so crazy, I thought you might do anything."

"Then I am sorry to say that we do not know each very well."

"No, we don't." Crombie paused for another swallow of beer. "But I respect your ability, Gus. And I'd still like to be in business with you—but only if you stay away from Webb. No good is going to come of being mixed up with him."

Sehlinger puffed away for a long moment. "With McQuaid dead," he said, "I do not expect there is any reason for me to be in touch with Mr. Webb. However, I cannot promise you that I would not try to help him again. If I can do something to stop men like Gleason and McQuaid, I will have to do it, Edwin."

"I have to be honest," said Crombie. "If you do, our partnership is over."

In a quiet voice, Sehlinger said, "Then I may have no job at all."

Crombie didn't understand. "What about Edison?"

"I have missed too much work. Mr. Edison is very unhappy with me, and somewhat suspicious. I have not been discharged yet, but I do not expect to be working for him much longer."

"Damn, I'm sorry to hear that, Gus."

"I do not mind. I did what I felt I must, and I am prepared to accept the consequences—from Mr. Edison or from you."

"Like I said, I'd still like to work with you." Crombie promptly added, "As long as you don't get mixed up with Webb again."

"How about if I tell you before I do? Then we can terminate the partnership and there will be no hard feelings."

"Fair enough," said Crombie. He hoped that Sehlinger would stay away from Webb at least long enough to make some improvements to the camera and devise a projection system.

CHAPTER 38

Marshall Webb found himself all alone Thursday morning. As far as he could tell, he didn't have an ally in the world.

Rebecca Davies was angry with him because he hadn't told her about the way he and Sehlinger had gotten Joe McQuaid to confess. She didn't object too much to their means—what they had put McQuaid through was tame compared to some of the things her girls had endured—but she was definitely peeved that Webb had kept her in the dark about it.

As for Gus Sehlinger, he had telephoned last night to say that he and Edwin Crombie would no longer be of any help to Webb. Since Sehlinger and his two musclemen had failed in their mission to get McQuaid safely to the police station, Webb didn't see that there was much that Crombie or Sehlinger could do now anyway.

What had to be done was to find a way to use McQuaid's revelations about Warren Gleason—and get the patrolman put behind bars. The late Josiah McQuaid might still be the key to doing that, Webb thought. Gleason might never pay for his role in Christina van der Waals's murder, but if Webb could tie him to McQuaid's death, that might serve the same purpose.

Webb believed the odds were strong that Gleason was the one who had killed McQuaid. The patrolman clearly benefited the most from McQuaid's death, and Bryant Park, where McQuaid's body was found, was only ten blocks from Gleason's station house.

He would have to do it alone, but Webb was determined to see if he could find evidence to back his instinct.

* * *

A little after nine in the morning, Webb walked through the door of Cutter's Saloon. Besides Cutter Smyth, who was lazily polishing beer glasses, the only other person in the place was the same old man who stood like a statue at the rear of the bar.

The compact bartender nodded a curt greeting at Webb but didn't offer a drink.

"Can we talk for a minute?" Webb asked him.

Smyth shook his head. "Nope, I got customers to take care of."

Webb laughed, thinking that the bartender was joking.

"I mean it," said Smyth. "I'm busy. Go bother somebody else with your goddamn questions."

Webb didn't understand why Smyth's attitude was so different from what it had been the last time they'd spoken. "It's important," he pressed. "I need to talk to you."

Eyeing Webb coldly, Smyth rested his sinewy forearms on the bar and leaned forward. "Listen, buddy. I've learned never to put much stock in what somebody says in a barroom—telling whoppers pretty much goes along with the drinking. But what you did was different. You didn't just spin a yarn to be entertaining or brag about yourself to impress a dame." His dark eyes narrowed. "You out-and-out lied to me when you said you was with Immigration—you tricked me into talking with you. Then you come in and tell Gleason you're a writer, doin' some story for *Harper's*. Why the hell should I talk to you now, when I know I can't trust you?"

Webb mulled that over for a moment. "I *am* a writer," he said, "but this isn't for a story. It's because Gleason is responsible for the death of a girl I knew." He went on, "And the reason you should talk to me is that you'll be helping yourself."

"What do you mean?"

"I saw what Gleason was like the last time I was here. He had everybody in the place terrified of him. You and I both know he'll end up driving your customers away. On top of that, he's charging you protection." Webb looked at Smyth directly and steadily. "Here's the truth, whether you believe it or not: I'm trying to put Warren Gleason away. And if he is put away, you'll never have to pay him another cent or give him another drop of free whiskey. You may not like the fact that I lied to you before, but you know it's to your advantage to talk to me now."

As the bartender thought about what Webb had said, he

poured himself a shot of rye and gulped it down. After studying the empty glass for a few moments, he said, "All right, I got nothin' to lose. What do you want to know?"

"Did you see Gleason with another man recently? The fellow's name is McQuaid; he's about fifty years old with a sleepy eye and a face like a basset hound." Since McQuaid had mentioned having once met Gleason at the saloon, Webb thought he might have come here again.

"I've seen him twice," said Smyth. "He was here about a month ago, then again Monday night." He smiled slightly. "I told you I never forget a face."

"You know what they talked about?"

He shook his head. "They went to a back table. I couldn't hear much. But it seemed to me like this fellow McQuaid was trying to explain something to Gleason. Gleason was mad—even more than he has been lately—and McQuaid kept apologizing, trying to make peace with him." Smyth reached for the whiskey bottle again. "That was my take on it, but I couldn't swear what was really going on between 'em."

Damn, thought Webb. McQuaid might have told Gleason about Rebecca. "You didn't see him again after Monday night?"

"Nope. You want to know if he comes in again?"

"He won't. He's dead." Webb then asked, "You have a 'take' on whether Gleason was mad enough to have killed him?"

Smyth paused, hefting the shot glass in his hand. "I wouldn't put it past him."

That was Webb's impression, too.

Rebecca could usually hold a grudge for much longer than was healthy, but it only took twenty-four hours for her to realize that she was no longer angry with Marshall Webb.

She excused the fact that Marshall hadn't told her about Josiah McQuaid by telling herself that the past few months had been trying ones. Marshall had clearly been doing his best to make things right, and she couldn't hold one failure of judgement against him.

Thursday afternoon, Rebecca invited Marshall to join her in visiting Liz Luck. Not only did Rebecca want to see how Liz was faring, she wanted Marshall to see the woman, too. She hoped he would be encouraged when he realized that their efforts were truly helping someone.

When the two of them arrived at the Kimball apartment, a cheerful Mrs. Kimball led them into the parlor before excusing herself to prepare dinner. As soon as she entered the room, Rebecca faced a couple of surprises.

One was that Liz Luck looked like a new woman. Vestiges of her injuries remained, but overall she appeared healthier and happier than Rebecca had ever seen her before. Part of the reason might have been the young Kimball girls, who were entertaining Liz with a puppet show. It was obvious to Rebecca that Liz had developed a fondness for the energetic children.

The second surprise was that Alice was there. Her sister, dressed in a fashionable brocade silk suit with velvet trim, looked completely out of place in such a humble home; she sat quietly in a corner chair and watched the children play. Alice regularly visited the sick and poor, Rebecca knew, as part of her charitable duty, but Rebecca thought her sister seemed genuinely interested in Liz Luck's well-being.

After speaking briefly with Liz, who appeared captivated by the puppet show, Rebecca and Marshall left her with the girls and pulled up chairs next to Alice. The three of them chatted politely for a while about nothing of any importance. Then Alice made the mistake of asking Marshall if he'd written anything interesting lately.

Marshall began to talk, first casually, then with increasing intensity, about the book he'd been planning to write about Christina van der Waals. He ended up telling Alice almost everything that had happened in the past couple of months. Rebecca hadn't realized how much it must have been weighing on him; it all burst out as if a dam had given way.

Alice maintained perfect composure, nodding occasionally and smiling politely.

After Marshall told her about Warren Gleason demanding protection money from Cutter's Saloon, Alice said, "That's awfully impertinent of him to take payments to which he's not entitled. I should think that his superiors would be most displeased with him."

Rebecca had to keep from laughing. Of all that Gleason had done, Alice seemed to think impertinence was his greatest crime. She looked to Marshall to see his reaction, and noticed a strange, serious expression on his face.

"I'm sorry," Marshall said to Alice. "I've talked too much. You've been very kind to listen."

"Not at all, Mr. Webb." Alice smiled prettily. "It was really most, um, interesting."

Marshall then caught Rebecca's eye and she gathered that he wanted to say something to her. "Would you excuse us for a moment?" she asked Alice. "I'd like to show Marshall—Mr. Webb—those charming prints in the hallway."

When Alice nodded, the two of them went out by the front door. "What is it?" Rebecca asked.

"Your sister gave me an idea."

"She did?" Rebecca couldn't imagine what it might be.

"Yes. About Gleason's superiors being displeased with him. I want to tell them what he's been doing. Could your brother-in-law contact Inspector Byrnes? I'd like to meet with him."

"I don't know, but let me talk to Alice about it." Rebecca left Marshall and went back to her sister. She returned to give Marshall the bad news. "Alice says she'll ask her husband, but she thinks the two of them are at odds right now."

"Why?"

"She's not sure, but she thinks they were involved in some investments that recently failed. Inspector Byrnes seems to believe that Mr. Updegraff was responsible for the loss."

Webb appeared disappointed but determined. "If Updegraff can't arrange it, maybe I can find another way," he said.

Inspector Thomas Byrnes was ensconced in his richly appointed office at police headquarters on Mulberry Street. He looked up at Webb from behind an imposing desk of polished mahogany. An enormous walrus mustache hung like a drape over Byrnes's mouth, obscuring much of his facial expression, but he made up for it with his close, piercing eyes—and they clearly betrayed his impatience. "Let me be sure I understand you, Mr. Webb. You are a writer for *Harper's Weekly*, but you want to speak with me about a story you're *not* writing?"

Rebecca's brother-in-law had been unwilling to try to arrange a meeting with the police official, so Webb decided to make use of his *Harper's* calling card. He'd simply have to hope that his editor didn't find out about it. "That's right," Webb answered. "I'm not doing a story on the police department, and I'm not here for an interview."

Byrnes studied him suspiciously. That was no surprise, since the New York police had recently been castigated in the press for corruption. "Then what is it exactly that you want to see me about?" He pulled an elaborately engraved gold watch from his pocket. "I am quite pressed for time."

"I understand. And I appreciate you seeing me, inspector."

Snapping open the watch cover, Byrnes said, "You have two minutes, Mr. Webb."

Webb wasn't sure how to make his case in so short a time. "I'm here to give you some information about one of your patrolmen, Warren Gleason, with the Nineteenth Precinct. He's corrupt, and a disgrace to the department."

Byrnes's gaze remained on his watch face. "One and a half minutes. What makes you think he's corrupt?"

"While working on another story, I've found that Gleason is running his own protection racket in the Tenderloin. He's shaking down bartenders and prostitutes." Webb didn't think the police department would do much to investigate Gleason's role in the murders of Christina van der Waals or Joe McQuaid, but they would probably at least kick him off the force if they learned he was undermining the department's system of organized corruption.

"Despite what the newspapers say, we do not tolerate corruption by anyone on any level," Byrnes said blandly. "I will ask Gleason's captain to look into the matter. You said the Ninteenth Precinct?"

"Yes."

"Very well. Are we finished?"

"No. There's more."

"Thirty seconds."

"Gleason has killed two people to cover up what he's doing: Josiah McQuaid and Christina van der Waals, who was only fourteen years old." Webb didn't want to use any of his allotted time to explain that Gleason hadn't killed Christina with his own hands.

The inspector finally looked up at Webb. "You have evidence of this?"

"No. It died with McQuaid."

"So then this is merely wild talk." Byrnes clapped the watch shut and put it back in his pocket. "In case you haven't read the papers, I have bigger problems to deal with than investigating reckless accusations about one patrolman. Our entire department is under assault, and I intend to defend it to my utmost."

"Officers like Gleason are the ones who reflect badly on your department. I would think that bringing him to justice would make it appear that the police are committed to getting rid of their bad apples."

Byrnes said derisively, "Thank you for your concern over our reputation, Mr. Webb. Good day to you, sir."

As Webb left the office, he tried to console himself with the thought that the visit had been a long shot anyway. But now he had no idea what to do next.

CHAPTER 39

Rebecca was working late at her desk Friday night, penning letters to acquaintances from Boston to St. Louis to Richmond. She was writing to anyone who she thought might be able to provide a position for Liz Luck. As happy as Rebecca was to see that Liz was recovering at the Kimball home, she knew that she still had to get her out of New York and into a safe, permanent situation as soon as possible.

A sudden, violent banging on the front door caused Rebecca to jump. The sound was one she had come to dread. Most often it signaled the arrival of an angry man looking for his wife or daughter; other times it was local police, who seemed to consider Colden House a haven for "suspects," and enjoyed rousting her residents. Before heading downstairs, Rebecca glanced at the clock: ten minutes until midnight. No one would come to the door at this hour with good news.

Her fears were confirmed the moment she opened the door. There stood two helmeted officers of the New York police department; both of them had their nightsticks in their hands and looked eager to use them. Rebecca recognized one of them as a patrolman named Darby; he'd been to Colden House before to harass her girls, and he took pleasure in doing so. The other, much bigger officer matched the description Marshall had given her of Warren Gleason.

Gleason demanded, "Where the hell's my wife?" He was tottering slightly, obviously drunk.

Maintaining her composure, Rebecca answered politely, "Miss Luck isn't here."

"I didn't ask where she *ain't*. I wanna know where she *is*."

Darby, a short man with oily skin and straggly black side-whiskers, spoke up. "You want me to search the beds, Gleason?"

Rebecca promptly repeated, "She *isn't* here." She did not want Darby or Gleason going upstairs.

Gleason's bristly red mustache quivered. "Then where the hell is she?"

Rebecca wanted desperately to get these men away from Colden House. But she had no intention of taking them to Liz Luck. "Near Union Square," she lied.

"Take us there." Gleason slapped the shank of his club into his open palm. "Now."

Darby said to Gleason, "I can't go all the way up to Union Square. That's too far out of my precinct." Rebecca had hoped Darby would refuse to go along, which was part of the reason she'd named that location.

His bloodshot eyes still directed at Rebecca, Gleason replied, "Then me and Miss Davies here will go all by ourselves. But if she's takin' me on a wild-goose chase, she ain't comin' back." He turned to Darby. "As for you, Nancy boy, you can go to hell if you're so scared to leave your beat."

Darby responded in kind, giving his fellow officer a vicious cussing before he stormed away.

Good, thought Rebecca. It was no longer two against one, and soon the odds might be in her favor. "May I get my coat?" she asked Gleason.

"Huh?"

"It's a chilly night, and Union Square is three miles from here. I'd like my coat."

"Yeah, sure." Unfortunately, Gleason stepped into the foyer with her, so she was unable to use the telephone.

Back on the street, Gleason waved down a passing hansom cab and rudely ordered its two elderly passengers to get out. "Police business," he said to the driver. "Take us to Union Square."

Marshall Webb was sleeping fitfully when someone began pounding at his apartment door.

"I'm coming!" he yelled groggily. He struggled into a shirt and trousers, but didn't bother with a collar or cuffs.

The order to "Open up!" came thundering through the door. Webb recognized the voice as Warren Gleason's.

When Webb did as the officer ordered, he was startled to see Rebecca with him. She appeared unhurt but nervous.

"You got my wife," Gleason said. "I want her."

Rebecca spoke up. "You misunderstood me, officer. I didn't mean that Miss Luck was *here*."

Gleason turned to her. "What are you trying to pull? You said—"

In a calm voice, Rebecca interrupted him. "Mr. Webb is actually the one who found your wife a place to stay. I don't know the exact address, but I believe it's down on Third Avenue. Mr. Webb can lead us there."

Webb tried to make sense of what was happening. Obviously, the reference to Third Avenue was so that he wouldn't reveal Liz Luck's true location. But where would they go then? He looked at the ruddy-faced Gleason, who was swaying slightly—drunk, Webb was sure. Then he looked at the revolver in his belt and the nightstick in his fist, and he had his answer: They had to go anywhere that might present an opportunity for them to get away from Gleason.

"Come in while I get dressed," Webb said.

Gleason grunted, "Yer dressed enough. Take me to Lizzie." He poked Webb with his nightstick.

The patrolman then marched Webb and Rebecca downstairs and into the dark, cool night. On East Fourteenth Street, he told a waiting hackman to take them to Third Avenue. When they stepped up to the cab, Gleason appeared a bit confused, unable to decide on the seating arrangement. He first sat between Webb and Rebecca, then swapped places with Webb so that he could more easily keep them both in view.

As the cab rolled along through nearly empty streets, Webb tried to think of a plan. First and foremost, he wanted to give Rebecca a chance to escape, and to do that he thought it best to keep Gleason's attention on himself.

"Convenient about Joe McQuaid getting killed," Webb said.

"Yeah, ain't it?" said the police officer. "You might want to keep that in mind as a warning of what happens when somebody crosses me."

"I will," said Webb.

As they continued down Third Avenue, Webb peppered Gleason with comments and questions until the patrolman was thoroughly irritated with him.

When Third merged into the Bowery, Gleason demanded, "Where the hell are we goin', anyway?"

"We're almost there." Webb called to the driver, "Let us off at Rivington."

The cabbie complied, pulling over at the corner.

As the three of them shifted to get out of the cab, Webb kept himself between Gleason and Rebecca. He put his mouth to Rebecca's ear and whispered, "Run! Go call somebody for help."

Without hesitation, she jumped down from the hansom and began running, her long skirts fluttering about her legs. Gleason made a clumsy move to go after her, but Webb blocked him.

"You get the hell back here!" Gleason bellowed. It was too late; Rebecca had already darted into a side street.

"Let her go," said Webb. "I'm the one you need. I'm the one who knows where your wife is."

Gleason roughly grabbed a handful of Webb's shirt and used it as a handle to pull him out of the cab and onto the sidewalk. He then drew his revolver. "You're gonna take me right there, right now. Don't even think of pulling anything like that dame just did."

Webb agreed to do as he was told—he had little choice with a .38 pointed at his belly. As he began walking east on Rivington, he saw there were more people on the street. This came as no surprise, for they were now in the Bowery, where the nights were long. Webb would need a real crowd, though, if he hoped to break away from Gleason.

With Rebecca safely away, Webb felt somewhat more at ease; he could bide his time and watch for his own chance to escape. He first decided to pick up his pace slightly, quick enough so that Gleason might begin to tire, but not so fast that the policeman would think he was trying to run away.

After a few blocks, Gleason was panting audibly. "Hold on," he said. "I got to wet my whistle." They were in front of Sneaky Pete's, an illicit saloon with which Webb was familiar.

"Whatever you say." This could be his chance, Webb thought. He partially closed his eyes, preparing them for the darkness inside.

"Yer damn right it's whatever I say." Gleason poked the muzzle of the revolver into Webb's back. "We're goin' in." He pushed Webb through the saloon door.

Through the smoky haze, Webb looked for the door to the saloon's back room. There was a cluster of roughly dressed men standing there. Perfect, thought Webb; Sneaky Pete's was just as he remembered. And this was his chance.

Webb spun quickly, knocking Gleason's pistol aside with his elbow. Then he made a break for the crowd, hoping that Gleason's eyes weren't yet adjusted enough to the dim light to take aim.

Hearing curses but no gunfire, Webb elbowed his way to the back door. He knew that a larger crowd was beyond it—one big enough to get lost in. He burst through the door and shoved his way past a plug-ugly who shouted, "It's a dollar admission, you bastard!"

The noisy, chaotic scene was perfect. The only light in the spacious back room came from a couple of bright, bare electric lamps hanging low over a fenced rat pit. A derelict in blood-splattered boots was trying to stomp as many of the squealing rodents as he could before they bit through to his feet. Dozens of men were clustered around the pit; they cheered or cursed every death, depending on whether they had bet on the rats or the man.

Webb tried to stay in the darkness. He worked his way along the wall, hoping to make it to the outer door before Gleason could catch up to him. If he could get out to the alley, Webb was sure he could escape the patrolman.

Then a gunshot split the air. "Everybody freeze!" bellowed Gleason.

Webb looked back and saw a few men running toward him, trying to make their own escape. Gleason's second gunshot brought everyone to a halt.

Webb briefly debated whether to make a dash for the door anyway. Then he spotted two more uniformed officers illuminated by the light over the rat pit. They'd had prime viewing spots at the edge of the pit. Now they angrily pushed their way to Gleason, their own revolvers drawn. Webb decided he might have a better chance with them than he would trying to outrun a bullet.

The two officers exchanged heated words with Gleason. After Gleason pointed in Webb's direction, all three officers walked over to him. Not one of them had holstered his weapon.

The tallest of the cops, a gray-haired sergeant, asked him, "You Marshall Webb?"

"I am."

"We're taking you in. Make it easy on yourself and don't give us no trouble." When Webb nodded that he'd comply, the sergeant said to Gleason, "You're coming, too. We'll get this straightened out at the station house."

The station house, at the corner of Delancy and Attorney Streets, was in the city's Twelfth Precinct. They had been there for almost an hour, and Webb still couldn't tell how the situation was going to be resolved.

Webb and Gleason, along with the two policemen who had brought them in, all sat in an interrogation room waiting for Captain Finnegan, the precinct's commanding officer. During the wait, both of the local officers repeatedly—and angrily—mentioned to Gleason how much money they had had riding on the ratting contest that he'd ruined. Webb wondered if there was anyone anywhere that Gleason hadn't antagonized.

Finally, a stout, clean-shaven man wearing captain's insignia and an irritated expression stormed into the room. The local officers hopped to their feet. Gleason didn't rise until the captain glared at him. "What's going on here?"

The sergeant answered, "These two came into Sneaky Pete's rat pit about one o'clock." Pointing at Webb, he said, "This one—name's Marshall Webb—looked like he was trying to get away, but he didn't cause no trouble." Pointing at Gleason, he said, "This is Warren Gleason, with the Nineteenth. He came in and fired a couple of shots, breaking everything up. Claims Webb is an escaped prisoner." He added sourly, "It was a helluva match till he broke it up. I counted forty-seven dead rats."

Captain Finnegan addressed Gleason: "Sneaky Pete's is in good standing with this precinct. You had no business disturbing their operation."

"I had to," Gleason said. "I was after this bastard." He jerked his thumb at Webb.

"You were bringing Webb in?"

"Yeah."

"In this precinct it's 'Yes, sir.' " He waited until Gleason made the correction, then asked, "What is Webb being charged with?"

"Murder. He killed a fellow named Joe McQuaid."

Finnegan asked Webb, "That a fact?"

"No, sir. Officer Gleason here is the one who killed Joe McQuaid. Inspector Byrnes knows all about it; you can ask him."

"At this hour?"

"Whenever you like." Webb didn't mind waiting. Compared to being alone with Gleason, he felt relatively safe here.

To Gleason, Finnegan said, "I will make a phone call to your captain. Wait here." He then ordered the sergeant to join him and left the junior officer to guard Webb and Gleason.

Webb didn't have a watch with him, but he guessed that the better part of an hour had elapsed before the captain returned, with the sergeant at his side. "We don't tolerate lawbreakers in my precinct," Finnegan announced. He nodded at the sergeant. "Take him to the holding cell until we can get a wagon to transport him to the Nineteenth."

Gleason gave Webb a sneer of victory. It lasted only until the sergeant pulled Gleason's revolver from its holster and said, "Put your nightstick on the table. You're coming with me."

Captain Finnegan said, "Mr. Webb, you're free to go."

Webb hesitated only a moment—just long enough to see the astonished, fearful expression that washed over Gleason's face.

CHAPTER 40

Rebecca rather enjoyed the sight of Marshall Webb asleep on the sitting room sofa with the morning sun on his face. His legs were too long to stretch out completely, so he was curled up, with one of the wool blankets from Tyner's Dry Goods draped over him.

Miss Hummel had had a far different reaction when she came downstairs in the morning to find a man sleeping in Colden House. She had run to Rebecca in a panic over the potential for scandal.

Under the circumstances, Rebecca had thought it entirely appropriate to let him sleep here for the night. Marshall had come to Colden House at three-thirty in the morning, worried about what had happened to Rebecca after she'd fled Warren Gleason. Mostly what Rebecca had been doing was worrying about Marshall, and she'd almost cried with relief when she saw him at her doorstep.

Compared to his experiences at Sneaky Pete's rat pit and the Mulberry Street station house, her night had been positively tame. She had immediately returned to Colden House after escaping from Gleason and had begun making telephone calls trying to alert the authorities about what the rogue police officer was doing. She'd called her sister to ask that a message be relayed to Inspector Byrnes; then she began contacting local precincts. She didn't know if any of her efforts had done any good, or if Gleason's transgressions were simply more than even the corrupt New York City Police Department was willing to tolerate, but she was certainly relieved with the final result: Warren Gleason was in custody and Marshall was safely in her home.

Taking one more long look at Marshall's peaceful face, she decided to let him sleep a while longer and went out for the newspapers.

When she returned, she learned from the front pages that Warren Gleason was being portrayed by the police department as an example of a previously good officer gone bad. And his arrest was being used as "proof" that there was no need for an investigation of the department, as Reverend Parkhurst and the editorial writers were seeking. According to Inspector Thomas Byrnes, "The arrest of Patrolman Warren Gleason should provide ample evidence that the New York City Police Department can police its own."

Neither Rebecca nor Marshall was mentioned in the articles. They all made it sound as if Gleason's arrest for extortion and murder had been solely the result of a thorough investigation by the detective bureau.

As she thought about Gleason's arrest, though, she wondered if police officials might have overlooked something: Since Gleason had nothing more to lose, he might decide to reveal what he knew about systematized corruption in the department.

The spit-and-polish sergeant who came to Webb's apartment Sunday morning was extremely courteous. He even managed to make the request that Webb accompany him to the Nineteenth Precinct station house sound like an invitation, although Webb could tell it was an invitation that he was not expected to decline.

The courtesy extended to driving Webb to the police station in a private carriage rather than a department patrol wagon. During the ride, however, the sergeant gave Webb no indication of the purpose of the trip. At the station house, the officer ushered him into the office of Detective Tom O'Connor. Then he and the other detectives in the room excused themselves, leaving Webb and O'Connor alone.

The graying detective appeared as stone-faced as when he had first interrogated Webb about Christina van der Waals's murder, but his tone was far more civil. "Thank you for coming," he said.

Webb wasn't feeling quite as polite. "Why am I here?" he demanded.

O'Connor offered a cigar, which Webb brusquely declined,

then lit one for himself. "I wanted to tell you personally," he said, "how sorry I am for our previous misunderstanding."

"'Misunderstanding?'" Webb repeated. "You locked me up, and then you did nothing to find the real killer of that young girl. That's not a misunderstanding. That's dereliction of duty."

O'Connor must have been under the same orders as the sergeant to treat Webb kindly. Although the detective looked rankled over the scolding, he held his temper in check. "You're right," he said through clenched teeth. "I apologize."

Webb decided it was best to accept the apology; nothing would be gained by remaining angry at the detective's failure to do his job. "It's over," he said. "Apology accepted."

"Thank you." O'Connor paused to draw on his cigar. "I also wanted to let you know that Officer Gleason will unfortunately not be going to trial for what he's done."

Figures, thought Webb. *The police are once again taking care of their own.* "Why the—"

O'Connor cut him off. "Officer Gleason is dead."

"Dead! How?"

"I'm afraid a policeman doesn't stand much of a chance in jail. He was found beaten to death in the holding cell this morning." O'Connor tried to look sorry about the loss, but he was a poor actor.

Webb didn't bother to express regret at the news, and he certainly felt none. All he felt was surprise. "Who did it?" he asked.

"There were no witnesses."

"No witnesses?" Webb remembered how crowded the cell had been when he was in it, and all the police lodgers who'd been spending the night on the basement floor. "But there must have been . . ."

O'Connor shook his head. "And with no witnesses, there's not much for us to investigate."

Webb recalled Rebecca mentioning to him that she wondered whether Gleason would inform against his superiors. They must have wondered the same thing. Webb was certain that if Gleason really was killed by a prisoner, it was either with the tacit approval or at the expressed request of the police.

The detective continued, "We are considering this matter closed. And the department assumes that you will have no further inquiries either."

Webb thought for a few moments. Josiah McQuaid was dead, and Warren Gleason was dead. Christina van der Waals could hopefully rest in peace, and Liz Luck would never have to suffer at the hands of Gleason again. As to the details of Gleason's death, Webb didn't care enough to want to know them. "I consider the matter closed, too," he answered.

CHAPTER 41

Webb was surprised when Rebecca reached out to adjust his necktie. He almost protested that it was already perfectly straight, but he enjoyed the small attentions she'd been giving him.

"How much are you going to tell your family?" she asked. The two of them were finally going to the Tyner home for Sunday dinner.

"The same as always: as little as possible."

She laughed. "You mean you don't want to regale them with your adventures in rat pits and holding cells?"

Webb stifled a shudder. "I think perhaps I'll discuss the weather." It had been a week since Gleason's death, but he hadn't quite yet accepted that he could now go back to a normal life. "I keep thinking there's more I could do," he said wistfully. "What about the girls at the tobacco farm? And the sweatshops on Ludlow Street? I want every one of those places put out of business."

"So do I," Rebecca said quietly. "But I'll be happy to save one girl at a time. It's better than waiting for the whole world to change."

"Maybe I should give that book we talked about another try."

"That's an idea. And what about the moving pictures? Is anything happening with those?"

Webb shook his head. "No, I telephoned Gus Sehlinger to tell him how things ended up with Gleason. He was glad that I called, but he said that Edwin Crombie still doesn't want anything do with me. Sehlinger even wanted to give back the film that I'd gotten for them, but I convinced him to keep it."

"At least one person is getting a happy ending," said Rebecca. "I've found Liz Luck a place in Philadelphia. She's still got a lot of recovering to do, but it will be a new life for her."

"She deserves a fresh start." Webb didn't think Liz's life could be called "happy," though, not with the memory of Christina's death and the knowledge that her husband was behind it.

Then Rebecca brushed a finger along his whiskers, although those, too, were perfectly in place. "Smile," she said.

Webb, delighting in her touch, couldn't help but do so. He thought to himself that maybe there was indeed a happy ending yet to be written.